The Women in Pants
Sidesaddle No More

Stan Himes

Cover design by Jeff Regenold

ISBN:
978-1-3707-0463-7

For Thane and Tasha

PREFACE

My name is Laurie Michaels. You'll meet me later as I don't appear in the story early on, even though I tell it (and, just to prepare you, often interrupt it). I was an eyewitness to and participant in most of the events in this book. What I didn't witness, I learned through interviews, figured out from some facts, or made my best guess. The point I'm trying to make is that I've done whatever I could to be as accurate and truthful as I can about what happened during that summer of 1878.

PART ONE
FORMATION

Chapter 1

Half-dozing at the bar, Charlie hadn't needed to look up to know that little, if any, business was coming in when Jonas entered. The slow, drawling squeak of the saloon door said it all. A thirsty man, or one hungry for a woman, always burst in. Still, these days anyone who broke up the boredom was welcome, and Charlie gave a smile.

"Jonas. Long time."

Jonas nodded back. His eyes swept the big room. No sign of life beyond Charlie and two saloon girls daydreaming their way through a card game. "Guess I picked the wrong place to look for cattlehands."

"Been bad," said Charlie. "Silver strike over in Leadville."

"Colorado?" Jonas's face darkened and there was a little twitch in his square chin as he clenched his jaw. He spoke through closed teeth. "How many went?"

"Just the damn fools."

"Which means everybody."

"That sums it up." Now it was Charlie's turn to sweep his eyes from one side of the empty saloon to the other. Once bright walls were dull with age and smoke and grime and mostly neglect. Usually bawdy patrons colored the view, but not now. "Though maybe I'm a damn fool for staying. Get you a whisky? Beer?"

A trickle of sweat rolled down Jonas's neck, but he shook his head. "Only drink to celebrate. Don't see that happening today."

The younger of the women, a sprightly thing named Ellie—with a bosom large enough her feet stayed dry in the rain—checked the exposed tops of her breasts for perspiration, seeing none but dabbing them with her kerchief just in case. Pearl, the wiser of the two, placed a black eight on a red nine and offered up quiet advice. "Waste o' time."

"For you, maybe."

Ellie cut off Jonas at the door with her lushest come-hither look. "Think I might be just what you're looking for?"

Jonas sidestepped her. "Only if you're a man who can drive cattle." This time the door's creak was quick and direct as Jonas strode through to the street. It was Ellie's first taste of rejection and they tell me that her jaw dropped, but I don't believe it since, like I said, she has a more than ample bosom.

This was all about three days before Mary came to my father's bank. After Jonas had hopped off their ragged wagon to head into the Castle Royal Saloon, Mary and Katie had taken the wagon on up the dusty main street to Mickel's General Store and received the same news.

"No men? None at all?" This was disappointing information to just about any 16-year-old girl, but especially to Katie, who only came to Secluded Springs a few times a year and now wore her newly made blue gingham dress that matched her eyes. What good was wearing a new dress if there were no men around to impress?

Mickel's General Store was the essence of efficiency, at least as far as storing items was concerned. Floor-to-ceiling shelves lined every wall and even bracketed the front window. Flour, sugar, coffee. Fabric, needles, thread. Handguns, knives, sheaths. From alpaca scarves for winter warmth to zinnia seeds for summer beauty, Edward kept it in stock and his tall, lanky granddaughter, Ernestine, kept track of where it was. It was a sight to behold, but Katie saw only Edward's that's-the-way-it-is-miss face.

Mary raised an eyebrow at Katie's forwardness. "It's not like we'd be buying men at the general store, sweetheart." There was also a hint of a smile at one corner of Mary's mouth. She remembered being a rather forward girl herself, but she had no intention of letting Katie think a brazen indecency was anything but improper. She gave a slight cough to hide the smile.

"I know. It's just… I thought I could at least talk to one."

"You should be more concerned about what this means for the ranch. Your pa came here looking for cattlehands."

"I'm sorry."

Katie looked toward the corner where Ernestine stretched her gangly frame to a high shelf and pulled down some burlap bags to hold the dry goods. "Don't you wish there were men to talk to, Ernestine?"

Ernestine was reserved to the point that she was known to even clam up around dogs. Most customers saw her back as she gathered items and saw the top of her head as she carried them, head bowed, to the counter. But her ears worked fine and while you might think the biggest bone in her tall body was a leg bone, it was actually her funny bone. The thought of her talking with a man struck her as the funniest thing she'd heard in a month of Sundays and she let out a shrill, piercing howl that had Edward glancing up at the glassware for fear of cracks. Katie related to me later that it was the first time she learned what a pretty smile Ernestine kept hidden behind her veil of shyness.

The thump of Ernestine plopping a bag of sugar onto the counter drew Katie's attention.

"That much sugar?" She took in the large amount of supplies her mom was buying. They hadn't been in town long, but the day was sure going every way but how she'd expected it. No men to show off her dress to. No men for her dad to hire. That meant no cattle drive, which meant no money, which meant... well, she didn't know what all it meant, but she knew it wasn't good. And now her mother was ignoring all the troubles by buying out the store. "Ma, there's no sense stocking up if there's no men to drive the cattle."

"You know your pa better'n that. He'll drive them himself if he has to." Mary waved a finger over the supplies, adding them up and marking them off on a checklist in her head. "Better add five more pounds of flour, Ed. Those Byerly boys are big on biscuits."

Ed snapped his fingers. "Almost forgot." A tiny area of the store was devoted to a telegraph machine and a basket for holding mail. Telegrams and letters to Secluded Springs were few and Edward didn't deliver them until at least a month had passed. He said he didn't sign up for deliveries, but I'm pretty sure he really just thought that holding onto them was another way to get people to visit the store. "Got a telegram for Jonas and another for Hank Byerly. Mind taking this one to Hank?"

Mary accepted both envelopes. "Sure will. And if anyone shows up who can drive cattle, I'm sure Jonas would want you to send them our way."

Katie picked up a box of supplies. "Even if they can't drive cattle, send 'em out anyway."

Mary almost dropped the envelopes. "Katie!"

"But it's so disappoi—"

"Katie Bartlett!"

"I'm sorry." She stared at the floor, knowing what was coming next.

"When we get home, young lady"—the words didn't roll off Mary's tongue so much as snap off like she was taking a bite out of each one—"the chicken coop needs cleaning, the root cellar needs swept out, and I'll think of more after that."

"All right," Katie resigned herself to her fate. But as she glanced up to see the twinkle in Ernestine's eyes as she stifled another giggle, extra chores didn't seem like too high a price.

The ride into town had been filled with expectations, the morning sun shining down like a beacon of hope. Not so heading home. The same sun now beat down on them as Jonas eased their dusty wagon past Sally's Seamstress Shop at the edge of town. Humidity hung in the air and dust from the road caught in the beads of moisture on the back of Jonas's hands. He couldn't help but notice Mary's eyes glance at the bright dress in the shop's window. He looked at the frayed one she wore. Even after 18 years of marriage and ranching, she still had her fine looks and a figure that should be wrapped in an outfit just as fine. If he couldn't find cattlehands, more was lost than a new dress.

Mary knew Jonas's mind better than her own. She patted his leg. "I'm comfortable with what I have."

He knew her mind, too. She was worried.

Anyone holding a telegram would be worried. The wagon was loaded with supplies, but the heaviest items on it were the telegrams. Telegrams brought bad news. Mary and Jonas—and me, too, if I may interject—never knew a single person who received good news in a telegram. Good news could wait a few months or even a year and drift in in a letter, but bad news needed to be delivered right away (except, of course, when under Edward's slow care in Secluded Springs).

Mary wondered if they should wait until Katie was out of earshot, but a nod of the head from Jonas told her to get it over with. If someone was dead, he wanted to get the news and then put it behind him. She tore open the envelope.

"It's from Zeke."

"I hope it's gonna shock me and say they're on their way." A gust of wind rattled through the brittle leaves on the brush as they left the town behind. The dirt street turned into a grimy trail.

"'Got in fight, stop. Lot of damages, stop. In Nogales jail next 60 days, stop. Unable to make drive, stop. Sorry, stop.'" Mary added the "sorry" herself.

Jonas crushed the reins in his tightening fists. "All three of them?"

"Seems so."

"Nothing left but the two Byerlys and me. Probably find them struck by lightning when we get home." He looked at the other telegram in Mary's hand. To Mary, it now felt even heavier. Sweat began to glisten on her hands as well.

Lightning did strike the Byerlys in the form of the telegram, but Jonas was the one burning. He stared down both Hank and Early beside the empty corral. They were young men who were good workers and good company, out here in Texas from Tennessee to get away from the farm that was now calling them back.

"I'm sorry, Mister Bartlett, I truly am," said Hank. "But family duty has to come first."

Just as he always had, Early followed his big brother's lead. "You do what you have to do for family."

Jonas's tanned face gave way to red. "My family could lose this ranch."

"We feel awful, we really do." Hank held out the telegram. "But Ma says Pa's sick and the farm is in trouble." He pointed at the small, unpainted barn as if it represented the family farm back east.

"You know we'd stay otherwise," Early added, one hand rubbing his day's growth of beard as the other pointed northwest. "It ain't like we're running off to mine for silver."

Jonas grunted. He knew the two had a family duty. He knew that was the only way they'd choose farming over ranching. They were born to ride.

"At least do this," he said. "If you come across any hands while you're riding east, send them my way."

To the Byerlys, it was like Jonas had kindly opened a door to let them out of the confrontation, and they ran through it. "We'll do it for certain," Hank nodded as he gave Jonas a quick handshake before turning away. Early called back as he followed his brother. "We'll leave right now and send over anyone we see. You can count on us."

If I could count on you, you wouldn't be leaving, Jonas thought, despite his understanding that leaving was just what they had to do. Talking to him about it later, I couldn't get him to remember exactly what he did as the men rode off. But Jonas was a contemplative man and I picture him leaning a tanned, muscular arm on the corral fence, staring ahead and seeing nothing but the worries in his mind. Over 600 head of cattle ready to brand and take to market. A remuda of horses ready to ride. He'd done everything right and had everything in place, and all he had to show for it was a list of cattlehands as empty as the corral.

Chapter 2

Without being conscious of it, Jonas had built the Bartlett ranch exactly as he was—sturdy, trim and efficient. The heavy-timber house had a kitchen and an area just off it that served as the dining room, living room, work room, parlor and anything else that involved an activity beyond sleeping. Mary had turned some old quilts into hanging blankets that separated the bedrooms from the main room.

Inside the house was Mary's domain, and now she and Katie worked to prepare a meal she hoped would soothe her husband's worries. Setting the table, she peeked at the kitchen as Katie pulled biscuits from the oven. Gently, carefully, as if baked goods had bitten her before, Katie lifted a biscuit from the pan. Half of it stuck to the pan and the rest crumbled in her hand. Katie had learned plenty about cooking and keeping a proper household, but concocting a decent biscuit continued to elude her. Mary looked away with a smile.

"I hope you didn't make too many biscuits. We won't need as much with the Byerlys leaving."

Katie shook her head and sighed back a dangling wisp of her blond hair. "Too many won't be a problem."

Mary lit a lamp and placed it in the center of the pine table. The evening sun was setting and tonight was not a night for gloom.

Katie salvaged as much of the biscuits as she could by placing the best ones on top of a plate, then looked at her mom with a curiosity that showed more was on her mind than a failed day and failed biscuits. "What makes them go?"

"Hmm?"

"Not just the Byerlys. Men. What makes them go away?"

"Oh, lots of things." Mary checked the coffee. Good and hot. "Runnin' to something. Money. Runnin' away from something. Sometimes not running at all, just lopin' off to find adventure." She wiped her hand on her apron and smiled at Katie. "Not your father, though. He's made this ranch his adventure."

"Even he's gonna be leaving."

"A cattle drive isn't like leavin'. It's earnin'."

Katie poured her glass of buttermilk and seemed to dream along with the swirls in her glass. "I know how I'd keep a man. Prudence showed me."

"I doubt that life lessons from Prudence will serve you well."

Setting her glass on the table, Katie dropped her chin a tiny bit and then gazed at Mary with wide, alluring eyes. "First, I look at him dreamy, then…" She batted her eyes. "Prudence says a man can't resist the look."

Mary pulled off her apron and gripped it in one of the hands she held on her hips. "You act like that and the man'll think *you* won't resist, either. Don't let me catch you flaunting yourself like that. Never. The only thing you'll catch is the wrong kind of man."

Katie figured that since she'd spent all day saying the wrong things, she might as well keep going. "At least it'll be a man."

"Will you hush? You're only 16."

"Near 17. Besides, you were married when you were 16." And with that thought now at the top of her mind, Mary's sulky, man-hungry teen floated back to the dreamy-eyed romantic that Mary adored. "Tell me again how Pa swept you away."

The day's heat still lingered in their bedroom, but it didn't stop Jonas and Mary from holding each other, their combined wills serving as a fortress against the uncertain future. The bed filled the bulk of the room, and after so many years of having Katie just a quilt-wall away, they'd become adept at hearing each other's whispers.

"Used to be the problem was not enough cattle," Jonas said. "Never not enough men."

Mary pressed her head against his strong shoulder. "They get tired of prospecting, they'll come back."

"No time. We don't leave by mid-July, risk bad weather up north slowin' us down. Maybe wipe out grazing. Plus there's the brandin'."

She hated to see his brow furrow. When things weighed on him, they weighed heavy and dragged him to low places. It troubled her less when Jonas was sick. An illness she could treat, but a burden like this couldn't be lifted with a cold cloth or some herbs.

On the other side of the hanging quilt, Katie lay still, straining to hear the whispers and wishing that she, too, had a way to lessen the burden. "I finally had everything in place," she heard Jonas continue his lament, a type of talk she had never heard from him before. "Full herd. Good prices up north. Could've paid off the mortgage, bought you that dress and had something set aside for Katie."

Being in her dad's thoughts brought a smile to Katie, who snuggled deeper into her bed, then froze as the bed frame let out a creak. They'd know she was awake.

Jonas continued a little louder. "But it all fell apart faster than one of Katie's biscuits."

"Well!"

Mary's voice knocked some dust from the ceiling timbers. "Katie, you go to sleep and keep your ears to yourself!"

"I'm sorry, Ma." Seemed like she'd been apologizing for her actions all day. But the smile never left—her dad still had his humor. That meant his mind was working fine, and that meant he'd find a solution like he always did. As she drifted to sleep, she wondered if she had any of her father's inner strength inside of her. How would she bear up under tough circumstances? I'd do all right, she thought—smiling again—especially with a handsome husband by my side.

On her side of the quilt, Mary didn't wonder how she'd bear up. Jonas had always had enough strength for the both of them. She not only knew her role of support, she cherished it. She rolled a little more and draped an arm across his chest, closing her eyes and entering the soft fade from simple rest to deep sleep.

Jonas stared at the ceiling for a long time before he found sleep as well.

Chapter 3

By sunup the next morning, Jonas had a plan.

"We can't wait for men to come straggling back from mining or for the Byerlys to stumble upon ranch hands," he said over the steam of Mary's breakfast coffee. "Sittin' and hopin' won't pay the bank loan."

Katie was never one for being bright-eyed in the morning, but her eyes widened and her breath held as Jonas reached for a biscuit. She near bubbled over when his hand came away with more than half of one. "See that, Ma! Only part fell off!"

"That's at least a third more holding together than yesterday."

"You're about to have more to do than improve your cooking skills," Jonas continued. "Soon as you're done, take the buckboard over to see... What's Prudence's brother's name?"

"Billy."

"See if Ruth can spare Billy to help me with the branding."

"He's only eight," Mary interjected. She expected Jonas to frown, but he'd made his decision to take action and couldn't be stopped.

"Then see if he's big for his age. Bring him back if he can work. And don't dawdle yakkin' with Prudence about boys, because as soon as you're back I need you and your mom to go into town again."

"Twice in the same month?" Now this was exciting. Katie thought perhaps the Colorado silver strike was going to pay her some dividends after all.

"I want you to put up a sign in Mickel's store advertising for cattlehands. Ask Edward to take another sign over to the saloon—that's likely the first place any men'll stop. Then send a wire to Briscoe, Clay and Archer. Maybe the men there decided goin' to Leadville was too far to risk. While you're gone, I'll get started on the brandin'."

Concern clouded Mary's eyes. "You can't do that by yourself."

"I'll be fine."

Jonas looked down at his biscuit remnant, but he could feel Mary's brown eyes locked on his face. Even her hair, usually a light sandy color that seemed as full of life as Mary, would somehow darken and give rise to an attitude whenever Mary assumed a judgmental pose. He knew she was remembering the last time he'd said those three words—right before Pitch, a wild black stallion, tossed him to the ground in less than a second. He'd wrenched his shoulder enough that Mary had to cut their wood for a week. But he didn't quit and soon made Pitch into a fine mount. He wasn't about to quit this time, either. He turned back to Katie.

"Let me know about Billy before you head into town."

The Hadleys lived in a one-room shack dug into the side of a hill and fronted with patched-together logs. Ruth liked to say that James lost all his gumption digging into that rocky hill. But my father (and just as a reminder, he ran the bank) said James was never one to step forward when there was work to be done. He suspected that Ruth did most of the digging, but her only response when asked about it was to tell me to tell my father that he should lock up his opinions in the vault with the money.

However it was built, the shack sported a short porch made of ash and a few nearby stumps where the trees used to be. As Katie pulled the wagon to a stop, she spotted Prudence Hadley seated on a stump and churning butter. Katie waved at her dear, dear friend.

"I'd wave back," Prudence sighed, "but I swear my arms might fall off."

"Hope your butter sets up better than my biscuits."

Prudence wore a gray dress dusted with dirt and splashes of cream from the churn. Her dark hair was tied back, but strands clung to the sweat on her forehead and neck like old Kiowa scratchings on a stone wall. Still, there was prettiness under the grime. Six months older than Katie and just as sure that she was destined to be an old maid, Prudence had a playful sparkle in her eyes that would certainly turn a man's head if only she'd ever get to go to town and there were actually men there.

Even in her ordinary dress, Katie felt a bit fancy standing beside Prudence and was about to get to eye level by plopping herself onto a stump when Ruth Hadley poked her head out the door. "Who are you – oh, Katie."

"Hi, Mrs. Hadley."

"Is your pa gone to Colorado?"

"No, Ma'am. Home with the cattle."

With a snort of disgust, Ruth slammed the door, startling Katie. For a slight woman, a true example of small-but-wiry, Ruth packed a wallop. Katie turned to Prudence and raised an eyebrow.

"Dad's gone prospecting for silver, and Ma's…"

"Not pleased?" Katie offered.

"One way to put it. Took Billy with him. Nothing left here but me, Ma and chores." With a fierce grunt, Prudence slammed the cream skimmer into the churn. "I swear, I thought I'd be married by 17, but I ain't saying 'I do' to nobody who's gonna run off."

Cattle are happy when chewing, drinking or swallowing. Any other activity is an irritation worthy of a low, whining complaint. Any activity that involves being roped, pulled to the ground, getting legs tied and then being seared with hot metal is downright cause for panicky bawling and angry shakes.

As Jonas released the third branded calf of the morning, the bellows were deafening. He didn't mind. He figured he had his job to do and the cattle had their noises to make. He was far more concerned about the pace. At this rate, without any help, the branding would never be done in time.

He was getting faster, though. His system for solo branding was to ride Pitch into the herd, rope a calf, then loop the rope around the pommel on the saddle. Pitch would pull the calf to two posts Jonas had set in the ground. Jonas would circle the rope around a post to hold the calf steady as he dropped from Pitch and flipped the calf on its side. With another rope, he'd tie the flailing legs, then, finally, he'd raise the Circle B brand from the fire and apply it to the wailing calf. It was the work of four men, and he still held out hope that Katie would return with Billy—and that Billy was big enough to help. He didn't even want to think about trying such a process with a larger unbranded steer.

Hoping doesn't get the work done, so, once again on Pitch, Jonas pulled another calf to the posts. A deep, moaning bellow rose behind him and he glanced back over his shoulder to see one of the cattle staring at him, black-eyed and stern. "Easy, mama," he said as he dropped from his horse. "You'll have your little one back right quick." The cow snorted back.

With practiced hands, Jonas flipped the shrieking calf onto its side. Catching a flailing hind leg, he twirled a rope around it and reached to snatch the other leg when the calf bucked and kicked. Jonas leaned back to avoid the oncoming hoof, losing his balance and slamming his backside to the ground. Whether it was the sudden movement of Jonas falling to a weak position or the bond between mother and child that drove the cow to action is hard to say, but regardless of the reason the black-eyed cow burst toward Jonas like the devil toward a lost soul.

Jonas saw the movement in time to roll onto his stomach and cover his head. He heard the harsh crushing of his hip before he felt the pain shoot through his body in every direction, agony flashing streaks across his eyes like lightning in a prairie. His scream barely registered as his ears filled with the pounding of his heart and another fierce crunch as the frantic cow stomped on his left knee, the weight driving the leg into the hard ground in a direction that God never intended knees to bend.

He writhed in pain and awaited another blast to his body, but the cow's action had spooked Pitch, who bounded to the side, dragging the calf with him. The cow ran past Jonas and chased Pitch, stopping as the rope loosened from the saddle and the calf broke free. As quick as the fury had risen, it quieted. The cow nuzzled her calf. It rose and walked with her, still bleating from fear, back to the herd, dragging the remains of the rope behind it.

Even if there was someone to nuzzle Jonas, he wasn't about to get to his feet and walk away. All the damage was on his left side, and the pain seared deeper than any brand. His hip, his knee—whatever was left of them—were torment and agony. Just the thought of rolling over intensified the pain, yet he knew he must check for bleeding. Teeth clenched, his mind braced for shards of pain, he turned his body. Lightning again flashed from his legs to his eyes before the bright sunburst of pain flamed into darkness.

His next memory was awakening in Doctor Galen's office.

Chapter 4

Doc Galen would never be rich, but he was the most valued person within forty miles of Secluded Springs in any direction. White-haired, the essence of calm as he worked, he'd delivered countless babies—myself included—and removed countless bullets. Mary couldn't pray right then, but she knew when she did later that she'd offer up thanks to God for providing Doc.

For now, Mary held Jonas's cold hands as Doc cut through the trousers to expose the wounds. For a moment, her mind shifted her worries to the price of a new pair of pants, but just as quickly she chastised herself for letting her thoughts move to anything but her husband's welfare. He was pale, unconscious. He hadn't even awakened as she and Katie had dragged and none-to-gently lifted him onto the buckboard as best as they could. Jonas. Her Jonas. His cold hands in hers. His blood on her dress.

His life in Doc's hands.

The doctor sensed the emotions rising in Mary. He'd seen it time and again. People take action when a tragedy occurs and do what needs done, but then the feelings rush back to the surface. Katie lingered at the back of the room, her sniffling now on the verge of weeping. With a soothing tone developed through years of experience, he stemmed the tide.

"Don't you ladies fret. He's alive. He's gonna stay that way. You did just fine getting him here in time."

Mary wiped back a tear. "If Katie hadn't ridden by…"

"But she did. And she got you. And you got Jonas here. You did everything right. Now it's my turn."

Peeling away the trousers, the doctor began to run his hands across the leg.

"Katie, how are you at making coffee?"

"Fair or better, I guess."

"I could use some, if you don't mind. Water and stove's in the other room."

Katie shuffled out as the doctor continued his examination. Mary noted that the leg was a rainbow from hip to ankle, purple, yellow, red. None of the colors pretty. She didn't like the look of it, and truly didn't like the way Doc lingered over the knee.

"He'll keep the leg," Doc said at last. "But let's hope he stays out cold. What I need to do to this knee won't be pleasant."

"What can I do?"

14

"You can hold him down if needed. I'd appreciate that, though he may not. Better send Katie somewhere. When Jonas wakes up, he'll be screaming something fierce and I know his pride won't want Katie to see him that way."

"I'll send her to Sally's."

"Good." The doctor rose up from examining Jonas and looked Mary in the eyes. "There's more. He won't be riding anytime soon. Walking either for that matter. So you're gonna need to look after both him and the ranch. If I know Jonas, he won't stay tied to the bed if there's ranch work."

"I'll do it."

"I'll help, too." They hadn't seen Katie come back in. Doc gave her a warm smile and Mary placed her warm hand on Katie's shoulder.

"Jonas surrounded himself with some fine women," said Doc as he reached for the coffee from Katie. "I'd say you're both stronger than you know." His eyebrows rose at the taste of the coffee and he gave Katie a wink. "Almost as strong as this coffee."

As the afternoon came to a close, Jonas was still unconscious and Doc Galen was pleased by it. "He's healing," he told Mary, "and you watching him won't speed it up. Go get some rest."

Mary was too tired to protest and knew chores were piling up at home, but leaving didn't seem right. Doc gave her the final push she needed. "I'm asking you to leave so that I can take a nap."

"But if Jonas wakes…"

"I'll tell him you'll see him in the morning. And I doubt he'll wake till then anyway."

So Mary returned to the wagon, intending to stop by Sally's to get Katie and then go home for the night. In the wagon she saw the two posters she'd written up for Jonas. *Cattle Ranch Hands Wanted. Apply at Bartlett Ranch.* No sense waiting a day to put them up. She needed help now more than ever.

In Mickel's store, she found Ed rearranging a shelf of hats and Ernestine trying each one on just for something to do. Both Ed and Ernestine turned at the sound of the door, ready to pounce on a rare customer. They settled for giving Mary sympathetic smiles and trying not to look at the blood on her dress.

"Terrible sorry to hear about Jonas, Mary. He's in good hands with Doc, though."

"Thanks, Ed. Would you mind putting this in your window?"

Ed took the poster, really just a small piece of paper, and looked it over. "Don't know who'll be around to see it, but I'll sure put it up."

"I appreciate it. And would you send a wire with the same information to Briscoe, Clay and Archer?"

"Bet they emptied out, same as us."

"Worth a try." In the light of the moment and her current situation, Ed's gray hair didn't seem so gray. "You used to ride, didn't you, Ed?"

"Don't even think it," Ed was quick to protest. "I became a storekeeper so I wouldn't have to be around smelly cattle and eat dust. I wish you luck though."

"We'll need it. I thank you for hangin' the sign and sendin' the wires." As she turned to leave, she noticed Ernestine holding a black Stetson hat. "Not sure if that hat's your color, Ernestine."

Ernestine put the hat to her mouth to stifle her high-pitched giggle.

As Mary left, she remembered she was supposed to give Ed the other poster to take over to the Castle Royal saloon. No, she thought, I'm going right by it and I need to be doing more things for myself. Besides, she'd always wondered what it looked like in there.

Charlie Firemark opened the Castle Royal in 1848 and now, 30 years later, Charlie Jr. ran the place. The original Charlie was killed during a robbery and Charlie the third, I'm sad to say, barely lived long enough to have a name. When Charlie Jr.'s wife lost her battle with unhappiness and died just a year later, Charlie was tempted to drown his sorrows with the stock inside the Castle Royal but instead made a family out of the saloon girls. It was a family built on survival rather than love, and the girls often left at a hint of a suggestion of maybe a promise of a possible life with a passing cowhand, but other girls would come along and join the family. That Charlie took a hefty cut of the money they earned taking men upstairs was accepted as the price paid for room and board. With the exception of baking pies for the funeral dinners, Mary knew little of Charlie's history. Jonas enjoyed a drink with the men every four, five months and had said Charlie was a good man. All she needed from Charlie right now was a place to hang the sign where hopefully some future Bartlett Ranch cattlehands would come upon it. Yet, standing on the saloon's wooden porch, so near to the faded "Drink Like A King" sign at the left of the swinging doors, she hesitated. The swinging doors were short, but they seemed to loom over her like giant barricades that should not be breached by the likes of her. The doors led to another world, a world where men drank and gambled and smoked and did whatever they could pay for with women. Mary was the first to admit that she was no fancy lady born into high society, but she was a decent woman who had no reason to lower her head. So she did what any decent woman would do at the doors of a saloon.

She knocked.

The sound of a knock at the door was so uncommon, perhaps even unprecedented, that Charlie almost lifted the week-old newspaper from his face and rose from his nap. Since uncommon didn't necessarily mean interesting, however, he chose not to move. "See what that is. I'm busy."

Pearl gave him a look that was wasted on the paper, but since answering the door was something she had never done before and was beyond a doubt going to be far more intriguing than her endless games of Solitaire, she glided to the front and pushed open one of the swinging doors.

"Oh." Seeing a woman like Mary on the doorstep... now that was interesting, especially since Mary was disheveled, tired and had blood on her dress. Pearl had never felt better dressed than a decent woman before. Still, she waited for the berating that was sure to come. Every now and then one of the town's women—often a group of them—felt the need to give Charlie's girls a piece of her mind. It usually started with "harlot" and went south from there until the woman ran out of steam. She braced herself for the tongue-lashing.

"Hi, I'm Mary Bartlett. Miss, uh...?"

"Pearl." Not only not a tongue-lashing, but calling her "Miss?"

"I was hoping perhaps Charlie might display this poster, Pearl. In case anyone passing through stops by."

Pearl took the paper, read it, and smiled back at Mary. "I'll see that he does."

"Thank you for your kindness." Mary nodded with a warm smile, then turned and walked away. Pearl lingered in the doorway, watching her go.

"Who was it?" Charlie asked from beneath his paper.

"Mrs. Bartlett."

Ellie bounced her chest and grinned. "You tell her we ain't hirin'?"

Pearl ignored the chuckles from Charlie and Ellie. She watched Mary get farther away and tried to recall the last time a regular woman had spoken to her in a way that hadn't made her feel low and ashamed. Nothing came to mind.

That night, while Mary's bed seemed big and empty, her mind was full. Katie had met her in front of Sally's shop and on the ride home she'd told Katie all that Doc had told her. Katie had promised to do her part, to take on even more chores and push her boy-hungry thoughts to the side while Jonas recovered. Mary was proud of her daughter's conviction, and she also knew it wasn't enough. She and Katie could not run the ranch without help.

It clouded her mind. She felt there was more she could do, yet she also knew that Jonas needed help, so it was only right that she should need help too. But from where? Would anyone see her posters? Would anyone come from the other towns?

She slid to Jonas's side of the bed and smelled his scent upon the pillow. She breathed it in deep. Nighttime was when Jonas had his best ideas. Perhaps the night would send her a guiding thought. She said a silent prayer of thanks for Jonas's life, for Katie finding him, for Doc Galen's knowledge, and for Jonas's scent upon the pillow. She drifted away wishing his head was on the pillow as well.

Chapter 5

The next morning found Mary at her small mirror, smoothing the wrinkles in her best dress. It was a flowered print that was saved for special occasions—or, as in this case, whenever her regular dress was splotched with blood. Her reasons for the dress went beyond necessity. She wanted Jonas to see her at her best. And she wanted to look nice for my father. He was the idea that came to her overnight.

She was adjusting her bonnet when Katie rushed in carrying a bucket. "Wagon's hitched, chickens fed, eggs gathered and Henrietta's milked, ornery old thing. Can we please go see Pa now?"

"Put the milk in the root cellar to keep cool. Might be a while before we're back."

Katie sighed but did her mom's bidding. In a little over an hour, they were in front of the doctor's office.

"You go ahead," Mary said. "I'll be along soon."

"Don't you wanna see Pa?"

"I want to bring him some good news. Most likely he could use some."

The Secluded Springs Bank was small but sturdy. There were two offices in the back, one of which housed the safe. There was one teller window in the front and due to circumstances beyond my control, I was the teller standing behind it. Now that you finally get to meet me, I suppose I owe it to you to describe myself. I was 20 then and had turned away enough gentlemen callers to know I was pretty (though my being the banker's daughter was likely the attraction for some). My hair was light brown with a tinge of red, and my attitude was decidedly unpleasant because I was as bored as can be.

Mary's smile and bright dress burned off some of the fog I was in.

"Good to see you, Mary. I'm so sorry to hear about Jonas getting hurt."

"Thank you, Laurie. Takin' over for Fred today?"

"He's like every other thick-headed man around here. Took off for Leadville to make his fortune. Daddy says I have to work the window until Fred wises up and comes back." I gave her my best there-has-to-be-more-to-life-than-this smile. "It's not exactly boiling over with activity."

"Then perhaps your father would have time to meet with me."

My father—Mr. Lawrence Michaels—is small and thin but with a voice and gestures bigger than any room he's in. He is also a patient, thoughtful listener and he gave Mary his full attention as she sat on the edge of the wooden chair across from his desk.

"So, as you can see, a slight extension of the mortgage is all I'm asking. Just enough to see us through fall and winter. Jonas'll be ready to sell the cattle next summer."

"Mary —"

"By then the men will be back and —"

"Mary."

Before my father could get going on a speech, Mary squared her shoulders and got to what was, for her, the bottom line. "You know we're good for it, Mr. Michaels. We've never missed a payment."

It was also the bottom line for my father.

"That's just the thing, Mary. It's Jonas that's made the payments, not you. It's Jonas that I've banked on."

"We're a family and Jonas —"

"And Jonas is hobbled. Maybe worse than hobbled."

"Doctor Galen is confident that —"

"Doc is a fine man and in any other year his confidence might be enough. My business is risk, calculated risk. And with so many folks taking out their savings for a wild silver chase, I have no room for more risk. I also have a responsibility to my shareholders. I'm sorry, Mary. I'm a banker, not a gambler. I cannot add to or extend the loan any further. Please understand that when the note comes due in its full amount in the fall, though I won't enjoy a second of it, I'll have to foreclose."

I'm trying to be as true to the facts as I can in this story, so I must confess to listening at the office door. When I heard my father's chair scoot back, I scurried back to my post, both understanding of my father yet sickened by his position. A banker's daughter can afford to see both sides, whereas a banker doesn't have that luxury.

The door opened and Mary strode past me with a quick nod. I wanted to reach out and tell her how sorry I was that life was piling up on her, but she was out the door just like that. I turned back to see my father standing in his doorway.

"I suppose you were listening at the door."

"Yes, sir. Just to hear Mary. Your voice carries enough."

He shook his head, turned back into his office and slammed his door, no doubt asking himself if any of the money he'd paid to send me to finishing school in St. Louis had been money well spent.

If Jonas had said "fine" when she asked him how he was doing, then Mary would have known he was in a lot of pain. But since he said "I'm all right," she knew the pain was considerable indeed. The more his emphasis on how well he was doing, the worse he was. That made it hard for her to fill him in on her plan to save the ranch by extending the loan, and even harder to let him know it didn't work.

"So no money from Mr. Michaels," she summed up. "But he does wish you his best."

"I can feel his kind thoughts healing me already."

Jonas shifted in an attempt to rise, but the clear burst of pain caused him, Mary, Katie and Doc to all wince. His tan had already turned to cream. Now any remaining color drained away.

"Now you just settle in for a long rest," said Doc. "There's no hurrying this. Kind thoughts are exactly what you need. Your own."

"My side tells me not to move, Doc. But the rest of me knows that layin' here won't pay the mortgage."

"Neither will doing something stupid and losing that leg. I can get you whiskey and laudanum for the pain, but the only cure for the damage is time. So let me put my doctoring instructions in the simplest terms possible: don't move 'til I tell you."

"Maybe the wires I sent will work," said Mary. "Or some hands will happen along."

"That's the spirit," said the doctor, his eyes bright and sparkling. "Who's the finest man in north Texas? Next to me, of course."

"My husband."

Doc turned to Jonas. "And who's the finest woman."

Jonas smiled. "My beautiful bride."

"Exactly. God won't let two fine people like yourselves stay down for long. Something'll happen, an idea'll come along."

Katie's voice was sad and thoughtful. "I could try to find a job, but I don't think there's a soul hirin' right now." Then she brightened. "Maybe I'll meet a rich young man!"

"There," said Doc as his smile grew. "New ideas are springing up already."

Mary and Jonas could only look at Katie with the mixture of love and weariness that parents everywhere understand but their children never do.

Katie immediately went on the defensive, hands on hips, nose in the air. "I might. I happen to be quite a catch."

Jonas tired quickly and it wasn't long before Doc scooted Mary and Katie out the door. Mary knew the injuries contributed, but that it was also the thoughts of losing the ranch that wearied her husband. They wearied her, too. She needed to talk and the fortunate thing about being in town was that her friend, Sally, was right down the street.

After sending Katie on an unnecessary errand ("Go down to Mickel's to see if anyone's stopped by. I'll be along soon." "But Ma, you were just by there." "Go anyway."), she made a beeline for the seamstress shop. Sally was working her sewing machine, but she took her feet off the pedals and rushed to meet Mary when she heard the door.

"Mary! Oh, it's so good to see you. I've been meaning to visit, I really have. It's just..." Her voice and smile faded for a flash of a second before returning. "Oh, pay me no mind. How's Jonas?"

"Bad. Better, but bad."

"His leg?" She led Mary to her sitting area.

"Doc says it should heal eventually. It's his spirits that worry me, Sally. He thinks he's let Katie and me down. I don't know of an answer to clear his mind of it."

Sally patted Mary's leg and gave her a small grin. "He's a worrier, same as you. It all comes from caring too much." There was always a calm practicality about Sally. She was what some people called a handsome woman rather than pretty, though that's a term I still think of as manly. There was nothing manly about Sally, except that a woman in her mid-twenties shouldn't look as weary as Sally often did. "Plus, all he has right now is time to think."

"Time to think'd sure be a luxury to me." Mary wiped back an oncoming tear. "My big idea is writing 'help me' on papers no one's around to see."

"I ain't much brighter, making dresses for no one to buy."

Silence in the presence of a friend is comforting, and the two basked in it for a moment. It seemed that each had more to say but lacked the energy to say it. Sally poured Mary a glass of water, then broke the silence as she lowered the pitcher.

"Henry left again."

"Oh, Sally. For the silver?"

"Before then. Just disappeared like before. No word."

"You poor thing." Mary took her hand and they drew strength from each other. "Where do dreams go? They seem so close and then..."

Now it was Sally's turn to wipe away a tear with the sleeve of her dress. "I don't know. Maybe it's up to us to go find 'em, 'cause they sure don't stay close."

The late afternoon sun shone red behind Mary and Katie as they rode the old wagon on the weathered trail toward home. Katie had never been shy about asking questions and she stayed true to form.

"What are we gonna do?"

"Same thing women have always done. Whatever it takes."

"What does that mean?"

"It means the cattle need to get to market to get us the money to save the ranch and care for your father. So we get the cattle to market."

"But how?"

That, of course, was the question for which Mary had no ready answer. As sleep overtook her that night, an answer still seemed far away.

At the dusty slide-click of a horse's hoof, Mary woke at once. Years on the range had taught her to distinguish unusual sounds even in the deepest sleep, and that sound didn't belong. A foot shuffled. Human. Definitely didn't belong.

Mary sprang from her bed and snatched Jonas's pistol from a holster hanging on a nail. Katie appeared at her side. "I heard it, too."

All senses alert, they pushed open the hanging quilts and strained to listen over the sound of their racing hearts. It was well before sunrise, that time of day where the glow has begun deep on the horizon but the moonlight, if any, still dominates. The moon was slight, and the two women could see no movement through the two small windows.

In the dim light that entered their home, Katie could see Mary motion toward the door with a knowing look. Katie understood. She lowered the rifle from the rack above the door frame and tip-toed back to her mother.

Even in the summer, the room felt cold to them after leaving their warm beds and the unknown cause of the noise increased the chill. Mary's mind raced through possibilities. Indians? The army and the Rangers had pretty much established an uneasy peace with the Mescalero Apaches, and their settlement was more than 70 miles away, but there was always the threat of a rogue war party. Bandits? Murderers? Worse than murderers? It was all guesswork and she needed answers.

Gesturing for Katie to take the far window, she crept up to the other. The weight of the gun kept her right hand from shaking. The left hand tapped at her thigh. She nodded at Katie and together they eased up and peered out. Against the small pink oval of the waking sun, they could make out several silhouettes. The two women must have been more visible than they thought, because one of the silhouettes began to wave with girlish joy.

"Hi, Katie!" shouted Prudence. "We're your new cattlehands!"

Chapter 6

"You scared us half to death."

Mary had everyone inside now. She'd changed out of her nightclothes, splashed water on her face and sipped some of the coffee Ruth had made. She gave all of us—Ruth, Prudence, Sally and myself—a look that was somehow appreciative and dismissive at the same time. We likely did look out of place in our dresses, fresh-scrubbed and ironed as if we were off to Sunday church.

"We might've been a bit overanxious about getting out here," said Sally. "But we were gonna wait 'til sunup before telling you our idea."

"Well it's the craziest idea I ever heard."

"I think we could do it, Ma," Katie spoke up.

"Now don't you start. Six women driving cattle." I thought she might spit, but she locked her gaze on me instead. "Laurie Michaels, why would you even think about leaving your father and the bank?"

"There's more to life than being the banker's daughter. Things I want to do, new towns I'd like to see." It was the first time I'd said out loud what I'd been feeling for the past few years. It felt good.

"Same goes for me, Mary," Sally chimed in. "I'd like to open a real dress shop, see rich ladies wearin' my designs…"

"We ain't moved a cow past the barn and you're already opening up a new store in a big city. We ain't there quite yet." She pointed the hand with the coffee cup at Ruth. "Don't tell me sixty days of eating dust and sleeping on the ground appeals to you, Ruth."

"It sure don't. But slavin' away here while that no-good man of mine is out adventuring… it galls me."

"You're barely 90 pounds."

"You're sellin' cattle, not me." Ruth squared her shoulders and made her stick-figure frame look as big as she could. "And I'm wiry — I'll hold up."

"Mrs. Bartlett?" It was Prudence's turn.

"I know, Prudence. You want an adventure and you want to find a man."

"Yes, ma'am. But what I really wanted to say was, we're all you got. We're here and we're willin'."

I must confess that Prudence was someone I'd never given much thought. She was pleasant in the times I'd met her, but she not only said things that didn't strike me as very bright, she also had a tone in her voice that always made her sound like she just woke up. Words came out slowly and had a kind of echo that implied they came out of an empty head. But in this particular instance I thought she stated our case as well as anyone. Everyone did, because heads were nodding all around. Even Mary had slowed her protest. She just needed one more little push to move her off her hard stance and I had the key fact to balance Prudence's simple statement.

"It's business first with my father, Mary. Even if he hates doing it, he will foreclose."

"We have to try," added Katie. "For Pa. For the ranch."

Mary looked us over, face by face, seeing nothing but earnestness and a desire for action. Her shoulders dropped slowly as her lips curled in a grin of resignation. "One day. We'll try it for one day."

That moment we became the first cattlehands in history to hug each other in excitement. We stood together, embraced in our bright dresses and in the bravery that women share when banded arm in arm. The now-orange morning sun poured through the east window upon our smiling faces, and we basked in it. None of us thought about how many miles we had to travel or how much dust we'd have to swallow. We didn't think about storms or rustlers or Indian Territory or snakes or hunger or any of the hundred other dangers we could very well be facing. Some of us, and I count myself in this category, had our selfish reasons for wanting to get on the move, but the top reason for all of us, the heart of our bond, was pure: we wanted to help our friends.

"You'll likely regret jumpin' in with me," Mary said with watery eyes. "I've never been farther than 30 miles from here since we started the ranch. But I love you all for this."

Of course that led to another round of hugs, perhaps not what normal cattlehands mean by "another round," but no one would ever accuse our troupe of being normal.

Sally had been the instigator. It had felt so good for her to talk with Mary. The pains in their lives were different, but their willingness to take each other's pain into their hearts had turned their friendship into a bond. A little over a year earlier, the second time that Henry had disappeared from Sally without a word, she went to the house and cried in Mary's arms. Up until then, only Mary had known that Sally was keeping company with Henry. No matter Sally's skills with a needle and thread, if the pious women of the town, the ones that shared tea with my mother, had known of Sally's unmarried relations, her business would've been lost. The gap between decency and scandal was the size of a wedding band. The difference between Sally's life and the life of a saloon girl like Pearl was her seamstress business. Sally could support herself with the shades pulled up.

If you understand what makes a woman love a man who doesn't deserve her love, then I question your honesty with yourself. I don't think there's any explaining it. For some women, there's just a pull inside, and Sally was pulled toward Henry enough that she left the back door unlocked. Whenever Henry tired of work on the tiny farm he'd run since his parents died, the doorknob turned. But Henry was just as apt to hop on his horse and ride in any direction the wind took him. A few years of that had worn on Sally, and when she'd blinked away the tears she'd cried in Mary's arms that day, she was struck by the most simple sight. Jonas and Katie were in the kitchen cooking eggs. He wasn't just there for his wife, but for his wife's friend. And he was helping, not demanding. She could easily have been jealous of her friend, but as you'd expect if you knew Sally, she was happy for Mary. Moreover, what Mary had was proof to Sally that it could be had.

So as Mary left the seamstress shop the day before we all surprised her at the ranch, Sally thought a lot about helping her friend keep together something so beautiful. Then she thought of a way to do it that would also help her break free of the sad pattern she was locked into. She came to the bank and asked me to have lunch with her. While Mary and Katie visited with Jonas in Doc's office, Sally told me her idea and asked about my willingness to help.

"Before you answer," she said, "let me say that I'm going no matter what. I need a fresh start, so whether it's on a stagecoach or a cattle drive, I'm goin'." I didn't know about Henry at that time, but I understood what she meant about needing a fresh start. If there was a means to get away from turning down the dullards more interested in my father's bank than me, I was for it. I suppose there's a chance I would have been happy to please my parents and settle down in Secluded Springs with the right man—about the same chance of a stallion preferring to pull a wagon rather than run free. I was no stallion, but I was also no pack mule. I was ready to run free, even if I didn't know where to or what for.

I gave Sally my best smile. "Either way, I'm going with you."

Adding Ruth and Prudence to the scheme was easy. Anything that had a hint of spite toward her wandering husband appealed to Ruth, and Prudence would do anything that got her away from their little shack.

Less than a day later, we were on horseback and heading toward the cattle herd.

The basics of driving cattle are as simple as it gets (which begs me to say that's why men are so good at it). Just box in the cattle and move them forward. We understood that. What we didn't appreciate about the task until we tried it was that cattle aren't always interested in being boxed in and moved forward. A long life of wandering around eating grass and brush would suit them just fine.

Also, while the idea behind the job was easy, we would soon learn that the hard part was the physical toll. Spend a full day from sunup to sundown in the saddle, baking under the hot sun, choking on the dust-filled air and inhaling the foulness that longhorns can produce, and the seemingly simple task of moving cows from here to there becomes anything but.

However, I'm getting ahead of myself. All we cared about that first morning was proving to Mary that she could put her faith in us. We rode past the corral and the empty bunkhouse out to one of the fields of grazing cattle. Most ignored us, but a few looked up with stern stares, mouths chomping on sweet grass, as if to say, "Keep moving. We're doing just fine on our own."

"There," Mary pointed. "That little group of eight. That's our test. If the six of us can't move a herd of eight from there to that ash tree yonder, then we surely can't drive cattle to market."

"Seems simple enough," said Sally.

We all nodded agreement.

And we all did nothing. I think it went through most of our minds that this was now something real. Not a single thing about it seemed all that difficult, yet it was a task and any task brings the risk of failure. As long as we didn't move, we couldn't let Mary down.

A different thought went through Mary's mind, a thought that was just as paralyzing. *They're waiting for me. I'm the leader now.* It was a role she'd never experienced or even ever considered. At that moment a spark lit within her. The flint was her home and family and the steel was her memory of telling Katie that a woman will do whatever it takes.

"Sally. Ruth. Loop around to the far side. Laurie and Prudence, take this side. Katie and I will push them forward."

Her voice may have warbled a bit, but I don't recall it that way. It felt good to have our first orders, and we all moved into position. We went from nervous to eager and the cattle sensed the change. Two drifted ahead of Sally, but she pushed her horse around to coax them back to the center. That movement startled a steer and it rumbled ahead—exactly in the direction we wanted.

"Follow that one!" shouted Mary from the rear of the grouping. The noise alarmed the remaining cattle and as we urged our mounts forward the cattle moved with us. We were doing it! We were herding cattle! It didn't matter that it took six of us to move eight steers maybe 75 feet to a shade tree. All that mattered was a taste of success.

I took a glance back at Mary. She was smiling, probably her first full smile since Jonas was injured. "Turn 'em left at the tree," she shouted. "Let's see if we can guide them back."

All that morning those eight steers were our guinea pigs. We moved them around the field and when one would try to break away, one of us always brought it back. Mary's confidence grew and we looped in two more steers. Then a cow and a calf. We wore a path in the pasture and likely had our horses wondering if we ever planned to go anywhere. By the arrival of the noon sun our dresses were soaked with sweat and we didn't mind at all. The calf squirted free between me and Prudence and I was about to chase it down when Mary shouted, "Let it go! That's enough for now."

Leave it to Prudence to ask the question on all of our minds. "What do you think, Mrs. Bartlett? Satisfied with your new ranch hands?"

Mary matched her movement from the early morning, once again gliding her head slowly from face to face. Then she nodded. "If you're still willin', then I am, too."

We were feeling more like cattlehands every second, so there were no hugs this time. Just smiles all around. Besides, we were on horses.

We rode in silence back toward the house, a sense of triumph in the air. To any observer, we'd sure have been an odd-looking team. None of us had spent much time on horseback, mostly riding on buckboards. Now the bulk of us rode sidesaddle like ladies. Sally had the longest dress and it wasn't easily noticeable that she straddled the horse like a man. Ruth's dress rode up a little more and it was obvious by the little bit of skinny white leg exposed above her boot that she also rode straddle. The cattle didn't appear scandalized by it.

At the house, Mary was the first to dismount. We all had sort of lined up behind her and she gave us a good, hard stare.

"I suppose I look as silly as the rest of you."

"What do you mean?" asked Katie.

"If you weren't covered with dirt and sweat, you'd look more like you're heading to a barn dance than a cattle drive. Not a one of us looks like a cattlehand."

"Maybe we need hats," offered Sally.

I pictured us looking splendid in fancy cowboy hats with wide brims and figured we might as well add another touch. "Oh, and a pretty little kerchief."

"Not what I had in mind," said Mary. "Something we need even more."

Edward's neck veins bulged like blood-filled ticks. "Pants?!!" His hands moved from his hips to the countertop. He needed the support. "But not for Jonas? For you?" He shook his head as if his brain had come unhitched and he needed to snap it back into place. "It don't make no sense."

Mary started to speak but Edward wasn't through trying to get his mind to comprehend what his ears were hearing. "You mean britches? For you? What are you, Calamity Jane?"

"No, and I ain't Joan of Arc neither. I simply want to purchase some work pants in my size." She gestured to the window where we women were peeking in with interest. Naturally I was closest to the door and listening to every word. Katie's eyes were wide. She wasn't used to seeing her mother so worked up.

"Oh, you mean material so you can sew up some work pants."

"No, I mean ready-made work pants. I'd love for Sally to sew us up a fine set, but there isn't time." She shifted her tone. "But maybe you've been so busy making sales lately that you don't need our business."

"Now there's no need to get on a high horse. You come in here asking for work pants that'll fit a woman, you gotta expect... well, it just ain't a phrase I heard before."

Ernestine had been looking on with interest. "There's those newfangled blue ones that came in from San Francisco, Grandpa." She turned to Mary. "They're called waist overalls. Made out of denim."

"They'd be good work pants at that," added Edward. "Thick. The miners call them blue jeans."

Mary pointed toward us at the window. "You got sizes for my cattlehands?"

"What? Oh, now, Mary, I don't have time for games. Business is tough enough these —"

"It's no game, Edward. I've got a ranch to save and the only ranch hands available are those you see right there. Now I need six pair of those waist overalls."

"Mary —"

"Do you have an extra skinny pair for Ruth?"

Edward threw up his arms in exasperation. "All right, I'll play along. Go pick out six pair." Mary turned toward the trousers but had to stop when Edward tossed out an ominous "However" that hung in the air like a frost moon. He laid out his conditions. "I need cash up front. I don't give credit for hare-brained schemes."

"But —"

"I thought Michaels was a bit harsh with his banking decision, but it seems a chunk more sensible now."

"Edward —"

"No cash, no pants."

Outside the store, we all surrounded Mary. First she was fuming. "He'll only take cash." Then she was forgiving. "Can't blame him, I guess."

"Should've robbed the bank before I left," I mumbled.

Cash money was always hard to come by, but especially of late with a lot less people spreading it around. We stood in silence for just a moment, not yet thinking but getting our minds set on the idea of thinking, when a voice came from just around the corner of the store.

"Mrs. Bartlett?"

We could see part of a woman's face peeking around, most of it in shadow. I caught a glimpse of chestnut hair and a blue eye, but had no idea who it was. Fortunately, Mary recognized her.

"Pearl? Pearl, come on out."

Now before I relate any more of that part of our story or the events that will follow, I feel compelled to offer up a warning. Up till now, things have been pretty cozy. You may have read about the harshness of Jonas's trampling or seen some grouchiness or wished my father hadn't taken a hard line, but overall everyone you've heard about has been cordial. That's not me writing it that way; it's just the way things were. And as I'm committed to sharing this story as close to the truth as my capabilities allow, I must warn you that some harsh language and some indelicate conversations and descriptions about the... well, let's just say the curvy parts of a woman... will begin occurring soon. I am a decent woman, but also a truthful one and I promised all involved that this would be a truthful account. I'm sure there's nothing in this story that an adult cannot abide, but I put out this warning so that if you're reading aloud to young ones you'll know in advance to replace some words or skip over certain parts. I thank you for indulging this interruption and return you now to Pearl's appearance before the women outside Mickel's General Store.

"Why it's that, that whore!" bellowed Ruth with a volume surprising from a woman the size of my leg. There was fire in her eyes and I think she might have hauled off and walloped Pearl in the nose if Mary hadn't asserted her newfound leadership status.

"Hush up, Ruth. There's no good to come from that." It likely also helped that Mary positioned herself between Ruth and Pearl. As Pearl stepped out from the shadow, Mary moved closer. Ruth was right on her tail.

"I'm sorry to be talking with you in public."

"It's fine, Pearl. Go on."

"It's just that... I'd like to join your drive."

Ruth's mouth was too dry to spit, but her scoff was loud and clear.

"I can ride good," Pearl continued. "I don't eat much."

"Ain't no room for the likes of you!" Ruth roared again. If we'd known more about being cattlehands, we'd have known to pull her away and let the boss handle things. But we didn't know much, so we watched as Mary silenced Ruth with a hard stare.

Though Pearl's eyes were on the ground, it was clear she was seeing the past. "I don't blame you for hatin' me, Ma'am. It's part of why I'd like to go where nobody knows me." She looked up at Mary with pure sincerity. "I'll work hard. And I can pay my own way." She reached into the top of her dress and pulled out a handful of cash. The whole lot of us had the same flashing thought: there's good money in sin. She held it out to Mary. "Ninety-three dollars I've saved. You can have it if you'll take me on."

Mary looked at the pile of bills, then into Pearl's eyes, then into our eyes. Then she smiled. "Come on, ladies. We're going shopping." She grabbed the money from Pearl's hands and motioned Ruth to the doorway. Ruth was too steamed up to give Pearl the cold shoulder.

The rest of us had varying reactions. Sally didn't pay Pearl much mind. I can't say I was comfortable with Pearl as a team member, but I gave her credit for being up front about her desires and in particular for having cash money. Katie just did whatever her mother told her and walked into the store without a look at Pearl. Prudence was unsure how to react, as part of her was thrilled about the money and part of her was troubled by her mother's reaction to Pearl. It was clear that Ruth would be the hardest to convince that adding Pearl was anything but the worst decision of Mary's life.

As we entered the store, Pearl held back. Mary was the last to enter and turned around to Pearl with an inquiring look. After a swallow of hesitation, Pearl spoke up. "Never been through the front door."

Mary smiled and held out her hand. "Come on. You're one of us now." The most vicious pain imaginable couldn't have brought tears to Pearl's eyes faster than that moment of tenderness. To be treated as a normal human being was a rarity for Pearl. But to be welcomed? To have a respected woman reach out to her? She had no memory of such kindness. Even if she never experienced it again, she'd hang onto this instant for the rest of her life.

She took Mary's hand and followed her into the store.

The last time Mickel's General Store had known such squeals of utter giddiness, a family passing through had brought their twelve kids in for candy. The waist overalls were made for men, but we combed through the shipment to find sizes as close to our needs as possible. We added cotton work shirts to our wardrobe and took turns changing in the back room. I had never known such comfort existed, and I wasn't alone in my thinking.

"No wonder men dress like this," said Katie as she admired herself in the single mirror.

We were all admiring ourselves and each other. You see, a dress that's tailor-made like one of Sally's can give you a reasonable idea of woman's figure. And certainly a floosie's outfit like Ellie wore in Charlie's saloon left little to the imagination. But most dresses were made to cover, not display. Mary had made pleasant dresses for her and Katie, but nothing that would show off their womanly features. Ruth was no hand at sewing and had little fabric to work with, so the dresses she and Prudence wore were only slightly more refined than sacks. My parents had purchased fine-made outfits for me, but you could bet the last nickel to your name that my father wasn't about to have his daughter in anything but the most conservative clothing. Now here we were, our new shirts tucked into our new trousers right at the waist. Even as tiny as she was, Ruth had hips! Sally's shirt sloped out from her neck and took a lot of fabric to slope back into her waist, where her pants sloped right back out again — as fine an hourglass figure as you can imagine. And Pearl! Oh my. It was easy to see how that wad of cash wasn't at risk of falling through.

Even Ruth was smiling for the moment. She couldn't take her eyes off Prudence and Katie. They'd walked into the store as girls, but now she saw them as women. "You two are a vision, I swear."

We all felt like visions, and poor Ernestine stood there with her plain face and plain dress feeling like an outsider in her own store. Mary was the only one of us able to keep a practical mind. "Hope they're durable. It's one outfit apiece for the whole drive." Edward's price of $1.25 per pair was hard to swallow, but not as hard as a cattle drive wearing dresses.

While Ernestine took it all in, Edward was half hiding his eyes and half unable to look away. He knew us all well, including Pearl, who he'd served through the back door on occasion. Something about seeing us in a different kind of clothing seemed to heat him up. Sweat dotted his forehead. His mouth was dry. He kept putting his fingers to his eyes and then spreading them apart to give us another gaze that, in turn, inspired more dots of sweat. When I later asked him to recall the moment, he said only that he must've been bothered by our shameful display. I think he was bothered all right, but in an entirely different way. Edward was old, but not that old.

In the back corner by the mirror, Pearl stood transfixed by her reflection. Though she was still a young woman, years of shame and self-loathing had left their marks. There was a hard edge to her cheekbones, a bit of hollowness to her eyes, a slouch to her shoulders. None of those traits disappeared because of new pants and a shirt, but the image of herself in that mirror had knocked back some of the walls she'd built around herself. She was lost in peaceful contemplation. She glowed.

Katie was drawn to her. "Miss Pearl? You okay?"

"I feel… I feel brand new."

Leave it to Ruth to break the reverie. She grabbed Katie by the arm and pulled her away. "Changin' her clothes don't change her ways. You keep away from that man stealer."

Once again Pearl lowered her head in shame, and once again Mary rushed in to quell the storm. "None of that now. We got a hard time ahead, Ruth. Let's not make it harder fighting with each other."

Ruth held her scowl on Pearl for another few seconds, then turned and gave Mary an almost imperceptible nod of concession. Tension still hung in the air, and I would have expected a quiet moment if I hadn't spotted Ernestine about to burst.

"I wanna go, too!" she shouted, unable to hold back any longer.

The shrillness of her voice, not to mention her words, drove Edward's temperature up another notch. "What?!"

"I want to be part of it! The drive, being with you ladies. Wearing pants and looking curvy."

"Now just a —" Edward stopped short when—bam!— Ernestine slammed her hand on the counter.

"I'm tired of being plain, Grandpa! Tired of putting things on shelves, taking 'em down, putting more up."

"It's a good living, Sweetheart."

"It's not living to me!" She stood her full height, straight-shouldered, the years of doing what she was told no longer weighing her down. Yet just as her body hardened, her tone softened as she tried to make Edward understand. "I've never even traveled as far as the Bartlett's ranch, Grandpa. I don't know anything of the world except for merchandise that gets shipped from somewhere and then gets bought and taken somewhere. Now I wanna go somewhere. And I'm going." She turned to Mary. "If you'll have me."

"You have to understand, Ernestine. It'll be a hard time."

"But it won't be boring," Sally added with a grin. She understood the longing within Ernestine.

"Then you can count me in! Grandpa, a pair of trousers in my size, please."

While all the fuss was going on in Edward's store, Jonas played checkers with Doc in the back room that Doc used for recovering patients. It had a large window that faced the flatlands and the setting sun. It was nicer than Doc's own room, but since a fair number of his patients were drunken cowpokes busted up in a fight, he preferred that they face away from the street and enjoy a peaceful vista.

The afternoon sky was a light blue with just a few puffy, white clouds floating about. To most it would indeed have been a peaceful view, but to Jonas it was a reminder that he was laid up inside instead of branding outside. Checkers with old Doc, no matter how cheerful he was, was a poor substitute for a good day's work.

"You forget how to play, Jonas?"

"Huh? Oh, sorry, Doc. Can't keep my mind on it, I guess."

"I've got some books if you'd rather read."

"No, books are wasted on me."

"Well, I'll have to leave you to daydream soon. Need to see how the Widow Wheelwright is coming along with her gout." Doc gave Edward a sly grin. "Always good to get there around dinner time. The woman always has the tastiest biscuits and gravy ready."

"Sounds like you're ready for romance."

Doc laughed. "No, my sparkin' days are over. But may my eatin' days never end." He rose from the unfinished checkers game and stretched by the doorway. From there, he could see out the front window to the street, and he noticed us women leaving the store.

"Mary coming in today?"

"No. We decided she'd visit every other day. Too many chores. And we'd like to have someone at the ranch on the slim chance some hands show up."

By now we'd moved closer up the street and Doc could see us in our new outfits. He was startled for just a second, then the startle turned to amusement as he understood exactly what he was seeing. Old Doc was a perceptive man.

"You say Mary's not visiting today?"

"Wish she was. I doubt she's having any luck recruiting."

"She's a resourceful woman." God bless Doc for not giving us away. "Might surprise you someday."

As we walked side-by-side down the street toward our horses—Ruth and Pearl on opposite ends—it didn't take long for our non-traditional appearance to cause a stir. Two elderly pillars of our society, Xander Benson and his wife, Gertrude, were entering the town on their wagon.

Gertrude gasped at the sight of us. "Well, I never!"

Xander's eyes lingered on our swaying hips as he muttered to himself, "No, but I wish you would've."

We felt like new women. But then again, not really. It wasn't that we'd changed so much as it was that our purposes had changed. Our immediate future had a task to accomplish and, for several of us, there was the prospect of new lives ahead.

Reaching our horses at the rail posts, we paused for a gaze at the town. Maybe now that we appeared different, we expected the town to be different, too. Or maybe we wanted to drink in the memory of the place we'd soon be leaving. I don't know. But we all stood there in quiet contemplation.

There was Mary in her unexpected role as leader, a searching look on her face that betrayed excitement overshadowed by concern. All she really wanted at that moment was her old life back. A simple life of making a home for her husband and daughter had suited her fine. She wondered if she'd ever return to it.

There was Katie, filled with youthful energy. The future was like a fairy tale to her. She'd take the cattle to market as a pauper and come home as a princess ready to meet her prince and live happily ever after.

There was Ruth, who saw the cattle drive less as hard work and more as a trip that was her due after all those times her husband had drifted. She loved him, but he was a rascal. Perhaps a season of drifting like a rascal would help her understand him more—and if he should return home to find her gone, maybe he'd think twice before leaving again.

There was Prudence, wide-eyed and anxious to do anything different than what she'd been doing. Somehow sleeping on hard ground and inhaling the odor of cattle had more appeal to her than another lonely night in the shack.

There was Sally, older and wiser than Prudence but with the same viewpoint—there had to be more out there. And there was more to her leaving, as she had no plans to return. She'd gather a few mementos and favorite supplies from her shop, then make a clean break from her ties to Secluded Springs and, in particular, Henry.

There was Ernestine, who had no idea what she'd just signed up for beyond wearing new clothes and sharing an adventure with a group of women she admired. Her combination of lanky body, plain face and shy ways kept her from thinking highly of herself. Some unspoken dream buried inside of her knew that another such opportunity to be anything more than ordinary would never arrive again.

There was Pearl, whose wishes for a new life were the easiest to understand. Even Ruth couldn't begrudge Pearl's desire for a fresh start. But the kind of life Pearl had led has a way of following one around. She hoped a parade of cattle would trample any ties to the past.

And there was me. I fell right into the center of the group with Sally and Prudence. I just knew there had to be more to life than making small talk with old ladies at my mother's tea parties or listening to my father talk about the many benefits of compound interest. It embarrasses me to think back to how I had no interests of my own at that time. I just floated. But I'm also proud to say that I recognized the need for change and had the willpower to push for it. What I wanted from that cattle drive was to discover what I wanted to do with my life. A lot to ask, I know.

Together, we were a sight. Together, we were excited and frightened and brave and scared.

Together, we were the women in pants.

PART TWO
PREPARATION

Chapter 7

We rode back to the herd and spent the rest of the day practicing. Pearl and Ernestine took a little while to get used to riding, but once they did we were able to move larger numbers of cattle. Our biggest problem was always getting the herd started as they continued to prefer eating grass to moving on it. Quite by accident we stumbled upon a unique talent within our humble group—a talent that meant we'd never again struggle to start the herd in the chosen direction.

At the time, we'd reached the landmark Mary had chosen as our goal and were in the process of trying to turn the herd around so we could annoy them by driving them back the way we came. Three steers didn't like the idea. While the rest of the herd was amiable about turning, the three steers kept moving straight ahead. Ernestine was on a bay mount and pushed it up a ways in front of the steers to cut them off. The steers didn't like that either. They moved faster toward Ernestine. Then one of them broke into an all-out run and Ernestine felt its black eyes lock onto her. It rumbled closer and closer. "Look out!" Mary shouted, but Ernestine was paralyzed and held her horse still. As the steer was almost upon her and the horse was about to buck, the fear building in Ernestine burst out in a shrieking wail any banshee would be proud to claim. "Aaaaaaaaaaaaaaaaaaaaaaaaaaaaa!!" The lead steer couldn't have turned around any faster! It spun and raced back to the herd with the other two steers right behind. Mary shouted, "Good work, Ernestine," and from that moment on she was the wailing wonder who sparked the herd when they needed a start.

As we headed for the house, the brightness of an afternoon's work in the sun and Ernestine's screeching success dimmed as we saw two figures on horseback waiting in the shadows. Katie saw them first. We were a dusty, tired but cheerful group moving at a quiet pace. Katie looked past the corral to the house, mostly black against the setting sun. She squinted at a movement.

"Someone's at the house, Ma."

We all strained our eyes. None of us recognized the silhouettes, but it was clearly two men.

"Think it could be new ranch hands?" Prudence wondered.

"We'll know soon enough," said Mary. Something about their presence troubled her, even though some decent cattlehands would be a huge help. It might have been the way the men sat in their saddles. A working man stays comfortable, but sits upright with shoulders square, partly out of pride and partly to breathe better. These men were slouched, the kind of posture you'd expect to see at a bar. Mary conveyed her uneasiness to us. "Stay mounted. Stay alert."

As we got closer, it became apparent that though we'd seen two horses and two heads, most of the second man was blocked by the enormous girth of the first. He was a bearded mountain. He could likely pick up a steer and carry it to market. He stayed in the shadow of the house as the smaller man eased his horse forward into the light to greet us.

"Could I trouble you ladies to direct me to the Bartlett ranch?" He had an Irish accent that was pleasing to the ear, but the yellow tobacco stains on his teeth and the odor from his unkempt clothes were anything but pleasing. He appeared to be in his thirties, though he might've been younger. It was hard to tell if the stubble on his chin was graying or dusty.

"You have business there?" Mary responded.

"Aye. My name's Sean O'Donnell. My friend, Brute, and myself were on our way to Dodge City when we heard of a cattle drive in need of cowhands."

"Brute?"

Mary moved her eyes onto the huge man. Brute edged his horse— besides carrying the big man's weight, the poor thing was scarred from heavy spurring—a couple steps ahead. He took a hard draw on the stub of his cigarette and held it in. As Pearl edged her horse forward to better scrutinize Brute, he blew smoke out through his nose onto black whiskers that had never known a razor.

Sean smiled. "Sure and he's forgotten his given name, you see? But 'Brute' seems to suit him and he answers to it." His voice was musical and soothing, I must admit.

Mary must have felt the same. She smiled for the first time. "Well, as it happens, this is the Bartlett ranch." She was about to continue when Pearl caught her eye, giving Mary a small but definite "no" shake of the head.

Mary didn't miss a beat. "But I'm sorry, all the cowhand positions have been filled."

His smile falling, Sean made a fuss about looking around the ranch in every direction, exaggerating his movements to show how thorough he was being. "Do you see any cowhands, Brute?"

"Nope." Brute's voice was deep and raspy, the kind you might expect from a bear just stirring from winter's sleep. A bear that smoked.

"My husband has them in the field," said Mary. She looked up at the darkening sky. "They should be here soon and I'm afraid we must tend to their supper. But I thank you for stopping by."

Sean rubbed his chin. He cast his eyes upon each of us, one at a time. When he got to Ruth, he paused, smiled and spoke. "I thank you ladies for your time. Please extend my good wishes to your husband and his crew." It was then that the rest of us understood why Sean had locked his gaze on Ruth. She had a Smith & Wesson .45-caliber Model 3 American pistol pointed at him. The kick of shooting it might have caused Ruth some pain, but not as much as Sean would have experienced on the receiving end.

Brute didn't seem to notice. At some point during the exchange between Mary and Sean, his eyes had fallen upon Katie and his lips had formed a ravenous grin. Katie felt his leer only after she felt the hair on the back of her neck tingle. She looked up to catch his expression and his eyes were so piercing that she couldn't look away. Brute took her return stare as a sign of interest and he pulled his cigarette down so Katie could see his full, hungry, yellow smile. She shuddered.

After a moment's hesitation, Sean turned back to Mary. "I don't suppose we could wait here and have a talk with your husband?"

"He's not much for talkin' after a hard day. And like I said, he's hired all he can hire."

Sean glanced again at Ruth. "Then we'll bid you good day and hope we meet again under other circumstances." He tipped his hat at us and pulled his horse to move away. "Let's be off, Brute."

Brute said nothing, but spurred his horse to follow. Lust flared in his eyes as he drank in one last look at Katie. Her face was bloodless with fear. Pearl, bless her, moved in front of Katie to block the view.

As the two men sauntered off, I was the first to turn to Ruth. "I didn't know you had a gun."

"When you don't have muscle, you better carry some. These shirts are good for hiding."

Mary kept her eyes on the men. "Did you know them, Pearl?"

"Just that big one. His name is no lie. Seen him near kill a girl once just for sport. Heard of him doin' even worse to others."

"Reckon the sweet-sounding one's not much better then."

Up until that point, we'd had a good day. Working like a cattlehand, well, I can't say it was fun, but it was different and energizing and we felt a thrill about helping our friend while satisfying some selfish needs of our own. The arrival of the two men was like a splash of cold water on our warm dream. We woke up to the reality of dangers ahead that we didn't have the skills and upbringing to face. Not everything could be solved with a gun hidden in a shirt. Should we run into Sean and Brute again, or others like them, it was doubtful we could take advantage of being underestimated.

But the problems of what might lie ahead paled in comparison to the immediate problem of something that seemed so trivial—getting off our horses. It's one of those indelicate situations I warned you about earlier. You see, we'd been on our horses for hours, most of us riding straddle for the first time. Our legs had been bowed out in the same position and had stiffened something fierce, though we hadn't noticed until we went to move.

Prudence was the first to dismount and she moaned as she slid to the ground, both hands on the saddle horn for support. "My legs," she whined. "Something happened to them."

"Mine, too," said Katie. She rubbed the inside of her thighs, trying to massage away the muscle pain.

"I take it all back," I said with a grimace. "Side-saddle is better." I pushed my legs back together, but they bowed back out into their new wicket shape.

Even the married and somewhat-experienced among us were struggling. Their legs may have been spread apart on occasion, but they hadn't been held that way for hours before. Ruth bent over like she was touching her toes, perhaps thinking it would line her legs back up with her hips. Mary and Sally were both taking tiny steps in hopes of working out the kinks.

The whole time, Pearl stifled a smile. Finally she slid off her horse with ease and began taking the reins from each of us. "I'll take care of the horses while you ladies walk off the ride." She led the horses away toward the barn like she was strolling to a picnic on a Sunday afternoon.

Ruth groaned as she straightened up, then shook her head in resignation as she watched Pearl walk away. "Don't like her profession, but I guess it's good for keepin' limber."

For the next week, a pattern developed. We worked on developing our riding skills and endurance, practiced moving the cattle, failed miserably at roping, and found an unconventional way to get more branding done. All of us worked every day except for Mary, who left every other day to visit with Jonas while he recovered.

On the days she went to town, she wore a dress. She debated about telling Jonas of the all-female ranch crew, but put it off. She told him only that she'd been able to get a small group together and that they were working hard. She felt it would keep his spirits up if he knew work was being done at the ranch, but that it would get him up on his bad leg if he knew just who was doing the work. When Jonas pressed for details, she changed the subject in that sideways manner of which so many wives excel.

"Where'd the men come from?" Jonas would ask. "Are they experienced? How many are there?"

"I'm sure they aren't as experienced at checkers as you and Doc," Mary would answer. "He says you play all the time. Who wins?"

She'd leave each time hoping that no one in town would visit Jonas and spill the beans. Having so few folks around probably helped. Also, anyone tied to us like Edward or my father was too embarrassed to bring up the subject.

At last the day came where Doc determined that Jonas had healed enough to ride home in the back of the wagon, provided Jonas agreed to run the ranch with his backside in a chair rather than on a horse. He made Jonas shake on it, though Jonas was quick to add "for the time being" to the agreement to give himself room to hedge.

Mary, clean and fresh in her dress, drove the wagon on the trail toward home. Jonas was settled in the back, his leg straight out and braced with wooden slats. His crutches rattled beside him as he inhaled the fresh air, felt the warmth of the sun, and stretched his neck and strained his eyes to look ahead. He wanted to see those ranch hands, see some certainty in his future. If he couldn't do the work himself, he wanted to boss somebody to feel part of the work. His curiosity boiled over.

"You can at least tell me how many. I don't understand why you're so secretive."

"Hard to believe nobody in town said anything."

"Easier to believe when you consider that almost nobody's in town," Jonas spit. "Doc said the few there were buzzin' about your cowhands, but he wouldn't tell me more. Said the surprise'll get my heart started, whatever that means. Crazy old..."

"I only found six," Mary said. "But they're taking to the work real well."

Jonas considered the information. "Can't drive the whole herd with six, but can move some. Enough." He stopped straining and relaxed a bit.

"You did well, Honey. I think we're gonna be all right."

Seeing him at ease warmed Mary's heart. Somehow that always made her playful spirit rise. A twinkle formed in her eyes. "Katie's keeping a close watch on them."

Jonas snapped up. "What?! You left that boy-crazy girl with six cowhands?!"

"She'll be fine."

"Wasn't worried about her. Just the hands she might scare off." Jonas had a twinkle in his eyes, too. Things were looking up.

Before Jonas could get a glimpse of work at the ranch, he heard it.

"Aaaaaaaaaaaaaaaaaaaaaaaaaaaaaaaaaa!!!" came the piercing scream from Ernestine. Even with a bad leg and hip, Jonas rose in the back of the wagon. "My Lord! Hurry!" he shouted at Mary.

"Now you just relax. It's only the crew doin' the branding."

"Branding what? That was a woman's scream. Let's go!"

Instead of hurrying, Mary stopped the wagon and turned to face Jonas. "I guess I can't put off telling you any longer. These ranch hands are... out of the ordinary."

"Mary, I heard a woman scream. We need to do something."

"It wasn't a scream so much as... well, as a new way of doing things."

"I don't understand."

"It'll be better if you just trust me and let me show you. But I promise that everything's all right."

Another "Aaaaaaaaaaaaaaaaaaaaaaaaaaaaaaa!!!!!" rose up in the wind, startling Jonas again.

"Trust me," said Mary before Jonas could start questioning again. She snapped the reins. "All's fine. Different, but fine."

The pit in Jonas's stomach felt anything but fine.

Mary brought them to a stop on a ridge overlooking the herd, giving Jonas full view of the activities below. At his first sight of the women in pants, he looked on without voicing a comment, though his wince and choking swallow said a mouthful.

The two posts he'd set in the branding area remained. Sally stood by one and I stood by the other, each of us holding ropes with lasso hoops at the end. Katie stood behind Sally and Prudence stood behind me, each of them holding onto the respective ropes as well. Ruth stood by the branding fire where the Circle B iron lay reddish-white in the coals.

Mary watched Jonas as he absorbed the scene, what little color his face had slowly draining away. He sat bolt upright as he realized what Ernestine was about to do. For the first time, he spoke, just a whisper. "Lord help that crazy girl."

Ernestine stood almost nose-to-nose with a steer that looked back at her in mild curiosity. With the other women ready in their places, she performed her role. She slapped the steer in the face. The steer jerked its head in surprise, then huffed in anger. As Ernestine turned and ran, it followed its natural instincts and stormed after her. "Run, Ernestine, run!" hollered Prudence. And run she did. Ernestine made a beeline for the two posts, rushing first between us women and then straight between the posts.

Boom! The steer pounded into the posts and as it bounced back a few inches, Sally and I looped the ropes around its long-horned head. "Pull!" shouted Ruth, and the four of us with rope duty dug in our feet and held the steer against the poles with all our might. The steer was still stronger than us and its legs were free. It jerked and kicked. We could only hold it a few seconds, but it was enough for Ruth to close in and sear its hide with the Circle B brand. Letting the angry beast go was almost as dangerous. There was no way we were gonna jump in any closer to try to unloop the ropes, so we just dropped them and dived out of the beast's way as it rumbled off. When it calmed later, we'd get the ropes off.

We stood there panting, checking each other for injuries. Once we'd all caught our breath and gathered up more rope, Ruth said the magic words. "Okay, Ernestine. Go slap another one."

Up on the ridge, Jonas was wide-eyed with horror.

Whew, boy, I'm here to tell you that the next couple of hours were a lot tougher on me than trying to hold an angry steer. Tougher on all of us. Before Ernestine could pop another cow in the nose, Jonas bellowed from on high. "Everyone outta there! Back to the house! Now!" We looked up to see Mary pulling the wagon away, shoulders slumped, head down, with Jonas in the back. Even from a distance, we could see that his face had turned bright red—we were sure it wasn't from embarrassment.

By the time we got to the house, Jonas and Mary had leaped past spat and squabble and launched straight into argument. Their voices cut through the humid afternoon air like a hot knife through butter, and there were no biscuits around to soften the blow.

"If the rustlers and Indians don't kill you," rang out Jonas's voice, "the cattle'll likely trample you to death!"

Inside the house, Mary sat at the table, her eyes sad but her jaw clenched in fury. Jonas stood on his crutches, fuming, spewing, berating. If Mary had worries about being a leader, she was proving herself right then despite not knowing it. She took the verbal thrashing like a man.

"Few days of wearin' britches and ridin' straddle don't make you cowhands!" Jonas steamed on. "Can any of 'em shoot or rope? Can they ride fourteen hours chokin' on dust? Cross a river?!" A wound-up man can't keep still. Jonas forgot himself and turned to pace, stumbling as a crutch caught the corner of the table. Frustrated, he tossed the crutch across the room. "All furied up and can't even pace!"

He hopped to a chair, snatched it out, and lowered himself into it. All the while his hell-bent eyes were locked on Mary as if daring her to even think about helping him. Then, as is often the case in any rising fury, he made it personal. "Why you didn't stop this loco idea is beyond me!"

That did it. Mary was a mountain lion. She sprang to her feet and uncoiled her attack. "Because I love this ranch as much as you do! Your sweat ain't the only sweat that helped build it!"

Listening outside was a brutal time for us all, especially Katie. Jonas and Mary kept jabbing and thrusting and parrying, and poor Katie was sick with worry. We all were, wondering if our futures were becoming uncertain once again. But it was more than that for Katie. "Never heard Ma and Pa yell before," she said.

Sally put an arm around her. "They haven't been this scared before. They'll settle it soon."

I voiced the concern of the others. "I don't want to go crawling back to my dad at the bank and my mom and her society women. What if they settle it so we aren't going?"

Ruth stepped toward the door with determination. "Time we settled it for 'em."

Jonas and Mary were at opposite ends of the table, each standing, hands flat on the surface, leaning in as the battle raged on.

"There's nothing silly about any plan to save this ranch!"

"I ain't questioning your intentions, just the foolish way —"

We burst in, Ruth leading the charge. "'Kay if I speak my mind?"

Jonas rubbed the bridge of his nose and sighed. "Never known you not to."

Ruth took one step toward him, stood as tall as her petite frame could go, and said, "We're doin' this."

Jonas waited for more, but Ruth simply nodded once, putting a period to her sentence. In her view, enough had been said. Jonas had other thoughts. "Well, your speech is like you, short and to the point and I appreciate that. But it don't —"

Finishing sentences was not a goal Jonas seemed likely to accomplish today.

"You gonna make me spell it out?" Ruth continued. "Fine. It's like this." She pulled up a chair and sat at an angle to him. He sat down again as well—a great relief to his hip, which was throbbing more than his temple. "We all got our reasons, but they don't matter much compared to this one: You and Mary and Katie are our friends and neighbors, and you need help." She leaned in closer. "And if that ain't as plain as the boards holdin' your leg together, I'll make it even plainer. Even if you say no, we'll just take the cattle and go anyway 'cause you can't stop us. We'll save your ranch in spite of you. So either help or stay out of the way." This time she put a period on her sentence by slamming her tiny fist on the table.

All eyes were on Jonas as he considered her words. "Wasn't short, but it was to the point." He took a long moment to look over each one of us. We had iron in our eyes, I'm proud to say. We were determination personified. He lingered on the steely gaze of Katie, a sight he'd never expected from the dream-filled girl. The silence was oppressive. I could hear a slight wheeze in Pearl's breathing. We all had a lot riding on Jonas's next words, but none of us more than her. At last, Jonas turned to Mary. Decision time.

"Have your cowhands ready to work by sunup."

"Wooooooooooooooooooooooo!!" Ernestine probably scared the cattle with her celebration squeal, but she spoke for us all. Smiles and yelps and jumping and clapping chased away the tension that had been fog-thick just seconds before.

Mary rose, walked around the table, and hugged her husband. Like so many disagreements in human history, all was right between the couple once the woman got her way. But I say that just for a chuckle. There was plenty more. This was a couple in love, a devoted pair if ever there was one. Their argument wasn't built on anger but on fear. Mary feared losing the life she loved. Jonas feared for the lives of his wife and daughter. The fears hadn't disappeared, but the commitment of two people united in both love and cause pushed the fears back. They had the hope of togetherness.

Jonas accepted the hug with closed eyes and an open heart. As his eyes opened, though, he reverted to his stoic ways, not at all comfortable with us ladies staring at the united couple. He waved his hands to shoosh us to the door.

"Rule number one: no cowhands in the house."

A while after the fact, I was able to ask Jonas what went through his mind at that moment. Before I share his answer, I need to make sure you understand just how things were. Jonas was the head of the family, the head of the household and the head of the ranch. His decisions were gospel. He was the man. If they'd ever gone to one of those fancy ballroom dances back east, the fellow who shouts out the names would have said, "Mr. Jonas Bartlett and his wife, Mrs. Jonas Bartlett." The man was the identity, the king, the ruler. Ruth may have blustered up a speech about how we were doing this whether he was behind us or not, but there was no cold truth behind her statement. If he had said no, we were through. Like I said, it's just the way things were. Jonas was a rare breed in that he talked over his decisions with Mary, but there was always an understanding that if he said this was how something was going to be, then that was how it was going to be. It's a tribute to his character and his love for Mary that he never abused that authority like many men do.

Some of the others didn't have men or didn't have them around to answer to at the moment, or things might have been different for all of us. Sure, some of us were clever enough to get our way. I could never lie to my father, but I'd learned to say only what was needed. So I'd told my parents that I was "going out to the Bartlett ranch to help out" because that was a lot harder for my father to find fault with than "I'm going to risk my life on an all-woman cattle drive." Word of what we were doing had likely gotten to him by that time, and on occasion I expected to see him riding out to bring me home, but he didn't. I consider myself blessed that he never spoke the words, "Laurie, I forbid you to go," because that would have put me in hard place of deciding whether to defy my father or be a dutiful daughter. I had considerably more history of being dutiful and suspect I would have done what I was told.

So not only could Jonas have ended our cattle drive with a simple no, he had every right to. The decision was his. Getting him to talk about himself was harder than holding a steer against a post, but with the right amount of prodding I was able to learn what it was that had settled the matter in his mind. It was two things, both revolving around Katie.

He cherished that girl and he worried about her. She was a joy to be around, but she had also always been flighty in her dream-filled ways, not grounded like her mother. Seeing a new determination in her eyes had given Jonas pause, and then seeing that Katie was shoulder-to-shoulder with Pearl pushed Jonas the rest of way. They were close enough in resemblance that she could've been Katie's older sister. He knew nothing of Pearl's upbringing and history outside of where she'd been working, but at that moment it occurred to him that the primary difference between Katie and Pearl was their means of survival. Katie had a home and family to care for her. Pearl was on her own, and her only asset was her body. If the ranch was lost, Katie would still have Jonas and Mary finding some way somehow to get by, but she'd be a lot closer to risking a life like Pearl's. A successful cattle drive ensured the success of the ranch, and the success of the ranch ensured a future for his family that removed any possibility of Katie falling into darkness for lack of means. The ranch must be saved. The risk must be taken. Decision made.

He said he didn't think much about Pearl at that moment, about how he'd be sending her back to the life she wanted to escape. But I don't buy that. In that particular instant, I believe Jonas considered everything. And despite all that we would go through, I also believe now as I believed then—he made the right decision.

Chapter 8

I'll try not to bore you with the activities of the next week. Suffice to say that Jonas drilled us in riding, roping, shooting and more. He probably made more speeches that week than he'd spoken in his entire life. Sometimes his words were directed at one of us, like telling Ernestine that "it's a cattle drive, meaning that you *drive* cattle, not slap 'em on the nose and run." Sometimes there were words to all of us that bordered on thankfulness. "Can't drive many with eight of you. Maybe 250, 300 head. But that's enough to save our ranch and get all of us a little money, so for that I'm grateful." Then he'd cut off our smiles with one of his warnings. "But 300 head is more'n enough to run you into the ground. And you'll sure be mighty temptin' targets for thieves, I promise you that. No way you'll learn enough to be ready, but you'll learn all you can in the few days we've got."

It went on like that. Jonas giving instructions. Us trying. Jonas making speeches. It was hard work and we loved it. We were learning our roles and, of course, Jonas had a speech for each one. "Mary'll be both trail boss and scout, out front, leading and looking ahead for water." "Ruth and Laurie will be pointers, taking the front position on each side, with Sally and Prudence behind them at flank." "Ernestine and Pearl'll ride drag. It's a dirty job, I won't lie about it. But it's what keeps the herd movin'." "Katie will serve as wrangler, keeping the remuda of horses together." In other words, he told us what we'd already worked out ourselves, but I believe it made him feel good.

There were times, though, when his statements would raise our curiosity. That's when having Prudence in the group paid an extra dividend. She hadn't had much schooling, but somewhere in there she had learned to raise her hand and ask questions. Jonas would say something and, whoosh, up went the hand. Like the time Jonas told us to expect to spend all day in the saddle.

"A cowboy takes pride in staying on his mount from sunup to dinner."

Up went the hand. "Mr. Bartlett?"

To his credit, Jonas was endlessly patient. To Prudence's credit, she voiced what we were all wondering. "What if I have to, um, go? Like to the privy?"

"Fact is, Prudence, you won't be taking in a lot of water, and most of it you'll sweat out anyway."

Up went the hand. "But should the need arise, may I get off my horse?"

"You do what you need to do. Just don't expect privacy on the trail."

Up went the hand.

By the end of the week, Jonas had turned everything over to Mary. "I'm in the way," he said, "and I don't mean that for sympathy. I mean that these women chose to follow you, not a fella on crutches. You lead the training just like you'll lead the drive." It was really the passing of the burden. The unspoken words were "our ranch is fully in your hands." Far more important were the unspoken words that built up Mary's confidence. Jonas's warm eyes said, "There's no one else I'd rather trust it to."

The other big transition of the week was between father and daughter. Remember Pitch? The black mustang that had thrown Jonas time and again until he'd turned it into a fine mount? He'd developed a relationship with that horse that was downright eerie in how well they communicated. If Pitch was roaming free, Jonas always knew where to find him. If Jonas wanted to turn onto a new trail, Pitch would move to it before Jonas could pull the rein. Perhaps it was because Jonas believed, unlike many a ranch hand, that breaking a horse shouldn't involve breaking its spirit. Or perhaps they were just two souls who understood each other. Whatever the reason, there was no more powerful way for a father to tell his daughter he loved her than when Jonas said, "Katie, you ride Pitch."

He held out the reins for her, and her eyes misted.

"Pa? Are you sure?"

"He'll go where you tell him, and the other horses will follow." As Katie took the reins, Jonas put a hand atop Pitch's head and said, "You take care of her." Maybe it was just twitching away a fly, but I swear the horse nodded.

Except for the undesirable Sean and Brute, not another man came to the ranch until a day we saw a wagon on the horizon. It was the day before the drive and we were out for the final roundup of cattle and horses. The wagon headed for the house, where Jonas was. We'd have to find out about it later.

Jonas watched from his chair on the porch, squinting to make out the wagon in the distance. "Right on time."

It was a sturdy chuckwagon with a fresh canvas top. Jonas frowned and grabbed his crutches as the driver brought the wagon, led by mules, to a stop in front of the house. The driver was a grizzled old man, but spry. He hopped from the wagon and used his few remaining teeth to smile at Jonas.

"Howdy. Name's Homer Edwards, but everyone calls me Clean Through."

"I was expecting Homer Edwards, but a much younger man."

"I'm his father. Came in his place." He extended his hand to Jonas.

Jonas took it. "Let me guess. He's off prospectin' in Leadville."

"Leadville, yes. Prospectin', no. Gone to sell picks, shovels and meals. I raised him a dern sight smarter than them dirt-diggers," he grinned with pride. "Don't worry. I cook better'n my boy. And I'm as healthy as they come, if you're worried about my age."

Jonas could only smile to himself. "No, seems fittin' at this point. Come on in and let me acquaint you with our situation. Be awhile before I have company again."

"Maybe I ought to go out and meet the hands."

"Better you get a drink in you first."

We were doing well with the herd, I thought. We had them gathered in a draw. Ernestine, Prudence and Pearl circled the herd, keeping it together. Katie and I kept an eye on the horses, counting to make sure we had four mounts for each rider as Jonas had ordered. Mary and Ruth were trying to count the herd.

"Be easier to count if they'd stay still," said Ruth.

"Got to be over 400," said Mary. "More than we need."

All of our heads turned at the sound of the oncoming wagon. Clean Through was driving and Jonas rode beside him, his splinted leg jutting out to the side. Clean Through saw us, pulled the wagon to a stop, rubbed his eyes, and looked upon us again.

"It really is girls. You weren't joshin'. That skinny one's about as big as my arm."

"You tell her that, you might lose your arm. The one beside her is my wife, Mary. She'll be your trail boss. If you'll go."

Clean Through considered. He'd thought Jonas was pulling his leg, but sure enough this cattle crew was all females. "You say you're not coming?"

"Wish. About an hour in a wagon is all my hip and leg can handle. Even if I tried to go, I think my wife or old Doc would shoot me to make me stay put."

"They any good?"

Jonas was a little surprised by the confidence that sprung from inside him. "Let me show you."

He waved us over and we gathered by the wagon.

"This here is Clean Through. He's about to sign on as cook once we show him what you cattlehands are capable of. So it's time for your final test."

Up went the hand. "What test is that, Mr. Bartlett," asked Prudence.

"Hand me your mom's pistol."

Ruth gave the gun to Prudence, who gave it to Jonas. He pointed it to the sky and fired three shots, startling us but especially the horses and the cattle, which scattered. We were baffled why Jonas would do such a thing, but Mary understood and her shout cleared up the matter. "Well go bring 'em back!"

We snapped into action and though our training had been short, we'd been good students. Even more, we had good insights into our talents. When Mary bellowed, "Go Ernestine," she knew exactly what to do. The rest of us raced our mounts to cut-off positions on each side of the herd while Ernestine rushed to the front.

"Aaaaaaaaaaaaaaaaaaaaaaaaaa!!!!!!"

That bone-chilling shriek of hers was like putting up an iron wall. The lead cattle turned and we began guiding them back into the draw.

"That's a strange girl," Clean Through commented.

"No argument here. But it works."

Clean Through gave a firm nod. "Guess I can cook for women as well as men, long as I get paid. But I ain't dryin' tears if'n they start crying. I cook, but I don't wipe noses."

"Welcome aboard."

By the time we'd finished securing the herd and corralling the horses, Clean Through stood by his wagon handing out biscuits and beans. Katie was impressed with the wholeness of the biscuits but whispered a concern of a different kind to Prudence.

"What kinda name is Clean Through?"

"Hope it don't describe the effects of his cookin'."

Jonas waved us over to where he'd drawn a map on the ground with one of his crutches. "I'm pleased to say that Clean Through is a veteran of the trails and he agrees with Mary and me that your best bet is to take the Western Trail." He pointed at the middle trail on his artwork. "It's the shortest one from here, almost straight north into Dodge City."

Up went the hand.

"Yes, Prudence?"

"If it's the Western Trail, how come it's in the middle?"

"It used to be the most west until the Goodnight-Loving Trail, this one here, got made. It swings around to Pueblo. And before you ask, the eastern-most trail is the Chisolm, which goes up to Abilene."

I didn't raise my hand, but I had a question. "Isn't Dodge a pretty rough town?"

"They all are. What's a lot rougher, though, is the 400 miles between here and there. For those of you planning to return, about 50, 60 days ought to see you back."

Fifty days. That meant maybe seventy if conditions got rough.

Every time we'd get to feeling good about the progress we'd made, a thought would come along to remind us of the harsh reality ahead. I could see shoulders sag a bit and felt added weight on my shoulders as well. But Mary, who'd known nothing but cooking and cleaning for a couple of decades and whose leadership experience had previously amounted to sending the dog out of the house, perked our shoulders back up. "We're ready."

A born leader, whether she knew it or not.

"Fifty days." The whispered words hung in the air. Mary and Jonas were together on the bed, Jonas propped up with pillows to ease his hip, Mary's head on his shoulder. A small beam of moonlight reflected in the moisture of Mary's eyes.

"Thought you'd be the one waiting for me to come home," said Jonas. "Not the other way around."

"Don't take it wrong, but it ain't loneliness that worries me, yours or mine." She rose onto her elbows and faced him. "Maybe… maybe Ruth should be the trail boss. She can lead."

"She's bossy, but no leader. Likely shoot Pearl."

Mary gave a chuckle, but her eyes saddened. She lowered herself back to the mattress and rolled over, her back to Jonas. "Followed Ma and Pa to Texarkana. Followed you here. Never been out front."

"Out front's good. First one there. First one home." Jonas caressed her shoulders. "Whether my leg's mended or not, I'll rush to meet you."

PART THREE
UNDERWAY

Chapter 9

They started arriving before sunup. Edward, Doc and my father arrived together. Charlie made it shortly after. Against the rising pink sun, serenaded by lowing cattle, little pockets of goodbyes were scattered about the field. It was too late for arguments or persuasions or pleading or any this-is-just-foolish talk. It was a time to open up hearts joined through blood and love and history and friendship.

Edward gave Ernestine a pewter necklace in the shape of a cross. "Your ma asked me to give this to you when I thought the time was best. Guess that's now." Ernestine, misty-eyed, took off her hat and looped the necklace over her head. She touched the cross as it fell into place. She embraced her grandfather.

Not far from them, I stood with my father. We had always had both a closeness and a distance between us. The distance was because our dreams and our views had never quite matched up. The closeness was because we loved each other despite the distance. I've likely given his caring side short shrift in this story while stressing his business ways. Maybe it's natural to poke that way at someone we're close to, maybe because their light ways aren't as interesting as their dark. Just as Jonas had braved the frontier to build a ranch and a home and a family, my father had braved it to build a bank and a home and a family. He will always be the finest man I know, and saying goodbye was no easy task.

"Mother?"

"She couldn't bear to part," he said. Then he gave me a knowing smile. "Couldn't bear to see you wearing britches." I giggled and teared up at the same time, then raised my eyebrows as he held out a small package. "It's a sheaf of paper and some writing utensils. I hope you'll write me and your mother. Often."

"I promise."

We hugged. His warmth and his cigar aroma triggered a flood of memories. Feeling him look around to see if anyone was watching our public display triggered many more. There would always be that closeness. There would always be that distance.

Doc was simply moving from person to person, shaking hands, wishing well, offering reassurance. He never missed an opportunity to remind many of us that he'd brought us into the world. "But it's your responsibility to stay in it," he said to each of us in turn. "So doggone it, be careful."

Charlie stood a few steps from Pearl, their relationship hard to define and impossible for anyone who hasn't walked in their shoes to appreciate. He pointed a lecturing but kind finger at her. "New lives have a way of not working out, so if you get into trouble you go see Madam Smith at the Dodge City Home for Women, and know that you'll always be welcome to —"

"I know," she cut him off. She started to tell him she'd die before she ever returned to that life, but decided there was no point to it. As men who used women go, Charlie'd been kinder than most. She could let him have his goodbye.

Prudence, Ruth and Sally were mounted and in place. Only Doc had offered goodbyes to them. Ruth held the faintest of hope that her husband would ride over the ridge to see her, though she had no idea if she'd go home with him or tell him off and leave. Prudence was still too sleepy to worry about goodbyes. "Let's get moving," Sally mumbled to no one. She wanted to move. Every second standing still was another second that Henry might drift back into her life. She wanted distance, both physical and emotional.

What Jonas, Mary and Katie shared with each other that morning I do not know. It's among the rare items none of them would pass along. "Some things are nobody else's business," was all Jonas would say. I suspect that tender words were spoken, the kind that might embarrass Jonas if read back to him, and the kind that Mary would want to cling to in a private place of her mind, words she could call upon for strength in bad times—those moments when a Bible verse brings comfort, but a loved one's words bring peace.

The time had come.

Mary climbed upon a blue-gray roan. Katie mounted Pitch. The rest of us took our places.

"Ain't no more to say, no more I can guide you on," Jonas said for all to hear. "It's time for doing. God be with you all."

He nodded at Mary. She pushed on her stirrups, rising high in her saddle. "Ernestine! Move 'em out!"

"Aaaaaaaaaaaaaaaaaaaaaaaaaaaaaaaaaaaaaaaaaaaa!!!!!!!"

The rear of the herd jerked forward, sending out a reddish-brown ripple from back to front. The cattle were moving with Mary in front to lead them. All of us chipped in our own versions of "Hi-yah!" and

"Hooooo!" and "Come on!" and more, adding to the impetus to stir the cattle forward. The goodbyes were behind us.

So I thought.

I had concentrated on my role during all of our training and, as such, hadn't paid attention to how slowly a cattle herd rumbles along. Minutes after we'd cajoled the cattle into motion, as the yelling died down and I settled into my gentle ride, I glanced back for a final wave to my father, who would be a small dot in the distance. But he was right there, still within shouting distance. We hadn't yet moved fifty feet. Starting the herd was like starting one of those large riverboats. It took a while to get it up to speed.

We could've moved them faster, of course, but running meat off their bones was the same as running money out of Mary's pockets. So an easy, steady pace it was. Our goal was twelve miles a day—about 14 hours of forward movement, allowing the cattle a mid-day graze and allowing a lunch rotation for each of the hands. Bedding down the herd and rotating night duties meant still more hours in the saddle. So it was a little unsettling to have the ranch remain in view close to two hours after we'd started. It didn't feel like progress until the men and buildings we were leaving behind faded out of sight.

Perched on a wagon, his back against the seat and his mending leg extended outward, Jonas watched us until the last steer and rider was over the ridge and out of sight. Charlie had taken his horse back to town earlier, and Doc, Edward and my father had followed shortly after. For a moment, Jonas felt everyone in the world was moving except for him, but he chastised himself for thinking like a selfish schoolgirl and snapped the reins for the ride back to the house. His duty now was to wait, hope and pray. Especially wait.

During our steady progress, Mary often looked back at us and the herd as if wondering if all would still be there. To the front and on the right, away from any dust stirring in the gentle breeze, Clean Through chewed on a blade of grass as he guided his mules and wagon. After about five hours, with the noon sun high and hot, Mary broke from her position at the lead and rode to Clean Through.

"About time to let 'em graze, don't you think?"

"Agreed."

"Ride up ahead and get the food going. I'll spread the word."

Clean Through snapped the reins and quickened the pace of the wagon. Mary rode to Ruth's point position and told her we'd be stopping the herd soon. Then she made a complete circle of the herd, giving the word to each of us, ending with me at the point on the other side. When the herd was stopped and grazing—a far easier accomplishment than getting them moving—Sally, Pearl and I rode in a circle around the herd to keep it in place while the others ate. Then they relieved us. From that first day on, it would all become routine.

Dinner the night before had been the last time we'd see a table for a while. For the mid-day meal, Clean Through handed us a plate with beef and beans wrapped in a tortilla alongside a slice of corn bread. The drink of choice was water from our own canteens. We could eat on the ground or on our horses—up on my horse seemed cleaner to me.

Late in the afternoon, the process was close to repeated. Instead of circling round to talk to us, though, Mary rode to scout a place to bed down for the night. It wasn't difficult this first night as Jonas knew the territory and had told her where to camp. Within two days, though, she'd be handling the duty on her own. Riding back, she described the location to Clean Through and sent him on ahead to prepare dinner. In the fading light of the evening, we brought the herd to a stop, took care of the horses, and dragged ourselves and our saddles into camp. Ruth and Prudence took the first watch with the herd.

Clean Through prepared a fine beef stew with biscuits. He ladled it out as we came by and it was the first of many evenings where his cheerful ways and trail experience eased the burden of the drive. We were sore and moving slow, but his near-toothless smile propped us up. "Fine first day, ladies," came his sing-songy voice. "Fine. Don't worry about feelin' stiff and pained. Pretty soon you'll be numb all over and it won't matter no more."

Katie picked up her biscuit and was both impressed and jealous that it hadn't fallen apart. "He sure cooks better than I do," she said to none of us in particular. Sally nodded as she gobbled her food and used her biscuit to sop up every bit of the stew.

"'Course," continued Clean Through, "this grass'll soon turn to scrub and dust. And sleepin' on the ground tonight is something you're gonna feel until the numbness sets in."

"Right," Katie brightened. "We'll be camping out from now on. Maybe sing, tell stories."

"You don't want to spook the cattle, you'll keep your voice low," said Clean Through. "And keep in mind that morning comes mighty early on the trail."

"How far you think we went today, Mary?" asked Ernestine.

"Twelve, thirteen miles."

"Might be the farthest away I ever been."

"Me, too," said Katie.

Mary lowered herself to the ground, wincing as her tired bottom hit the earth. Despite the soreness, her face had a wistful glow. "I was farther once since coming here, when Jonas took me to Lubbock to find a preacher."

"Yes," said a grinning Katie. "That's the kind of story I was talking about. Tell 'em how Pa proposed to you, Ma." She turned to Ernestine with an ear-to-ear smile. "It's the most romantic thing you'll ever hear in your life."

"No," said Mary. "I should finish up and take over watch from Ruth."

"You can tell it quick."

"I'd like to hear it," said Ernestine.

"Me, too," I added, "if you don't mind."

Mary sighed and smiled. "All right."

Clean Through gave an exaggerated roll of his eyes and tended to the dishes. This was clearly not going to be like any drive he was used to.

Mary said, "My folks and I were living in Texarkana and there was a barn dance. Jonas came in, looked over the girls real quick, picked me out."

Katie was bubbling over and jumped in. "He told me he could see that Ma had somethin' special about her. Not just that she was the prettiest, but that there was more to her. Doesn't that get your heart going? I mean, just from looking at her!"

"Calm down," said Mary. "I'll tell it." Her eyes were bright with memories coming back. Warm. Tender. "After the dance, he told me he was building a ranch and needed a wife to help make it a home. He looked me up and down, then he looked into my eyes and said, 'You'll do.'"

Wait a minute. That's the romantic story? Perhaps not so warm and tender after all. Sally, Pearl and I stopped eating and stared at Mary, waiting for more. Nothing came.

"Hold on," said Sally. "'You'll do?' My, that is romantic."

"Don't sound like much, I know, but somehow the way he said it… it was the most welcoming, approving, inviting thing I ever heard."

I was still expecting a bit more. "He didn't talk about your eyes or your hair or get down on a knee or at least hold your hands and smile?"

"No, just that welcoming 'You'll do.' Fell in love right then and haven't regretted it a single day of my life."

Katie was stunned by our reaction and never took a breath to let us know it. "Don't you see? He walked into a room full of girls and picked out Ma to marry as if he'd known her all his life and she fell in love too and she was his and he was hers and all it took was for them to look at each other and… honestly, I can't be the only one who understands romance." She waited a moment for us to… well, I don't actually know what she expected from us. Anyway, whether it was being fired up about her mom's story or excited by the prospect of sitting under the stars and mooning on about love, she wanted to keep the evening going. "How about someone else? Who has a love story to share?"

The talk was too much for Pearl, who'd never been close to a love story in her life. She rose, took a last sip of coffee, handed her tins to Clean

Through and walked toward the tethered horses. "Reckon I'll go relieve Prudence."

Mary realized the talk had made Pearl uncomfortable and she rose as well. "And I'll send Ruth back. Don't let 'em all sit up talking, Clean Through. Daybreak comes early."

The fire reflected off Clean Through's front tooth as he offered a reassuring smile. "Don't you worry, boss. My biscuits start layin' heavy after a while. They'll lie down all right."

Sally and I each had some biscuit remaining on our plates. We exchanged glances, shrugged, and popped the remainder into our mouths. After a tiring day, we likely didn't need anything to help us sleep, but the biscuit tasted fine and our bodies would need every ounce of fuel during the journey.

We didn't stir during the night.

We sure stirred at first light, though. Clang! Clang! Clang! Clean Through's wooden spoon rattling inside a pan was just as shrill and annoying to us as Ernestine's shrieks were to the cattle. A yellow-orange wisp of sunlight danced on the horizon, but Clean Through was fresh and spirited like a new morning that was all the way here. "Rise and shine! Come on, now!" We rubbed our eyes and silently cursed the man as he kept banging that pot. "I let you ladies sleep in this one time, but we can't afford luxurious livin' for long."

"Sleep in?" questioned Prudence, too sleepy to raise her hand.

Ruth rubbed her stiff shoulders and back. "Luxurious livin', my foot."

The light was dim. The air was cold. The aches of the night before had magnified into a deep, heavy soreness. It was unlikely we'd be leaving our blankets anytime soon.

"Better shake the spiders out of your bedrolls and check for snakes."

We sprung to our feet almost in unison, like dancers reacting to a cue. Old Clean Through was a sly one, but at least he greeted us with coffee, bacon and biscuits.

Chapter 10

"You will meet bandits, wide rivers, Indians and rustlers." Before we'd left Secluded Springs, Jonas had used one of his worrisome speeches to tell us of the dangers on the trail. For a fellow who needed our help and didn't have any replacements for us in sight, he sure seemed to go out of his way to scare us off. I suppose he was just an honest man fearful for his family and friends, but, whew, it was tiresome at times. "I'd like to think that all the bad men rode to Leadville for the silver strike, but it's an unfortunate fact of life that the bad ones among us are disinclined to perform hard work."

Jonas wasn't sure how Prudence could have a question, but up went the hand. "My pa went to Leadville and he's not inclined toward work."

Before Jonas could respond, Ruth fired in her opinion. "Don't you go talkin' poorly about your pa. If anyone's gonna call him a lazy, good-for-nothing, sloth of a man, it'll be me and none other. You mind your respect!"

With Prudence sufficiently chastised, Jonas continued. "If there's bandits, they'll be north, just shy of the border. They won't go into Indian Territory. Rustlers'll be closer to Dodge—they want to take the herd and move it as little as possible."

So it broke down like this. The trip to Dodge City should take in the neighborhood of five weeks. We'd angle northeast and sometime in the second week we'd cross the Canadian River into Oklahoma to pick up the Western Trail. (With Prudence still mollified, it was Sally who asked, "Why's a river in Oklahoma called the Canadian?" She didn't get much of an answer. "It just is.") Up until we crossed that river, the danger of bandits was the highest. Then the next couple of weeks would see us across Oklahoma, where Indian tribes may or may not require a toll. Then in the homestretch to Dodge City, the risk of rustlers was high.

As such, we were outfitted to the best of our ability, and I'm not talking about our pants. Along with her pistol, Ruth had scrounged a shotgun for Prudence. Sally brought an early model Colt revolver. I couldn't afford a Henry rifle but had used my savings on an Evans repeating rifle and a scabbard for my saddle. Clean Through kept both a rifle and a shotgun in his chuckwagon. And Jonas put a rifle—I don't know the brand—in holsters on the saddles of both Mary and Katie. If he'd had his way, there'd have been cavalry units in front of and behind us.

The most interesting weapon of the group belonged to Pearl, simply because we never saw it. When Jonas offered her a pistol, she shook her head and said, "I'm armed in my own way" and left it at that. We hoped she had some sort of gun on her, because during our training Pearl had proved to be the best shot among us. Ruth speculated that Pearl had a Derringer stuffed in her bosom, another between her legs, a third down her back and a fourth tucked in her boot. "A woman of her sordid experience don't mind things rubbin' her all over." That was one time I was pleased Prudence didn't ask a question.

We kept the herd moving and kept our eyes peeled for any signs that might indicate outlaws were around. Katie had the lustful stare of that big man, Brute, seared in her memory. The rest of us remembered the sheer size of the man. He could snap any of us in two and maybe even make a toothpick out of Ruth.

"I wonder how many shots it'd take to bring down a man that size," said Sally at the campfire on the third night. "He's built like a buffalo."

"Best hope we never have to find out," I replied.

For once, Pearl added a comment, and it came in a cold, dark tone that chilled my spine. "Shoot the chest, then the brain. Anything else and he'll keep on coming." Suddenly we all hoped to be partnered with Pearl whenever we pulled night watch duty.

Our initial troubles, however, didn't come from Sean and Brute, but from three vile men whose names we never learned. It was late on our sixth day. The sun was lowering, but plenty of daylight remained and the sky was clear. Yet we never saw them coming.

They must have been watching us for at least a day because they knew exactly when to strike. Mary had gone ahead to find a suitable site to bed down the herd, and Clean Through had moved his wagon up as well to be ready to set up for supper at Mary's signal. The grassy prairie had turned to a stretch of scrub brush and loose dirt, with a steady breeze blowing the dust to the east, partially obscuring Sally and giving Pearl all she could handle just to get a decent breath.

The riders came from behind and to the left. The biggest of the three snatched Ernestine from right off her horse, cracking her dizzy with the butt of his pistol when she latched her foot in the stirrup and resisted. The second grabbed Prudence from her saddle as well, silencing her with three quick words: "Quiet or die." The third man held his gun high, covering the others and ready to fire should there be any pursuit.

But we were unaware.

How much time passed I can't say. Not much, I think. It was good fortune that Pearl had decided she'd swallowed all the dirt she could handle in one day. She chose to drop back and glide a ways to the left for relief from the thickest stream of dust. It was like riding through fog that clears at a sudden edge. Her first sight was the rambling herd beginning to spread out to the left. Her second sight was Ernestine's rider-less horse.

"Ernestine?!"

No response. She looked forward to Prudence. Another rider-less horse. She could see me up ahead.

"Laurie!" I couldn't hear her. She urged her mount to a high gallop and I heard it before I heard her. "Laurie! Help!" I raced back to meet her, my eyes absorbing the drifting of Prudence's horse and the wide scattering of the herd. "Ernestine and Prudence. Both gone!"

"Go tell Katie and Sally to stop the herd, then bring back Ruth. I'll go take a look."

"Alone?"

"Just 'til you get back. Hurry!"

Pearl rushed away as I pulled out my rifle, hoping Mary was on her way back, wishing Clean Through was a young marshal, and praying that Ernestine and Prudence were all right. I scanned the trail behind us. No movement. No signs of bodies on the ground. I began a slow backtrack. I had no tracking skills, and even if I had, the hoof prints and droppings left behind by the herd would likely have obliterated any sign. My best course of action was a steady speed, steady eyes and a steady finger on the rifle's trigger.

Looking to the southwest, I saw where the sage scrub brush blended into a thin section of salt cedars, juniper and honey mesquite. If the girls were hiding, that's where they'd be. If the girls were stolen, that's still where they'd be.

I headed that way, keeping the horse slow and quiet.

Three sets of tracks headed directly into the trees, even I could see that. That cleared up one mystery. They were taken. By three or more than three? Were they hurt? Dead? No shortage of mysteries yet to solve.

I am not proud to say that fear paralyzed me. Having dismounted, I watched from the cover of a thick juniper, lock-kneed, feeling the weight of the gun in my hands but unable to inch forward and use it.

In the grove, the three men had bound and gagged Prudence and were now at work on Ernestine, who was still dazed. "Now we'll start adding the others as they come lookin'," said the apparent leader of the group. He was thin and angular, with a powder burn on his cheek and the tattered remains of a Confederate jacket wrapped around his soiled shirt.

"What about the herd?" said the short, pug-nosed one.

"Ain't wasting time with it. Women like these are worth a hell of a lot more. Damn sight more. I know a comanchero across the border who'll pay a thousand dollars apiece for these young ones, maybe five hunnerd for the used ones."

"Hell yes we forget the herd," the third one chimed in. He had a twitchy cheek, like flies were landing on it. "Money like that? Damn straight we forget the herd."

"Damn straight," echoed Pug Nose.

Prudence shook with tears and terror. Ernestine had regained her senses enough to scowl at the men with a hate which I had not known her capable of but for which I believe her to be entirely justified. She tried to pull her hands out through the ropes that bound her, but succeeded only in tightening the bond.

"Hoofbeats! At least one's moving this way," Powder Burn alerted the others. I could hear them, too.

"Another thousand dollars," said Twitchy.

"She ain't our'n yet. Get back behind them mesquites. Let her come to us. Don't shoot 'less you have to."

Fear for myself held me in place. Fear for Prudence and Ernestine and whoever was riding up told me to move. I backed out of the grove away from the direction Powder Burn was watching, grabbed my horse's reins and moved into the open. Affording myself a quick glance back, I was relieved to see that Sally and Ruth had seen me and were high-tailing it my way. I moved to meet them. A group plan seemed wiser than shaming me with inaction a second time. Until I heard Ruth's plan.

"Let's rush 'em!"

"Hold on," said Sally. "We go in with guns blazing, we might hit Prudence or Ernestine."

"Prudence'd rather be shot than what might be happening to her. I'm goin' in."

Before I could even warn that we were being watched, she urged her mount into the trees, pistol drawn. Like it or not, that was our plan. Sally and I spread out behind Ruth and rushed forward, weapons ready as well. Everything about it felt wrong, but I didn't have time to think on it. In retrospect, what was wrong was that it was stupid. We had no idea what we were doing. Jonas had given us shooting lessons, but retrieving stolen women wasn't something we had practiced.

For all the wrong reasons, the plan turned out to be brilliant. No, I take that back. It was still stupid. We were lucky.

Ruth increased her speed and we matched it.

"Holy Christ! They're charging in!" shouted Twitchy. They might've expected us to be stupid, but not stupid and brave.

Ruth burst into the mesquite with Sally and me just seconds behind.

"There!" bellowed Sally, spotting the girls on the ground.

At the same moment that we reined in the horses, arms shot out from behind two trees and grabbed at Sally and Ruth. Sally spun in her saddle and fell, but Ruth ducked under and urged her mount toward Prudence. I pulled my rifle to my shoulder to shoot at the man hovering over Sally, but more hands grabbed the gun's barrel. It was a wrestling match for the gun and I lost it in seconds, dropping from my horse in the same motion. As Ruth yanked her horse to a halt and hopped down to Prudence, the loud cock of a gun ended the charge.

"That's far enough!" rang out Powder Burn's voice. Ruth's hand shuddered around her gun. "Don't do it. Drop it. No one needs to die."

Boom!

Boom! Boom!

Three men dead.

Pearl stepped out from behind a pecan tree, Katie's rifle in her hand. "Not the way I see it," she said.

Chapter 11

"Every person deserves to meet his maker with words said over him. So I'll just say that these terrible men were dealt with justly in this life, and I have no doubt they'll be dealt with justly in the next. Let's give them no more thought except to hope that their arrival will have taught us to be more vigilant and that their deaths will teach others to let us be."

So began and so ended Mary's speech beside the three shallow graves. You'll pardon my language, I hope, but I thought it was a damn fine one. Had she topped it off by spitting on the graves, not a one of us would have found it out of line. Ruth would have been happy to dig them up and shoot them again.

We were calm, quiet, yet our emotions were running full speed in every direction. There was fury that men would try to steal us and sell us. There was terror that it could be done. There was worry about what trials lay ahead. There was the bonding of a team pulling together to help each other. There was relief that we were indeed still all here. Above all, there was gratefulness that Pearl was a good, fast shot.

After alerting me, Sally and Ruth, Pearl had ridden to Katie. She took Katie's rifle, sending Katie on ahead for Clean Through and Mary. Pearl had then galloped back but hadn't seen the tracks to the trees. She'd pulled up wide of the grove and it was only by stopping that she'd been able to hear the crashing branches and yelling voices from when the three of us charged in. She entered from the other side, took aim, end of story. All had hugged her for it, even Ruth.

Once freed, Ernestine had sobbed hard for more than an hour, droplets of fear and anger and humiliation washing clean streaks through the trail dust on her cheeks. Prudence cried as well, but recovered quickly by taking strength from the support of all. Drying her eyes, she rose up and kicked the dead body of Pug Nose in the gut. "Anybody messes with us don't get no second try."

Mary and Katie rode up to the scene, ready for a fight that was over. Clean Through was last to arrive and, while relieved that all was well, I could hear an edge of disappointment as he said, "Pulled my gun and there's no one left to shoot."

Sally, Ruth and I returned to the herd, and Katie went to gather the horses. Mary kept Prudence and Ernestine with her as she, Clean Through and Pearl dug the graves. We all returned long enough for Mary's words, then it was back to business.

As we left the graves, Clean Through left a paper on the upturned earth and placed a rock on it to hold it down. It read: "Kilt For Steeling Women."

Attitudes were different at the campsite that night, quieter, more contemplative. Clean Through heaped the plates a little higher—cornbread, beans with bacon mixed in, even apple pie—but we didn't relish it the way we normally would have.

Prudence ate her pie first, like she just wanted something nice. Her anger at what had happened had faded into new thoughts. "That's about as scared as I ever want to be, I'm not ashamed to say. But when I think on what might've happened..." The lingering heat of the day didn't keep her from shivering.

Ernestine tore off a piece of cornbread and dipped it in her beans. "I'm done with being scared. Ain't nobody takin' me unawares again." She popped the cornbread in her mouth and gulped it down. "Let 'em try and they'll see Pearl's not the only one here who can shoot." She turned to Pearl, who sat near the fire, legs folded, reddish dirt on her pants. "I know I thanked you fifty times already Pearl, but it still don't seem like enough."

"For sure," Prudence chimed in. "You'll be in my prayers tonight. Every night."

Pearl was the teary-eyed one now, though I don't know if it was sadness from reflection on the killings or her hard life or warmth from her growing acceptance in the group. I only knew it was no time to disturb her.

Then Sally started laughing. Slow at first, then growing into one of those shaking-all-over laughs like when you remember the stupidest thing someone did as a kid or when someone fell in a puddle or something ridiculous like that. At last she got her breath long enough to spit out, "That ugly man said 'no one needs to die' and then, pow, there's Pearl saying 'not the way I see it!'" She was shaking with laughter again and it was contagious. I joined in and Ernestine howled and Clean Through cackled through his few teeth and suddenly everyone felt that Pearl gunning down three sneak-thieves was the funniest thing in the history of the world. Katie and Mary, who had been feeling bad about being removed from the action, were chuckling away. Even Pearl had a laugh and I think if Ruth hadn't been out with the herd she wouldn't have minded Pearl being part of the group. Well, just this once.

Maybe if Ruth knew more about Pearl, she'd have been less angry. But learning about Pearl was a chore even for me with my inquisitive nature. ("Nosy" was what my mother called it, but I always preferred "curious.") Little by little, I learned just that—a little—about Pearl.

Pearl's mother lived long enough to nurse her once, dying a day after what the doctor had described as a "fierce, hard childbirth." I've heard of many instances where a father blamed the child for the mother's death, but Pearl's father took to her just fine. He sharecropped a small Georgia farm with his brother and sister, leaving Pearl in her aunt's care most of the time. Despite the loss of her mother, Pearl had been born into love. But her life was destined for change within a few short years.

Depending on where you're from, you either call it the War of Northern Aggression or the War of the Rebellion. However you refer to it, it was a dark time. Darker still for Pearl, who saw her father and uncle leave but never return. Her aunt took to nursing in hopes of learning about the fate of the men, and in doing so left Pearl in the care of an elderly neighbor woman.

Life with the elderly woman, known to Pearl only as Nadine, was the last stroke of good fortune in Pearl's life. Nadine owned one book, a copy of Jules Verne's *Journey to the Center of the Earth* that a passing salesman had given her in exchange for a meal and a night's lodging, and from that book she taught Pearl to read. There came a time when the aunt stopped visiting, whether from death or distance or lack of interest is unknown, and Pearl's world consisted solely of Nadine, the book, and helping Nadine bake bread to sell.

Pearl was still but a child when a rider, a yellow-haired man with a black beard, saw her walking on a trail in the early morning light to deliver a basket of rolls. He snatched up both Pearl and the rolls and rode away. By the time they camped, Pearl's tears had dried.

"What'd you bring me out here for?"

"Thought you were older."

"I don't understand."

"Some day you will."

"I'm hungry."

"That's too damn bad."

He was just going to eat the rolls and let her starve! Even when there wasn't much food, she and Nadine had shared it. The small meal they'd shared the night before seemed like forever ago.

Hunger leads to desperation, a theme that would rule the next decade for Pearl. When the man looked away for just an instant, Pearl charged, grabbed a roll with each hand, and rushed away in what she thought was the direction of home. The man must have been satisfied with his remaining bounty or was too tired to care. He let her run, and he had not the decency nor the inclination to holler that she was running in the wrong direction. Even if she had been going the right way, they had ridden the entire day. More than likely, she was 40, maybe 50 miles from Nadine's. She would never see the kind-hearted woman again.

The happenings of the next few years are unclear. Pearl lived by stealing food and now and again stealing a dress as she grew. Every so often she'd be caught by a farmer's wife and put to work to pay for what she'd stolen, but as she grew older and her pretty face topped a comely body, there wasn't a farmer's wife who wanted her around for long. She was never in an area long enough to make a friend, and none who caught her ever showed sympathy or took the time to drop her off with a sheriff or a preacher.

So she drifted and drifted, gaining skills in sneaking up and running off. On the outskirts of Hattiesburg, Mississippi, Pearl came upon the campsite of a couple that was heading west. She watched to see where they stored their jerky, waited until they were asleep, and then entered the camp. She hadn't noted their dog, and the hound's bellow woke the family, the husband catching Pearl before she could get away. Pearl's best guess is that she was about 15 at the time, and I'd say it's a fair bet that she was plenty developed by then. So when the wife, not bright enough or interested enough to see her husband's lusting eyes, suggested they keep the girl to help with chores, the man was more than happy to oblige. They tied Pearl to their wagon, and the woman told her they would talk in the morning about how Pearl could come along with them, but that she'd be expected to do chores to earn her keep. Even tied up, Pearl thought it was the finest offer she'd had in years.

The man went at her that night. Weak, tired, and roped to a wagon, Pearl had no chance at all. She lacked knowledge of the ways of men—bad men, I should say to be fair—and didn't understand at first when he set himself down beside her. As his hand clamped over her mouth and his other hand lifted her dress… well, she learned quick. Her womanhood was taken before she even knew what it was.

Adding to the horror of the situation was that the wife hadn't minded at all. "Keepin' him off of me is worth a plate of food" was her only comment.

Pearl, without any say in the matter, endured the situation for another week. They kept her tied up and gagged in the wagon during travel time, then kept her tied to the wagon at night, never camping within earshot of a town or homestead. The woman fed her. The man went at her. Then it was on to the next site. Her wrists and ankles chafed under the ropes and, of course, other parts of her ached from the experience.

Far worse than the pain was the shame that washed over her. Though it had been a long time since she had had any form of a moral upbringing, she was no fool. She knew what was being done to her was wrong—after all, they had to tie her up to do it, plus the woman seemed happy that it wasn't being done to her. Pearl knew she had lost a part of herself, knew she didn't like how she was being used, knew she hated being bound and gagged, knew the man's smell and whiskers were repulsive, and yet the part that shamed her was that she knew how much she enjoyed having a meal brought to her, so much so that it almost seemed worth the hurt. She had scrounged and stolen for so long that a plate of food had more value than a bag of gold.

As her hunger dissipated, her mind cleared and her strength returned. By the week's end, her hatred of being used overcame her want of food, and she resolved to escape. That she was cleverer than both the man and woman combined was something of which she had no doubt. As night came, dinner was over, the woman bedded down and the man came at her. For the first time she didn't fight him. Less than five minutes after she said, "I'd like it more if I could put my arms around you," she was running free with a bag of jerky and potatoes, and the man lay woozy beside a dented skillet.

She had learned a range of lessons during that week, not the least of which was that her body could be traded for food, perhaps even money. It wasn't something she wanted to experience again, but a full belly felt good. In her own way, in her uneducated and morally untrained mind, she had prospects. But later, after she put plenty of distance between herself and the couple, her mind began to work over what she had been through. All at once she realized that she was rocking back and forth on the ground, hugging herself and crying.

Hunger remained a powerful motivator, and over the next few years she offered herself in barter for food and coins. Frequently she was chased from town by the law, more often by other women. Her shame grew, her self-worth dwarfed, and her way of life became routine. Sometimes someone would give her enough money for a stage ride, and she would move on.

Once she became a companion to a gambler who thought she brought good luck, and for a time she had a reason to smile. He taught her to shoot, reasoning that it can be handy for a gambler to have an unsuspected gun around. But her gun was never needed—he choked to death on a tough steak and she was on her own again.

More of the same followed. Drifting. Selling herself. Living in the wrong part of town. Spurned by most women. Denounced by most men when out in the street, but craved by those same men in the alleys and back rooms. Occasional beatings. Occasional kindness. Constant loneliness.

Eventually Pearl ended up in Secluded Springs. Now she was laughing by the fire with us, once again leaving a town behind, once again hoping to leave the past behind.

As for me, I can truly say that my life changed that night by the campfire. I had mixed feelings, being mostly down on myself for what I'd perceived as cowardly hesitation and a tiny bit pleased with myself for somewhat rallying to the cause. Staring into the fire while studying my feelings had little appeal to me, so I decided it was a good time to heed my father's wishes and write a letter. I had something exciting to tell, and I thought working up a paragraph or two would keep my mind occupied. The next thing I knew, three hours had passed and Mary was tapping my shoulder to join her on watch. I'd spilled my thoughts onto 17 pages, some about me, some about life, some about our journey and some about my friends. Writing had never interested me before, but I supposed that I hadn't experienced much to write about until then. Anyway, it felt freeing, and as I rode out to relieve Sally I resolved that writing was something I would continue to explore. I also resolved to write my parents a real letter soon.

The night passed. For once the clanging of Clean Through's wooden spoon against the pan was a welcome sound. Routine was returning.

One routine I didn't care for, however, was dealing with a cow I had nicknamed Uncle Angus. It was a poor name for a female, I admit, but her lackadaisical attitude reminded me of my mother's late brother, Angus. Much like Uncle Angus, this cow just wandered as it darn well pleased with no concern over the consequences. It was neither skilled at leading nor following. If we put her up front, she drifted and the cattle would start spreading out. If we put her in the middle or in the rear, she paid no attention to the rest of herd and moved off in any old direction. Aimless. Just like Uncle Angus.

While Uncle Angus the man had drifted his way into the wrong end of a jealous man's pistol, Uncle Angus the cow seemed determined to drift her way into anything but the proper direction. I spent an unfortunate amount of time driving her back toward the herd. Now here I was trying to think through the events of the previous day, what I did right, the many things I did wrong, how interesting it had been to write and how I couldn't wait to sit down and write some more, and there was Uncle Angus breaking my thoughts by roaming away like a butterfly in the wind. I circled my horse to her left and guided Uncle Angus back to the herd, but I had hardly started thinking again before Uncle Angus was drifting away toward a sinkhole. I cut her off and gave myself some peace of mind by roping her and pulling her along with my horse for awhile.

By mid-day dinner, enough time had passed that emotions were replaced by scrutiny. We wondered if the three men had stumbled upon us or had known about us in advance. It didn't seem that they were simply lying in wait for the next herd to come by, because not only had we not yet reached the official trail, but also their intent was to take us, not our belongings. By evening supper, we were leaning toward the idea that they knew we were coming. By mid-morning the following day, we confirmed the possibility.

Pushing forward ever closer to the Canadian River and Indian Territory, we spied a covered wagon at the edge of a field. A negro family had a fire going and meat cooking. That was unexpected enough. But the real surprise was that their five children were all lined up on a bench, watching us. They smiled and waved.

With caution on her mind, Mary told Clean Through to stop the chuckwagon and keep his gun handy. Then she rode over to meet the family.

"Good day to you, ma'am," came the welcoming voice of the husband. The wife's smile was just as warm.

"Good morning. Wasn't expecting to see anyone here."

"We're on our way from Arkansas to California, where I been promised railroad work."

"Long trip."

"Yes'm. We'd stopped in Wichita Falls for supplies and the storekeep said we just might be crossing paths with the women in pants."

"The town was cacklin' all about you," added the wife. "And please pardon my man. My name is Hattie, my husband is John, and these are our children."

"I'm Mary. Pleased to meet you all. You say people in Wichita Falls were talking about us?"

"Sure were," continued Hattie. "When we got this far and hadn't seen tracks, John thought we might be ahead of you. Then he shot that venison and it seemed like a fine idea to smoke it right here and hope you all might come along. It was a sight we wanted to see."

"And you didn't disappoint, no ma'am," said John. Then he shook his head as if he still couldn't believe it. "Women drivin' cattle and wearin' pants. My my. Thanks be to God that my children could be free to see such wonders!"

Mary smiled at the children, who smiled back, never stirring, never saying a word. I haven't seen better-behaved children in my life.

"We'd be pleased if you'd join us for a visit and some venison," said Hattie.

"You're very kind, but we must keep moving. I hope to reach the Canadian soon."

They were in sight for more than an hour as we walked the herd past. We likely stared at them every bit as much as they watched us. I had seen negroes during my time in St. Louis. Mary had seen them in Texarkana and it was a safe bet that Pearl had seen negroes, men at least. But it was the first time for the others and rare for all of us. Since the war, small groups had traveled into Texas and farther west, but most hadn't come through our particular area. Katie noted that while John was very dark, Hattie was only slightly darker than the deeply tanned among us, like Jonas. Above all, what we enjoyed most were the smiling children. They never moved from that bench the entire time we were in sight.

"Didn't they realize they'd be adding to our danger?" fumed Sally at that night's campfire.

Concern and speculation were running rampant. We wondered who had spread the word about our trip, and we wondered if more outlaws were lying in wait for us. Remember how I said no one ever got good news in a telegram? Well now that same telegraph service was spreading news about us and the only ones around to hear it were the people we least wanted to know.

"Could've been anyone in town," said Ernestine. "Maybe a reporter or maybe just someone gossiping about our scandalous clothes. Long as they paid, Grandpa'd send the message."

Mary changed the tone of the conversation. "Don't matter who. All that matters is word is spreading, so we need to be as vigilant as possible. Not likely that a kind negro family is all we'll run into." She was confident we'd reach the river the following day and move into Oklahoma the day after. That would lower the risk of bandits, but bring its own set of concerns. "Let's do triple watch tonight. Two-hour shifts. We'll worry about sleep once the river's at our backs."

While we were staying awake and scanning for bandits, Jonas was lying awake and staring at nothing. Sleep had been difficult for him since our departure. With his limited mobility, he wasn't doing much to tire his body out. And while his constant worrying was wearisome, his mind refused to rest.

Nighttime was the worst. Thoughts swirled without pause, wondering if Mary and Katie were safe, how the drive was going, how far they had gotten, if Ruth had shot Pearl, if buyers in Dodge would treat us fair—it was an endless parade of negativity brought on by the simple fact that the entire future of his family and his ranch was out of his control. That's hard for a man to take.

His main solace was thinking about Mary. He thought back to that dance in Texarkana and how superior Mary had seemed compared to the other girls. Just 16, she carried herself like a woman. She didn't pretend she was anything but what she was, which is something teenage girls often did in the hope of impressing someone. No, Mary was happy being Mary, and that impressed Jonas. He liked her looks, of course, but he'd need more than a pretty face and comely shape. He needed a woman with an inner strength to handle difficult times. Even more, he needed a woman with a mind that could envision what he envisioned, a fine ranch that would take at least a decade of work to become reality, probably longer. Mary's eyes forecast intelligence, and her conversation proved her eyes true. By the end of the dance, Jonas was convinced that his instant attraction had depth beyond infatuation. He shared his dreams with her. She responded to them with excitement and understanding. He asked her to marry him.

She said not yet. She said he must get her father's blessing.

Such an answer made Jonas sure she was the one. She had emotions, but she wasn't ruled by them. Impressive.

The next morning he called upon her parents, told them about the land he had purchased in north Texas and how taken he was with Mary and she with him. It was likely the most talking he'd ever done until he started making speeches to us. Her parents deemed him a fine man and a good match for their daughter, but the timing didn't suit them.

"It's this way," said her father. "Mary is sixteen. We realize that on the frontier, that's a woman's age. But in the east, where we're from, sixteen is still a girl. I am not comfortable letting a girl marry."

Jonas appreciated the candor, but said he hadn't the time for waiting. He needed to take possession of his ranch and commence the building, and he wished to have Mary by his side from the start so that the ranch would always be theirs together.

It's odd that mutual respect could create such conflict, but the more Jonas conversed with Mary's father, the more each of them liked the other and also the more each became further entrenched in his position. However, the growing respect ultimately provided the solution when Jonas presented a compromise based entirely on a handshake.

"Do you feel you can trust me, sir?" he asked.

"Yes, son, I do."

"Then let me offer up a promise that's respectful of all our wishes. Mary and I will marry, if this possibility is agreeable to her and to you, and begin to build our life and ranch together. However, our first year of marriage will serve as a courtship. We may hold hands and be affectionate, but that is all. Her virtue will remain intact so that, should her feelings have changed after the year, she'll be free to leave and will be unspoiled."

Jonas held out his hand. Mary's father looked at Mary. She nodded agreement. He took Jonas's hand and accepted him as his new son.

Mary's parents wished to see the land, so the next day the four of them set out on the trip. Once they'd reached the land and listened to Jonas outline his plan to build, any remaining reservations were gone. The circuit preacher was in Lubbock, so they headed there and the wedding took place.

For an entire year, Mary and Jonas slept side by side and often held each other throughout the night, but that was all. Both of them showed extreme willpower and dedication to a promise. So if Jonas had to trust his future to a woman, he knew there was no finer choice. She was resolute. She was determined. She was stronger than she knew. She accomplished what she put her mind to. No man could ask for more.

He tried to cling to those comforting thoughts, but the worries always crept back in. If only the rest of the world was as fine as Mary...

Sleep would eventually find him. It was a troubled sleep.

PART FOUR
THE RIVERS

Chapter 12

Whether it was God or Mother Nature or some other divine intervention, whoever put America together did a fine job of placing rivers right where somebody might need one. At least that was true in our case. Hot weather and thirsty mouths had about emptied Clean Through's water barrel, and none of us had full canteens. As the grass had turned to brush and small cedars, the cattle and horses were also getting dry. The herd was getting sluggish and progress was slow. Mary had ridden ahead to check the distance to the Canadian, but before she returned the herd began to pick up speed.

They could smell the river. It breathed new life into them.

Their dragging walk became a rumble, then a rush. We skipped the mid-day meal and let them go. Mary directed us toward the area she thought best for camping.

"Let them reach the river and drink their fill, but keep 'em on this side. We'll rest up tonight and cross in the morning."

It was no real challenge to keep the herd together. Even Uncle Angus went straight for the river. Once they hit the water, they stopped to splash and drink. The only thing moving them was each other as more cattle piled into the water. We'd left the ranch with near 375 in the herd, figuring that we'd lose some, trade some, and that some might die, the goal being to bring 300 to market. At that moment, I don't think we'd lost a single steer, cow or calf. We'd lost some women for a while, but all the cattle were accounted for.

Clean Through pulled his wagon upriver from the cattle to fill the water barrel with clean water. The rest of us attended to our duties, watered our horses, and filled our canteens. Then Ernestine spotted a rider and we were on instant alert, weapons drawn, eyes searching for more.

The plain was open leading to the river and we saw no other riders. Plus, this one rider was taking his time and coming straight toward us, not hiding his presence at all. We held our guns tighter nevertheless. Memories were too fresh.

"Howdy!" he hollered when close enough to be heard. "I'll be!" he shouted when close enough to make out our shapes. "You ain't men at all!"

"Keep your guns ready," Mary said to us as she urged her horse forward several steps. "Are you alone? What is it you want?"

The man rode to within ten feet of her, then stopped and smiled. "I was alone until I seen you people. Thought you might spare some jerky, maybe a biscuit." He was perhaps 25, with a scruffy beard and dust-covered clothes. He had ridden with his hands held high and he kept them high now. He had no sidearm and his saddle sheath held what looked like a shovel. "Say, is you all women?"

"Where did you come from?"

"Rode all the way from Ellsworth, Kansas, to Leadville to try my hand at prospectin'. After just two days of laborin', I said 'Dusty'—that's my moniker—'Dusty,' I said, 'you didn't like diggin' in the dirt when you tried farmin' and you don't like diggin' now.' So it's back to Ellsworth for me with the hope I can get my job back at the livery." He smiled. "Now you know my life story. I'd sure be proud to hear yours."

We kept scanning the horizon. There was no sign of other riders and we deemed his story true. Mary let him visit with us for a shade under an hour before Clean Through gave him some biscuits, bacon and beans and we sent him on his way, his hands once again held high as he rode. He was chatty and perhaps a bit jealous of Clean Through for being surrounded by women. I don't think he ever fully grasped that we were doing men's work; he seemed to think we were out for a joyride with cattle.

He was helpful—if not frustrating—in letting us know that there are two Canadian Rivers. We were about to cross the first one. Then we'd continue northeast to reach the Western Trail. Once we were northbound on it, we'd meet the North Canadian River, which he said wasn't as wide as this one, and then later the Cimarron River, about which he confirmed Jonas's opinion that it would be the widest.

What interested me about him the most was when he said he planned to stop at the Shattuck Trading Post and quench his thirst for a beer. I didn't care about the beer, of course, but I saw an opportunity to post a letter to my parents. I asked how much a beer was and he said probably five cents, then he cursed the operator for gouging travelers with high prices. I gave him ten cents to post the letter and have his beer on me, and he could keep whatever was left over. He was quite agreeable to such a proposal and scanned the others hoping they'd have a favor to buy as well. He was a thirsty man and a pleasant one, too. He didn't mind that no one else offered to set him up with a beer.

He was a nice reminder that there were decent people out there, and he was also a reminder that we could come across anyone at anytime. Watching him cross the river with the water barely above his mount's belly gave us confidence for an easy ride in the morning.

As it was, we were making the earliest camp of our journey. Ruth and Ernestine were happy to take the first watch, figuring it would lead to a solid break and night's sleep later. Clean Through was using the extra time to add some pies to the menu. Sally had her sewing kit out and was showing some techniques to Katie and Prudence.

Mary, Pearl and I sat together. Looking up to scan the horizon had become a good habit that we all indulged, though having the river on one side of us gave some relief. Marauders coming from the north would have to splash their way to us, giving us time to react. We had no desire to dig more graves and hoped to simply be left alone to do our jobs. I'm sure that's true of all cattlehands, not just a group of female ones.

"Pearl," said Mary. "I don't think I ever fully thanked you for what you did back there."

Pearl's least favorite topic was herself, and she deflected the praise with practiced grace. "You would've done the same. I thank you for bringing me along."

Mary laughed. "If it hadn't been for you, we'd be out here in dresses riding side-saddle. And you didn't just pay your way. You've earned it with hard work. I'm glad you're here."

"What are you writin', Laurie?" Pearl deflected once again.

"Another letter already?" added Mary.

"No," I said. "Just writing whatever comes into my head about the drive, the people and anything else. I can't explain it except to say that I find it enjoyable."

"Like a journal?"

"I suspect it is. I never kept one before, but I guess that's what I'm doing."

"I read part of a book once," said Pearl, her guard down just a bit. Maybe because Ruth wasn't around. "I can't say I understood much of it, but the imagination of it was sure something."

"What was the book?" I asked.

"Don't remember the title. It was about a man who entered a cave and was taking it down into the earth, all the way to the middle. I never got to finish it, so I don't know if he made it or what he found."

I wanted to pour out questions about Pearl's upbringing, find out how she learned to read, where she was from, how she ended up in her current state—and as you know by now, eventually I would—but right then I knew questions would close the crack in the doorway she'd opened. "I think I've heard of that book," I said instead. "It's by Jules Verne. Haven't read it, though."

"Sounds fascinating," said Mary. "I'm afraid reading isn't something I get to do much of. Sometimes a Bible reading on Sunday."

I swear, nature must view a calm moment on a trail drive as some kind of sin, because our quiet moment was shattered by a crack of thunder that knocked us all near out of our skins. Even Clean Through jumped so high he tossed a ladle thirty feet. We'd been so intent on watching for riders that we hadn't noticed a massive black cloud moving in from the west. This time we saw the scatter of lightning before another reverberation of thunder roared by seconds later.

We were still in sunlight, but the storm was coming on fast and the western plain was in shadow. Clean Through rushed over to us. "Beg pardon, Boss, but might I offer up some advice?"

"I'd be glad to hear it," said Mary, her neck and shoulders now stiff with tension.

"If it pours like it looks it's gonna pour, that river ain't gonna be none too shallow come morning. We best pack right back up and cross tonight."

"Do we have enough daylight left? I'd hate for our first crossing to be in the dark."

"I understand. But if we don't cross tonight, it may be days before the water lowers."

Mary was slow to mull but quick to action. She considered Clean Through's advice, thought about her inexperienced team, thought about being stuck on this side of the river, and made her decision. "All right. Katie, help Clean Through pack up and get the wagon across, then both of you get the horses to the other side. Everyone else, pack up, get fresh mounts and get in position to move the herd. Let's get crackin'." God must've been listening, because he sent a clap of thunder that put a deep, crackling period on Mary's orders.

It was a tribute to how well we had learned the ways of trail work that not a one of us hesitated or gave a thought to supper. Duty called.

Sally and I started packing our gear, and Pearl and Prudence hustled to pick out mounts and saddle up. Mary rode to tell the plan to Ruth and Ernestine. I'd just gotten my papers safely secured in my saddlebag when the big droplets began to fall.

The day was still hot, but that wouldn't be the case for long. The scattered droplets were cold, a precursor of the front edging ever closer. We could see heavier rains coming in and a rainbow formed where the storm danced against the sunlight. The cattle were growing nervous, lowing and rumbling along with the thunder.

Mary walked her horse into the river where we'd seen Dusty cross. She poked a long stick into the riverbed as she moved downstream. Satisfied that the footing was solid, she waved Clean Through ahead. I had wondered at the reason for the tall wheels on the chuckwagon, but seeing the mules pull the wagon through the water with the floor of the wagon hardly skimming the surface cleared it up for me.

As Clean Through hit the halfway mark, Katie rode Pitch into the river. Just as Jonas had said, the rest of the remuda followed where Pitch led. They were spread out more than Mary liked, so she guided her horse back and forth to form a line and keep the horses together.

The bank on the opposite side of the river was steep. The mules exited fine, but it took all their strength to raise the chuckwagon over the ridge and onto the bank. Again the tall wheels played a role by easing the angle. With some snaps of the reins and encouragement from Clean Through, the mules pulled the wagon onto the bank and ahead to flat ground. As Clean Through set the brake, the sky unleashed its fury.

All was darkness now. The thick clouds blocked out the sun and if we'd had time to think we would have thought it was night, not barely evening. Rain pelted down, stinging our faces, within minutes turning the topsoil to mud.

"Now, Ernestine!" roared Mary between thunderclaps.

"Aaaaaaaaaaaaaaaaaaaaaaaaaaaaaa!!!" The skittish herd needed little encouragement to move, but the cracks of thunder and slaps of the puddling rain outlasted even Ernestine's shrill cry. Cattle scattered in every direction, slamming into each other, some plunging into the river, others turning back. Ernestine cut off the retreaters and screamed again, turning them to the side. Pearl then cut them off and urged them forward. Most went. Some raced past Pearl. The storm loomed above us and a glowing shaft of lightning snapped down, scaring the cattle—and us— once again. Those that had raced by Pearl turned once more, bellowing, roaring, slinging mud with every sloppy step.

With Sally and I on one side and Ruth and Prudence on the other, we pushed the cattle forward into the river. Katie and Mary galloped back to help Pearl and Ernestine. The gray sky offered little light, and it was difficult to see how far the herd was spreading. The lightning became both enemy and friend, terrifying the cattle but providing us with glimpses to get our bearings. Clean Through shouted encouragement and the cattle responded to his voice, plunging their way toward the river's edge.

A sizzling bolt struck our former campsite, panicking a steer to ram sideways into the herd, its horns goring a cow, tumbling it to the ground. The horrific roar of the cow and the smell of blood distressed the herd even more, and controlling them was almost impossible. They were spreading too wide and rambling in too many directions.

"Form a wall and fire your guns," shouted Sally and the idea caught on fast. Katie joined us in the river and the three of us fired into the air. The herd tightened from our side, and at the same time, Ruth, Prudence and Mary fired from the other side. Then Ernestine fired from the back and we had re-established a form of order. We had no idea about strays, but the bulk of the herd was moving forward and crossing the river.

The minutes ticked like hours, so it was another shock to the system when the storm passed and the sun was still hanging low in the sky. The reddish-orange glow reflected in the multitude of puddled hoofprints on both sides of the river. The herd was antsy and lowing, but still for the moment as their fear had outlasted their energy.

Across the river, where we had camped for less than two hours, three strays roamed. Probably more were long gone. Four cattle carcasses dotted the landscape. I was surprised to see that Uncle Angus was not among them. She had crossed with the herd, no doubt saving her energy for future aimless wandering.

Mary and I went to retrieve the strays. Clean Through took a horse across the already-rising river as well, planning to examine the carcasses to add to his meat supply—a veteran's way of turning near-disaster into some small level of success. As long as there's a semblance of a herd and as long as the cowpokes are upright in the saddle, the drive goes on.

Prudence stood on the shore of the river, staring at the dead steers, wiping her eyes. As Ruth held her tight, Prudence was again the one to give voice to the thoughts shared by the group. "I don't know if I want to do this anymore."

Chapter 13

We were too tired to complain or whine or fight. The herd was too
exhausted to scatter, but nothing would've been done had they started to
roam every which way. There was no watch that night, and Mary's only
order was sleep. It was an order we followed without hesitation.

Morning came without Clean Through's clanging. Mary had told Clean
Through we'd camp here the entire day and start fresh the next. She'd
searched his eyes as if seeking approval of the decision. He just nodded—to
him, the boss had spoken. No approval was needed. He left us to wake up
on our own to get the rest we needed, though we all woke early wondering
why we hadn't been roused.

In the morning light, our path across the river looked like we felt.
Beaten. Sopping. Dirty. A shambles. Wisps of fog hung in the air. We could
see just how wide the herd had spread before we'd reestablished a modicum
of order. Overnight, the rain-soaked land had begun to shed its water,
filtering it into the river that was now close to three feet higher than the day
before. The rain and cattle had stirred the river to a heavy-clouded brown
with floating debris. Even though we hated to admit it in the light of all
we'd gone through, the decision to cross had been the right one.

I can't say we missed the three men we'd buried, but at least we
understood them. They had frightened us and threatened us and put the
drive at risk, and they were dead and in the ground because of it. We could
fight back against people. But you can't shoot a storm. You can't shoot a
rising river.

Above all, we couldn't shoot what would quite possibly be the biggest
opponent we would face: doubt. We'd had our lingering doubts from the
very first day, but our desires to help and to change our lives had pushed
those doubts aside. Our growing confidence in our skills and in each other
had driven those doubts still farther away. Now doubt had come raging
back, looming over us like an army of dark clouds, penning us in, laying
siege with barricades of fog.

You can't shoot fog. It has to burn off.

Mary gave us a day to rest, but the unplanned brilliance of it was that it
was also a day to burn off the fog that now enveloped our minds as well as
the landscape.

As Clean Through stirred the embers of the fire and banked it with a
new load of wood, Sally overlooked her unfulfilled dreams and an
unfulfilled heart to seek comfort in the past. "I never thought I'd miss
Secluded Springs, but at least there I had a roof and dry clothes." She

wrapped her arms around herself. Henry may have been a back-door lover, drifting in and out always at his whim and never hers, but sometimes he held her like she wanted to be held now.

"All my chores seem easy compared to crossin' that river," Prudence said. She tried to brush a clump of mud off her shirt, but her effort just smeared it. "I'd rather churn ten hours of butter."

Ruth patted her daughter's shoulder, a rare show of affection. "I know it ain't been easy for you, there or here. I admit our little shack looks pretty good about now."

Ernestine held out her hands to the fire and joined the brooding. "I used to wonder if all I'd ever do in life was reach up to get things off a shelf." She moved her left arm around, trying to loosen her aching shoulder from a spill she'd taken during the storm. "Reckon it wasn't so bad."

"Wasn't so bad?" Katie was the first of us to show any spunk. "You all couldn't wait to get away. You talked Ma into it, Ruth, remember? You, too, Sally."

Ruth just nodded. Sally just mumbled a soft, "You're right. I know," and then went back to staring at nothing.

"It seemed like an adventure back then," was all Prudence had to say. It being a statement instead of a question, she didn't raise her hand.

Not only had Katie's energy failed to spread to them, but their moping seemed to take the spirit out of Katie. She, too, stared at nothing or perhaps at a memory. "Wonder how Pa's doin'."

Pearl was not one to vocalize her thoughts. She had no intention of ever going back. She'd coughed up enough river water, though, to have deep concerns about how far into her new future she was going to get.

I was strangely thankful, not that we were alive, but that my saddlebags had kept my sheaf of papers dry despite the pouring rain and rising river. With the discovery that writing down my thoughts had awakened an energy inside of me, my life had already begun to change, whereas the others were basing the changes in their lives on reaching a destination and getting paid. Whether I returned to Secluded Springs or finished the drive and moved on to places unknown, my life would be forever different. My doubts were that I'd have the chance to experience it, but I guess I was the one person in the group who was feeling positive. If I'd realized how Mary had been churning inside as she listened to her doubting team, I would have spoken up.

Rising from the stone where she sat, Mary squared her shoulders, stretched her stiff neck, and faced us. "I have no doubt yesterday was brutal. I have no doubt that more difficult times are ahead. If you want out, then God bless you, go, today's your day to leave and I'll never hold it against you. But if you're still here at dinner, then you're in it 'til the end come what may. We are the cattlehands of the Circle B brand, and there's no room for quitters in our outfit. Back out now, or never think of it again." She picked up her saddle and started walking toward the horses. "No need to reply. Your presence will be your answer. I'm gonna go check on the herd."

We watched her toss the saddle onto a bay with a splash of white above its eyes. She tightened the cinch, climbed on, and trotted away without looking back at us. Whatever doubts she had, and I'm sure they were many, rode off with her.

Katie rose. "Think I'll check on the herd as well."

"I'll join you," said Pearl.

I got up next. Then Sally, Ruth, Ernestine and, finally, Prudence.

As we rode out to give the herd more attention than it could ever deserve, Clean Through called out, "There'll be pie when you get back."

Again in my spirit of honest representation, I must say that I believe Clean Through's cooking bedded down the nerves more than Mary asserting herself. With more time to cook and with a full understanding of current needs, he'd prepared a beef stew that included potatoes, more boiled potatoes on the side, black-eyed peas, skillet corn bread, sourdough biscuits, and apple pie. He added fresh coffee rather than reheating the morning grounds. Most of us never ate that well at home, and if we did, it meant the preacher was visiting.

We had reaffirmed our commitment to Mary, we had full stomachs, and we'd caught up on some rest. Our clothes were still soiled, but they were dry. The mood of all had greatly improved.

In fact, it wasn't until weeks later that it occurred to one of us (I forget who and curse myself for failing to write it down) that Mary had never offered up what would happen if any of us tried to leave after her offer expired. Mary refused to tell me what consequences she had in mind. Her toughness had risen to the surface that day, but I had my doubts that Mary herself had any thought of coming up with a punishment. I think she knew we'd stay together.

After all, we had pie.

We would later learn that about the same time our spirits were rising, another herd far north of us was crossing into Kansas on its way to Dodge City. The cattlehands were attacked and the herd was stolen. An army patrol found a single survivor who lived long enough to say that the gang of rustlers included the largest man he had ever seen.

Chapter 14

Some called it Oklahoma Territory. Some called it Indian Territory. Some said they were two separate areas and others said it was all one and the same. Regardless of how you drew it up on a map or named it, it offered an almost-straight northward trek to Dodge City. The earth was as red and often redder than what we'd left behind in Texas. It was soft earth, too, never seeming to pack down despite the trampling of herd after herd.

We reached the Western Trail and turned north without incident. No bandits. No rustlers. No Indians. Not even a sign of gawkers out to see the women dressed like men. Perhaps the news hadn't spread this far, or perhaps no one cared. Weather had been cooperative as well, which helped keep our spirits up. The cattle enjoyed the rich grass on the Trail—it must have been a hearty species to bounce back so green and tall after numerous herds chomped and flattened it. If our calculations were correct, it was now August 1. We had been on the drive for three and a half weeks. We felt seasoned, as if it had been three and a half years.

Then there we were, camped at the second Canadian River, this one referred to as the North Canadian River as if that made it unique. Under other circumstances, we might have spent more time wondering what the obsession was with naming rivers after a country more than a thousand miles away, but the memory of our previous crossing was too vivid.

Everything seemed to be in our favor this time. There wasn't a cloud in the sky, and believe me, we checked every few seconds just to be sure. We'd reached the river during the afternoon, giving us ample time to refill our water supply, settle the herd, and fill our stomachs. Still, we kept looking skyward, waiting for a lightning bolt to skip the need for a storm and just strike us down directly.

The same day, Doc rode out to see Jonas. If the examination went well, and if Jonas promised to keep using the crutches and to keep his backside off of a horse, Doc would remove the splints on Jonas's leg.

"Just cut the darn things off," grumbled Jonas as Doc poked at him.

Doc ignored him. "Can you feel that?"

"That you're jabbin' your finger into my hip? 'Course I can feel it." Jonas raised his eyebrows and his tone lightened. "That's good, right? I mean, I should be able to feel a bony old finger stickin' me in the side, hmmm?"

"Just relax." Doc never did like to answer questions before an examination was complete. He put Jonas through a series of tell-me-when-it-hurts tests, pulling his leg in different directions, swinging it at the hip, having Jonas flex his toes, and a whole bunch more. When Doc pulled out his stethoscope, Jonas had a fit.

"If you think a trampled leg messed up my heart then you need more doctor schooling! I'm telling you, I'm fine. Cut the darn things off!"

"When you calm down, I'll share some good news with you."

"I'll be a lot calmer when you get these boards off my leg." Jonas quieted as Doc stared at him with practiced patience. "What good news?"

"Two things. First, I believe you've healed enough that I can remove the splints." He held up a quieting hand to make sure he had Jonas's full attention. "That doesn't mean I believe you're ready to walk on your own, and certainly not to do any lifting or riding. As it stands, you may always walk with a limp, but if you put too much strain on that hip too soon, you'll be hoping that a limp is your only trouble. Crutches for two more weeks, maybe three. Do we understand each other?"

"I can't say I'm in full agreement with your view of what makes good news, but I'll abide by what you say. Ain't easy sitting all the time, though, knowing there's work to be done."

"The work'll wait. I came past your remaining cattle on my way in. They know how to chomp on grass without you watching them."

"Thinkin' that way is why you're a sawbones instead of a rancher. What's the second piece of good news?"

Doc grinned and reached into his pocket. "Laurie Michaels sent her folks a letter and they were kind enough to let me bring it out for you to read." He handed it to Jonas. "You can look at it while I cut off these splints."

Jonas gazed at the letter, longing to know the news it must bring about Mary, Katie and the drive. Yet he handed it back to Doc. "Mind reading it for me? I… I misplaced my spectacles."

That pretty much confirmed something Doc had wondered on for quite some time. Jonas couldn't read. Doc hadn't said anything when Jonas always turned down reading material in his office, and now he let him hang onto his pride and opened the letter that I'd given Dusty to post before we crossed the river.

"'Dear Mother and Father. The drive is going well, though I must say we've had our adventures. We have reached the Canadian River. All of us are well.'" Jonas let go a sigh of relief. "'We had a scare when some bad men stole two of us — not me…'"

"Stole 'em!" So much for the sigh of relief.

"'…But we tracked them down and Pearl killed the men. All of us are together again and safe. A man passing by has agreed to post this letter for me. I hope it finds you well. Thank you again for the paper. I find that I like writing and will try to send more letters. Love, Laurie.'"

"That's it? She didn't say who was taken. She didn't —"

"She was sending a letter, not a report. Now you know that all are safe. Heck, by now they're likely far into Oklahoma. You can't ask for more than that."

"I can ask to be there, but my doctor won't let me ride a horse."

"You're darn right he won't."

They squawked with each other for a while longer, but underneath it all was the comfort of knowing we were well.

Despite Dusty saying otherwise, the North Canadian River looked wider than the Canadian, but it seemed less intimidating without the storm clouds overhead. Mary had already ridden across and back, deeming the footing solid and the water level only about waist deep except for a slight dip in the center. The current was gentle. All signs were positive for a good passage across in the morning. That made us nervous.

Whereas before we were so busy watching for riders that we hadn't noted the oncoming storm, now we were so busy looking for any wisp of a dark cloud that we were fortunate when Ruth spotted a rider heading in our direction. I suspect it was because she's shorter than the rest of us and watching the sky still encompassed more of the horizon line for her than us.

It was a man with just under a dozen tethered horses trailing single file behind him. He'd clearly seen us and approached directly with no sign of ill will or outlaw intent. Our hands were on our guns anyway. Just because Dusty and John had been friendly, it didn't mean everyone would be. As it stood so far, the bad had outnumbered the good three to two.

"Evening, ladies," he called with a broad smile. Though he was somewhat silhouetted against the late-afternoon sun, it was still early enough in the day that there was plenty of light to see him. He was young, 19, maybe 20. He pulled his horse to a stop a friendly distance outside our camp. The trailing horses stopped as well and he jumped down. "I heard about your presence on the trail and wanted to offer my —."

You may not believe me, but that's exactly how it went. He was fresh and energetic and outgoing and he stopped in mid-sentence at the sight of Katie. I do not want the truth doubted at all, so if you bring a stack of Bibles I will swear upon them loudly and without hesitation that he went one hundred percent lock-jawed when he laid eyes upon that girl. Just stood there gaping. And I don't mean for one or two seconds, I mean that he might still be there if Clean Through hadn't finally tossed a ladle of cold water on him and said, "Easy, son."

For her part, Katie was staring right back. I didn't believe in love at first sight before that moment, and I still don't since infatuation can come to a screeching halt when mouths open and you find out your potential love is none too bright, but these two came as close to it as I believe possible.

He didn't seem to notice that the rest of us were there, that Katie wore a layer of trail dust and soiled, mud-spattered clothes, or that her once-lively hair had been matted down by her hat and by perspiration from the hot sun. Likewise, she couldn't see that his clothes were tattered and that he had a large splotch on his cheek from wiping off sweat with dusty fingers. They were twenty feet apart, maybe thirty, and lost in each other's eyes.

"I thank you kindly for the cool water," he said to Clean Through. "Guess maybe the sun was getting to me."

"Must've been it," said Clean Through, his hand over his mouth.

Mary stepped in front of Katie. "You mind telling us who you are and why you're here so we'll know whether or not to shoot you?"

"Of course, ma'am. I apologize." He wiped the dripping water back over his face and slicked down his hair with it. "I'm Parker Hagen. I raise horses. Takin' these to a buyer up in Caldwell."

"That's who you are. Now how about the why?"

"Don't be rude, Ma," whispered Katie. Mary ignored her.

"Heard rumors of women moving cattle north. Wasn't sure if you were on this trail or over on the Chisolm. Hopin' I'd cross your path. Figured I might never see something like this again."

"Seems reasonable, Ma."

"We'd be a lot more welcoming, young man, if you'd hand over that shooting iron."

Parker grinned. "My pa always told me never to give up my gun, but he also told me you can't win an argument with women. As long as we're agreed that I get it back when I leave, I'll oblige."

"Of course."

He lifted his gun from its holster using two fingers to grasp the handle. He held it out to Clean Through, but Katie pushed past her mom. "I'll get it." She took the pistol with a gentle touch, lingering in front of Parker long enough that Clean Through was reaching for the ladle again.

"Bring it here, Katie," said Mary with an impatient tone. "My goodness. Give the young man room to breathe."

Parker was the very definition of a strapping young man. Tall. Broad-shouldered. Forearms the size of Ruth's waist. If he had looked at Katie and said, "You'll do," I have no doubt she would've swooned. Yet what struck me most of all was his polite manner. He was the embodiment of western ideals in a man raised right. All of us could see he was beyond smitten with Katie, yet there was nothing about his ways that had us worrying he would snatch her up and ride off like the wrong kind of western man. He was respectful.

He had originally come to visit just so he could say that he'd seen the women in pants, but that plan had swiftly changed. He intended to win Katie's heart and, just as essential, Mary's approval to do so. He spoke of the business he was growing, of how the horses he raised in Amarillo with his uncle were often purchased by people as far away as Pueblo and Abilene. He wasn't boasting so much as making sure Mary and Katie understood that his prospects were good.

It was fascinating to see love bloom so quickly. Katie and Parker had known each other less than an hour, had never been alone together, had not taken part in anything more than a superficial conversation, and the only physical contact between them was when their fingers brushed slightly as he handed her his gun. As we pumped Parker with questions, he was agreeable to answer—and the way he often extended those answers made it clear that they were really meant for Katie.

"So you're takin' horses all the way to Caldwell?" Sally asked.

"Yes, ma'am, sure am." His eyes flicked to Katie for just a flash and his voice took on a richer tone. "Got a real good business going throughout this whole territory. Very good prospects for an unattached man of nineteen."

It went on like that. I experienced a strange kind of detachment that I'd never known before. It was like I was two separate Lauries, one participating in the conversation and the other serving as an observer of all involved, noting the nuances of communication between Katie and Parker and enthralled by the effect of their unspoken but obvious love on the rest of us.

The clear esteem for Katie that shined in Parker's eyes reminded Sally of her early days with Henry. This was before he became a back-door boyfriend whose arrivals were unpredictable and, some would say, immoral. He couldn't get enough of her during those times, and he not only went to see her by entering through the front door, but he also went out in public with her. They would have dinner, perhaps walk down the street holding hands. It was a courtship. Sally's memories were warm, but reality had tainted them into melancholy remembrances. Henry's eyes had wandered. In trying to win him back, Sally had left her back door unlocked and the covers of her bed turned down. She had settled for a fraction of the man's love and time, and as she watched Katie and Parker she said a silent prayer that they would be devoted to each other always. Sally is a kind-hearted woman.

I noticed that Ruth, however, eyed Parker with a hint of suspicion. At the same time, both Prudence and Ernestine seemed to hang onto every word Parker said and spent a good deal of their time glancing at Katie to make sure Parker's words met with her approval, though there really wasn't much doubt of it.

Mary was able to concentrate on the conversation much better than the rest of us. She had flashes of memory about her first meeting with Jonas and she had a mother's protective instincts regarding Katie, but she was also trail boss, scout, drover and owner of the herd and Parker had information that might prove useful.

"We know we're in Indian Territory," she said, "but we have yet to see any."

"You likely will soon. Where you picked up the Western Trail skirts right up the edge of Cheyenne and Arapaho tribes and now you're in one of the Cherokee areas. You won't see them until you cross the river, but I've no doubt they've seen you."

The thought of running into the Indians was chilling for all of us. Parker was quick to offer reassurance when Katie asked, "What will they do?"

"Don't fret. They're a proud people, but their leaders believe in peaceful ways. You'll have to make an arrangement with them, of course."

"Arrangement?" asked Mary.

"You see that I brought eight horses? I'm making deliveries for two contracts. One calls for two horses at the Woodward trading post, and three others are for my sale in Caldwell. Two of 'em I ride and use for packing. The last one is for safe passage. I make this trip often, and it's agreed that I'll provide a mount to the Cherokee one trip and to the Tonkawa the next."

"So my husband was right. We'll be asked to pay a toll."

"It keeps the peace, and it's fair, too." He smiled. "Now I'm not saying they won't frighten you, because you won't know they're there until they want you to know. But as long as you pay what they ask, most likely two, maybe three of your steers, they won't be a worry." He looked directly at Katie, his smile fading to concern. "What worries me and should worry you are the gangs this side of Dodge."

"Have you fought with them?" Katie asked with a catch in her voice.

"No, just heard stories. Several gangs and all of them ruthless. I wish you were on the Chisolm. Still have rustlers, but not as fierce or as rampant."

Mary shook her head. "We'll take our chances. Jonas selected the Western because Dodge was more direct than going all the way to Abilene."

"Why the A, T & SF runs through Newton now. You wouldn't have to go to Abilene or cross the Kansas River. Don't matter now, I reckon, since you're on the Western. But keep it in mind for your next drive."

Mary groaned and smiled at the same time, and her groan was echoed by several of us. "Oh, Lord, please don't put me on another one of these. If all the men disappear again, I'll just point the cattle north and hope they make it on their own."

The conversation continued a while longer. In all, Parker was with us a little over an hour, but what an hour! He'd made quite the impression on all of us—Katie especially, of course—and I believe we made quite the impression on him—again, Katie especially. If he hadn't needed to keep moving because of his delivery schedule, I expect he'd have been happy to stay there talking with us forever. As it was, he thanked us for the conversation and the slab of cornbread that Clean Through had offered up, and then he asked Mary and Katie to walk with him to his horses so that he could speak with them privately.

"My father always told me to be direct, and my uncle is the same, so I guess it's the only way I know how to be. If it's agreeable to you, Mrs. Bartlett, and not offensive to you, Katie, when we have all finished our jobs, it is my intention to come courting."

"Why, Mr. Hagen, I'm afraid that I'm already married," Mary couldn't resist saying.

"Ma!"

Parker took the joshing in stride and also as a sign that he was not objectionable. "You're right, I should make my meaning clearer." For the first time, he took Katie's hand. "I aim to win your heart, Katie."

Unlike the storm we'd suffered through at the river crossing, the lightning bolt that ran from Katie's hand through her arm and into her heart was pure pleasure. Her throat tightened and her voice was just a whisper. "I'd like that."

"I'd say you already have," added Mary. Then she stepped up and gently pulled their hands apart, much to the dismay of both. "But for the moment, we all have jobs to do. And though I may be taking Jonas's place here on the trail, have no doubt that he's the head of the family. Trust me, before any blessings can take place he will size you up like you've never been sized up before."

Katie's eyes went wide, but before she could speak, Parker chimed in. "That is more than fair, Mrs. Bartlett." His eyes moved to Katie. "Provided you'll let no one else come along and try to steal your heart."

Katie's eyes misted over. She could not speak. She looked at her mom for help and Mary rose to the occasion. "It appears there's none of her heart left to steal." Katie nodded.

With that, Parker released the breath he was holding and took to his horse. As he started his band of horses in motion, he turned back and said, "You stay safe." Katie knew the meaning ran deeper.

As I said, Parker's appearance and his instant attraction with Katie stirred memories and feelings in us all.

Clean Through was a hard man to read. He was always jovial, and he had that air of earthy wisdom that comes natural to some old men. He looked like he wasn't interested in the distraction, yet he hung on every word. When I asked him what seeing Parker and Katie made him think of, all he said was, "That I was young once." Later that night, I heard a small clinking sound coming from his wagon, where we all knew he kept a bottle of whisky for medicinal purposes.

The rest of what happened that night was instigated by Katie. Clean Through had stuffed us with a big supper, and Mary had insisted on an early bedtime for all. She wanted everyone rested for the crossing in the morning, and she took the night watch by herself so that we all could be ready. Shortly after she'd gone and after Clean Through's snores rose from under his wagon, Katie shook Prudence from the hazy sleep she was falling into.

"Katie?"

"Sshhh!!"

"What the devil?"

"Hush and listen. Am I pretty?"

"Of course you are."

"How was Parker to know it with me covered with so much grime and my clothes soiled through?"

"But he did. He took right to you."

"What if I was lucky? What if next time he sees me he can't see past all the dirt? What if all he sees is a filthy cowhand? That ain't what a man wants in a wife."

Prudence was now wide awake and offered reassurance to her friend. "I don't think he'll ever see you as anything but fresh as a daisy. What's the name of the chubby thing with the love arrow?"

"What? You mean Cupid?"

"That's it. It was like Cupid emptied his whole quiver into that boy. You're worryin' over nothing."

"Just the same, I ain't goin' to let him see me like this again. I'm goin' down to the river and wash myself but good. Clothes, too."

"The river? We're supposed to be sleeping."

"I can't sleep knowing Parker seen me like this."

"I'm tellin' you, he didn't mind. And what about your clothes? How are you gonna get them dry by morning?"

"It's still hot here, same as in Texas. I'll wring 'em good and hang 'em on a tree."

"It is hot, and it's all gone to your head."

"Come with me."

"No. Huh-uh, we're supposed to be sleepin'."

"Think how well you'll sleep after a good wash. Come on."

Katie turned and tiptoed toward the river as fast as she could without making noise. Prudence did just what most teenage girls are apt to do. She followed her friend.

At the river's edge, Katie whisked off her boots, trousers and shirt. Only a quarter moon showed that night, but it was still bright in the clear sky and the stars radiated like diamonds, the light dancing on the river and upon Katie's exposed white skin and her undergarments that had at one time been white as well. She moved into the water and held her clothes under for a good soak.

Prudence arrived and began to undress. "I suppose we might have thought to do this earlier in the day if Parker hadn't been such a distraction."

"It was a distraction I'll never forget."

Prudence joined her in the water and thrust her clothes into the river. "Should've brought some lye soap." Then she squatted into the water so that she was drenched to the neck. "Almost isn't deep enough for a bath. Feels good, though."

It's funny how we could be out in the open range with empty miles in every direction and still struggle to find time alone with a friend. They lounged not only in the water but in each other's company.

Prudence leaned her hair back into the water. "Wonder if I'll catch the eye of a handsome horse trader."

"I assume you mean one lookin' for a wife, not a horse."

Prudence shoved out a hand to splash water at Katie. "You know what I mean. I wonder if I'll ever live in a real house. Not a shack, but a real house that don't whistle when the wind blows. With a husband that's not too handsome but just regular and solid and appreciates me. Don't seem like that's askin' too much from life."

"I bet there's a man out there right now hopin' you'll come into his life. You'll see."

"Hope he don't like a lot of butter, though. I do despise that churnin'."

As their relaxation and excitement both grew, they were unaware that their voices were rising and their splashes getting splashier. So they nearly jumped out of what little they were still wearing when I said, "Can we join you?"

A moment later, Ernestine and I were in the water, too, trying to stay quiet but carrying on like schoolgirls. With her arms bared, we could see how trim and fit Ernestine was. Growing up carrying boxes and stocking shelves had benefits I'd never imagined. We talked more about the feelings that rose up while Parker was there.

Ernestine was moved to similar dreams as Prudence, except she didn't want a rugged man. "A storekeeper would suit me just fine."

"Was your dad a storekeeper like your grandpa?" Prudence asked, a rare question from her that didn't involve first raising a hand.

"Sure was. My uncle, too. I have a picture of 'em. They always look so much cleaner than most other men, even the preacher. Storekeepers are friendly and mostly quiet. Grandpa hardly yells at all except when we take inventory and he gets tired."

Prudence seemed to like sharing in Ernestine's dream and urged her to continue. "Would you help him in the store?"

"Sure. But he'd be taller than me so I wouldn't be the only one who could reach the top shelf. Smart, too. We'd read books and talk about them, and I wouldn't feel awkward at all. Wouldn't that be somethin'?" Her voice had thinned to a whisper, but then it rose as she looked at me. "You think you'll ever get married, Laurie?"

"Yeah, maybe."

My lack of enthusiasm made them all stop splashing. "Don't you want to get married?" Katie asked with a clear level of dismay in her tone.

"It just doesn't seem all that exciting to me."

"I guess it might not be to you, havin' been to St. Louis and all, but it would be to me," said Prudence as dreams washed over her again.

I got up to hang my clothes on the tree. They almost looked clean in the moonlight. "It would be exciting with the right man, I suppose. But I've sure met a lot of dullards, most interested in Dad's bank more than me. I want more than that. I want to see places. I want to rely on myself like Sally's able to do."

"Did I hear my name?" We looked up to see Sally and Pearl wading into the water. When we had first put on our pants and shirts in Edward's store, I thought they revealed our figures and our curves. They did, but not like wet garments that are generally unmentionable. Pearl's underthings were old and in two pieces, a chemise that might have been wool and a set of drawers that, well, that could be removed swiftly. Wet and clinging to her body, it was easy to see why men sought her out and why Charlie had hated to see her go. Maybe someday a decent man would cherish the person inside that body. Sally had a newer one-piece garment, most likely crinoline and most likely one she made herself. Once wet, it took on the full curve of her hips. I'm sure she looked beautiful, since she's a lovely woman, but all I could think about was how comfortable that undergarment looked.

"Sally, even your underwear is perfectly stitched. You won't have any trouble setting up a new store."

"Just the same," she smiled, "I hope folks don't ask to see my underwear."

"I know cowhands are to supposed to celebrate the end of a drive with liquor and gambling," said Ernestine, "but I agree with Laurie. A new set of underwear sounds pretty good."

Katie noticed that Pearl was sitting at a little distance from the circle that had formed. "Come in closer, Pearl. Sit by me."

You might have read a dime novel or even a "penny dreadful" story where a harlot has a heart of gold. Well, Pearl did not have a heart of gold. She had plenty of justifiable bitterness in her soul and she certainly showed no signs of forgiveness or hesitation when she turned a rifle on those three bandits. But for some reason, her heart was as unselfish as a heart can be where Katie was concerned. Maybe Katie reminded her of what she could've been. I don't know and Pearl doesn't say. What I do know is that the smile she radiated as she moved in beside Katie was brighter than the moonlight.

"That Parker seems like a nice young man. I'm happy for you."

"Why thank you, that's very kind," Katie replied, matching Pearl's somewhat formal tone.

A moment later Ruth arrived, and Prudence assumed she was in big trouble. Instead, Ruth threw off her clothes and waded in to the relief of Prudence and the laughter of us all. "I may be a bit older than you all, but I ain't forgot girl talk."

The conversation continued, but the tone changed as Ruth chimed in. Where the others had leaned on dreams, Ruth leaned on advice. "He looks like a fine man," she said to Katie. "But you watch out. You be sure."

She didn't say much more despite looking like she wanted to. But when the talk circled back to dreams, Ruth gave Prudence a hesitant look, then a stillness came over her that caught the attention of us all, a stillness of a decision made, of a need to share, of deep wisdom wrapped in deeper hurt.

"This is not somethin' I should say in front of you," she began, her eyes looking through Prudence and into memories, "but I reckon it's best you understand it now. Seein' that young man, it made me think of when James came courtin' me. We were poor, my folks and us kids, as poor as they come. Ma and Pa didn't want me marryin' James on account of he was poor, too. They wanted somethin' better for me. But I was used to bein' poor and figured I might as well be poor and loved. And James did love me. Still does in his way, I know it in my heart. He ain't a talker, but he ain't one to lie neither. So the first time I smelled another woman on him, I demanded the truth and he gave it to me all right." She shivered despite the warm night air. "'It's you I love,'" he told me, "'but sometimes I need to hold a woman with more flesh on her bones.'"

"Oh, Ma," Prudence whispered, but Ruth kept going.

"It hurt somethin' fierce. I knew I ain't been blessed with a body that bounces and wiggles, but I had thought I was woman enough for him. But his roamin' eyes and cathouse ways..." She wasn't looking toward Pearl at all, but Pearl lowered her head just the same. "I can't count the times I've cursed myself for lovin' him anyway."

If you've been picturing Ruth as a scrawny stick, you've been correct in your assessment. It was even more apparent with a wet, petite petticoat hugging her wiry frame. Yet she was womanly. Everything about her was tiny, but the curves and proportions were there and had you seen her you'd have cursed James for seeking comfort in other women. How could a man know he's hurting his wife and family, yet do it anyway? How less poor could they have been if he hadn't wasted so much money on bubbly whores?

"After a time I got used to his ways, and I think that bothers me more than the hurt he caused. I lost my pride. Thought maybe this adventure would bring it back. Then that boy today… sparkin' after you like he did, Katie. So much came rushin' into my head. If my two eldest boys had lived, they'd be about his age or maybe a year older. What would they be like now? Would they treat a girl respectful like that Parker boy treated you? I like to think so. I hope they wouldn't treat a woman like their pa treated me." Prudence wiped away a tear. Ruth brushed the water with her hand as if letting the memories ripple away, then gave a sad smile first to Prudence and then to Katie. "I deserved better than the life I've had, and you girls deserve so much more." Her smile at Katie broadened. "I have a good feelin' about that Parker boy. All I'm sayin' is, be careful before you give your heart away."

"I will, Mrs. Hadley. Thank you for sharing that."

"Well, I didn't mean to turn everyone sad. But at least we stopped talkin' about Sally's underthings." She splashed water at Sally and just like that we were happy and playful again, though I have to say Prudence looked at her mother in a new light. Soon she, too, was laughing again. With no thought of the time, we soaked and splattered each other and cackled some more.

Next thing we knew, there was the snort of a horse on the bank. Mary sat in the saddle, trying to stare us into shame but unable to control the twinkle in her eyes that betrayed her amusement.

Katie spoke up before Mary could say a thing. "Hi, Ma. We're doing the washing."

"A woman's work is never done," added Ernestine. I don't know whether it was her squeaky voice or the irony of her words in the middle of a cattle drive, but Mary was moved to a smile. Moments later, one more set of clothes was hanging out to dry.

We talked and splashed for close to another hour, thankful that Clean Through's nip at his medicinal whisky kept him snoring the whole time. Ruth's burden seemed lessened and she joined in the merriment as if she had let go of her stories eons ago. For that little bit of time, we were women out of pants, our work clothes and our worries tossed aside.

It was a time of pure, carefree joy — the last such time we would have. Looking back, I wish we had savored it more.

Chapter 15

"You ladies are sure draggin' after gettin' a good night's sleep." Clean Through banged and clanged that nasty wooden spoon in that nasty pot for the third time. He ruffled his gray whiskers and smiled his near-toothless smile. "Look at me. I'm fresh as a dewdrop on a cactus flower on a fine spring morning." I wanted to tell him that he likely hadn't looked fresh in forty years, but I held back. We were dragging. It wasn't his fault we'd stayed up cackling in the river.

Once you've sat in a river in your undergarments—assuming it's by choice—that river doesn't seem so intimidating. The memories of the previous river crossing had been washed aside by the memories of the previous day and night. Young love. Relaxing in cool water with friends. Despite the sadness Ruth had shared, the entire evening had passed without her calling Pearl a harlot a single time. Even the visible reminders of our rough adventure had been wrung from our clothes and hair. Though still far from clean, we felt renewed in the morning light. We shook off our sleepiness with the help of Clean Through's strong coffee and the knowledge that we had spent the evening both beside and in the river without disaster. That there wasn't a rain cloud in sight was the final piece of our confidence puzzle. Not only were we ready to move the herd across the river, we were ready to take on anyone who might dare try to stop us.

While Mary ordered us into position, Clean Through snapped the reins to get his team of mules going. I'd always heard mules were stubborn, but these two always did what Clean Through asked—probably because he kept them well fed.

Next, Katie took the remuda across. Again she rode Pitch and again the horses followed. Mary trailed the horses to encourage them to keep moving. Once they were across, she took her place at the front of the herd and we awaited the sound that had marked the beginning of our work day for quite some time.

"Aaaaaaaaaaaaaaaaaaaaa!!!!!!!!!!!!"

Ernestine was in fine voice and the herd responded exactly as planned by trying to get far away from her. They moved forward into the water, whining and bellowing with a touch of sadness that might have been from leaving the river but might also have been because Ernestine was louder than they were.

The river that had seemed so wide when we were nervous now seemed like a creek when viewed through confident eyes. No doubt its width is somewhere in between. Mary crossed and then moved to the side to watch the herd and holler orders. At one point she shouted, "Keep 'em moving! Don't let them drift down where it's soft!" It reminded me of Jonas making speeches about things we already knew. Sometimes the one in charge just has to say something to feel involved in what's going on. Then I realized that Uncle Angus was indeed drifting off and I moved to turn her back with the herd.

All of our heads snapped up at a passing shadow, but it was just a hawk floating in a circle above us. At least it's not a vulture, I thought. Or a storm cloud.

Ruth and I were the next to reach the bank. We stayed at the edge, acting as a funnel for the herd to move through. The cattle had no difficulty moving across. The water was still low and gentle, and the bank had an easy slope they could walk right up as if God had built a ramp onto the prairie. Their gait and progress was so mild and steady that the water had muddied only to a light brown similar to tea with milk. A frog even leapt up to sun itself on a stone.

Up ahead, Clean Through brought the chuckwagon to a stop and turned to watch the progress. The horses were content to nibble a grassy patch, so Katie left them and moved back to the river's edge, ready to offer support where needed. But all was proceeding according to plan.

Except for the hawk. It had other plans.

Like the lightning from our previous crossing, the hawk struck. It tucked in its wings and sped downward, snatching the sunning frog with its talons. Rising again, it soared past the face of Pearl's horse. Frantic, the horse reared back, throwing Pearl into the water, her limbs flailing, her head cracking on a stone. The horse rushed off. Pearl lifted her head, dazed. She pushed at the riverbed with her arms, trying to stand, but blackness clouded over her. She managed a staggering crawl, but the blackness was too overpowering. She collapsed into the water, limp, face down.

On and near the shore, none of us had noticed. We were caught up in our duties, and the lowing and splashing feet of the cattle had drowned out—a poor choice of words, I know—any noises Pearl and her horse had made.

"Keep them headed straight. Nice, easy pace," Mary directed. Ruth and I kept the cattle moving onto the bank. Sally, Prudence and Ernestine kept driving them.

Thank God for Katie's eyes. She spotted the rider-less horse springing upstream. Alert, she scanned the river.

"Pearl!"

She snapped Pitch into action, rushing toward Pearl's prone body. How long had she been there? What had happened? Was she alive?

Sally and Mary saw Katie's mad dash and looked ahead to Katie's destination. Pearl! They raced in to help.

Ernestine, at the back of the herd, close to the river's edge, saw the commotion from the corner of her eye. She raced to help as well.

Katie reached Pearl and sprang from the saddle. She dropped to her knees and scooped Pearl's head from the water. Blood trickled down Pearl's ear. She was pale and still.

"She's not breathing!" called Katie as Mary and Sally arrived. They plunged in to help, though not knowing how. Ernestine arrived next.

Together, Mary and Sally rolled Pearl onto her back, her head now resting face up on Katie's lap, the blood seeping onto Katie's pants. "Pearl!" shouted Mary, rustling Pearl's shoulders. No response. No movement. "Pearl!"

"Let's get her to shore," Sally said. Mary nodded agreement and she and Sally began to slide their arms under Pearl.

"I got her," said Ernestine, gliding in and scooping Pearl up with ease. She hustled the body to shore, Mary and Katie right behind. Sally gathered the horses.

For the first time, Clean Through saw what was happening and Ruth, Prudence and I saw Clean Through point. We couldn't tell all of what was going on, but we could see Ernestine setting something on the shore and the others kneeling beside it. We abandoned our duties, leapt off our mounts and sprinted to help. We could hear overlapping voices—"She's not movin'!" "She's not breathin'!" "She's bleedin' something fierce!"—but did not know who or why until we were close enough to see Pearl's prone, lifeless body.

"Oh, Jesus," whispered Ruth, her differences with Pearl cast aside in the harsh reality.

My mind raced, wondering what could have happened. We had done everything right, I was sure. In the heat of the moment, I was angry. Bad things shouldn't happen when you don't do anything wrong. Of course I knew that life doesn't share that viewpoint, but life had me pretty steamed at that particular moment.

Mary gave Pearl's shoulders another shake. "Pearl!" Nothing. She put her ear to Pearl's chest.

"Oh, Ma, tell me she's alive!" begged Katie.

"I can't. I don't know," Mary's voice cracked.

"There!" shouted Prudence. "Her arm moved! I know it did!"

None of us had seen it, but none of us was about to argue. If there was a sign of life, we'd rally to it. Mary shook Pearl again, then gave her face light slaps. "Pearl. Pearl." She looked up at Sally, who was closest. "Help me put her on her side."

They propped Pearl up on her left side, and for the first time I saw the gash on her head and the clotting blood. Without warning, Mary slammed her fist between Pearl's shoulder blades. The body shook and all of us watched for any sign of life. "I swear I saw her arm move. I swear it." Prudence's voice was almost too soft to be a whisper.

A cough!

Pearl lurched to life, choking on the water that filled her lungs. Mary hit her again, softer this time with just the heel of her palm. Pearl coughed again, spewing up water. Her body racked and convulsed, retching out more water, brown, ugly, tinged with blood. A gurgling, crusty sound echoed from her lungs as they worked to eject the water. On her own, Pearl rolled onto her hands and knees, vomiting, coughing, aching life back into her body. Her chest cleared. Her breathing quieted. She slumped onto one elbow, and then with a gasp she rolled onto her back, unconscious again but breathing.

We were all standing or kneeling around her, onlookers grateful for the life that had returned to Pearl yet unsure what to do next. The answer came in a renewed trickle of blood. With her breathing once again steady and her heart again pumping, wet, sticky blood pushed through the wound that hadn't completely clotted over. Mary brushed back Pearl's hair and we could see the gash. "Better she stays out while we take care of that."

Mary looked up at Sally with a hard, knowing stare. Sally understood. She nodded, swallowed and spoke. "Move her up into better light." While several of us pulled Pearl farther up the bank, Katie swung her saddle of off Pitch and placed it down for us to prop Pearl against. Some of her color had returned, though the color seemed deep under her skin like her face was encased in wax.

Sally returned with her sewing kit and Mary once again brushed back Pearl's hair to expose the wound. As Sally threaded a needle, Prudence clutched her stomach.

"Oh, Lord, I'm gonna lose my breakfast."

She turned away, facing the river, bending over and fighting to regain control. Mary gave her the control she needed.

"Better get back to moving the herd. Have Clean Through go on ahead and look for an early campsite. We'll be along."

Prudence welcomed the words, but hesitated as we all did. We wanted to get out of there and we wanted to stay and help. None of us knew at the time what had happened to Pearl, but we all knew it could have happened to any of us. There was really nothing more we could do, so we followed Mary's directive and went for our horses. The air seemed fresher as we moved farther from our injured companion, leaving just Mary and Sally to care for her. She was breathing. She was in good hands. We had work to do and after our initial hesitation we warmed to it. The herd was a fine distraction.

Prudence kept down her breakfast.

I glanced back long enough to see Sally pulling the thread through Pearl's skin. Pearl, thankfully, remained unconscious. Mary winced with every stitch, but she kept her arms on Pearl's shoulders to hold her steady should she awaken. Sally concentrated on her work. She had always taken pride in her even stitching and now she wanted to be more perfect than ever—this was a sewing job that would be seen for life. Pearl had enough scars on the inside.

As we were left wondering how once a again a river—this one calm, shallow and sundrenched—had been the site of potential disaster, Parker was all smiles as he delivered his horses to the Woodward trading post. He also posted another letter I had written (I doubt that I had ever written two letters in one year, let alone two in one week) and as he accepted payment for the horses he told Will and Ethyl McKendricks, the long-time proprietors of the trading post, about the beautiful girl he planned to marry. They offered up some pie to celebrate and asked him a lot of questions about her and about what his plans were. At the time, he couldn't provide much detail about Katie except that she was pretty, pleasant, kind, and had captured his heart. If he had known about Katie beginning the rescue of Pearl, he would have added "brave" with pride. As for his plans, he needed to complete his delivery in Caldwell, then—what? By all rights, he should return to the ranch to help his uncle, who would be expecting him. But Katie was headed to Dodge City. Should he go there first rather than straight home? It was worth considering. Maybe he'd be fortunate enough that a short courtship was agreeable to all, despite Katie's father not being there, which, he admitted, bothered his sense of the order of things. And he didn't like the thought of Katie being around the outlaws and barkeeps and drunkards and general rascals in Dodge. But he had a duty to his uncle and to his half of the business. It was a lot to mull over. He had a little time. Once he got to Caldwell, then he could decide whether to say yes or no to his impulse to go straight to Dodge City.

For the moment, he did not say no to a second helping of pie.

North of us, in our destination of Dodge City, it was reported that a young woman had been found dead in a nearby field. She had been beaten to death, and the doctor who examined the body was quoted as saying that "the beating might have been a relief after all she'd been through." There were no witnesses—at least none that came forward—and the law had no leads beyond some deep hoofprints, perhaps from a horse with two riders or one very large man.

PART FIVE
DIVIDED

Chapter 16

Clean Through's years of experience on cattle drives served us well. He led us ten miles that day when we might easily have stopped before the mid-day meal. "Things happen on drives," he said, "but the drives don't stop until the cattle is in the stockyard. Best remember that."

I'm going to try now to give you a good idea of where we were, because it's important that you understand how far we had traveled, how far we had to go, and what our location was in relation to the trail system. The problem is that, while I think I'm holding my own in telling you the story through my writing, I have no artistic skills whatsoever and feel nervous about attempting to draw out a map. If you put a straight-edged piece of lumber on some paper and asked me to trace along it to make a straight line, I would mess it up. So please don't hold it against me if the map I'm about to sketch out for you looks like a child's drawing and is in no way an accurate representation in terms of scale. If it's true that a picture is worth a thousand words, then this one is probably worth two hundred at the most. It's just supposed to give you enough information that you think, "Oh, all right, I see what's where." Even with that understood, I hesitate to draw it out because I just know I'll end up being called that woman who can't draw a decent map rather than that woman who wrote about those women on the cattle drive.

Nevertheless, and with respect and apologies to any cartographers who may see it, I present my Here's What's Where sketch:

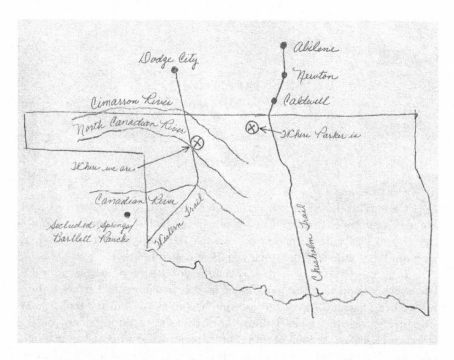

Again, my apologies. You may have been better off with the thousand words. But perhaps this little sketch will give you some reference for the many activities that I'm about to describe and that were happening close to the same time.

As I noted, we were about ten miles north of the North Canadian River. Clean Through started a fire while the rest of us settled the herd and the horses. By suppertime, Mary, Sally and Pearl had arrived. Now Pearl rested by the fire after eating her fill of something Clean Through called cornfritters. They were like hotcakes, but thinner and with corn inside, and as he fried them up in butter they sent out an aroma that I have since decided Heaven must smell like. He said it was a family recipe handed down from the Pilgrims, who had originally named the concoction "corn oysters." Not only were we impressed that Clean Through knew about the Pilgrims, we were even more impressed with the taste of these fine treats.

"Why haven't you made these before?" asked Prudence, her arm in the air. "They're tasty as can be."

"Been savin' my corn," he replied. "Waitin' until we needed an extra cheer. If you was men, I'd pass around the corn whiskey. These'll have to do in this case."

"Having tried whiskey once," I said, "you can keep it. But don't hesitate to stir up more of these fritters any time."

100

Clean Through acted like he wasn't paying attention, but I know he soaked up compliments the same as his biscuits soaked up gravy. His back was to me, but I was certain his near-toothless grin was in full form on the other side.

Sally took a moment to ease back Pearl's hair for a closer look at the stitches. Mary handed Pearl coffee and sat down beside her. "Might be a little scar," said Sally with approval. "Not much."

"I hadn't planned to be your next sewing job, but I sure do appreciate the mending."

Sally patted Pearl's arm. "Just be glad you slept through it. It was a queasy time for us and we weren't the ones in pain."

Sally rose and headed back to the chuckwagon. If there was a problem with those cornfritters, it was that the smell they left in the air kept you hungry for more even when you were full. We felt blessed to have full stomachs on a cattle drive and, despite the troubles we'd encountered, to all still be alive and generally healthy.

Pearl moved her head around, keeping it slow to hold off dizziness, but clearly searching. "I need to find Katie so I can thank her."

"She's on first watch," said Mary, who had settled down beside Pearl. Mary sighed. "I should have seen you right away, but I was caught up watchin' the herd. I'm sorry. Ain't much of a leader."

"I'll be fine after a night's sleep. And you're leadin' just fine."

Mary scoffed.

"It's true," Pearl continued. "I mean it. You know how I know?"

Mary shook her head.

"Because everyone's followin'. Don't take no more than that."

Pearl's words brought out a gentle smile from Mary. "You're the one who's hurt and here you are comfortin' me."

"Makes me feel good to talk with you, and the way some of the others treat me. Ruth, she don't like me and I can't blame her." Pearl hesitated. When Mary said nothing to fill the void, Pearl kept going. "Her man... well, he's paid for me a dozen times at least. It shames me to see her."

"The shame's on her husband first." Mary's voice was stern, then it softened. "Though I do hope you find a new line of work."

Pearl sat up with a look of determination, any possible pain or dizziness cast aside as she spoke to Mary with pure heartfelt sincerity. "I will. I swear to God and anyone else who's listening."

She winced as the pain flared in her temple. Mary eased her back onto the saddle. "There now."

"At the end of this trail's a new life for me. Has to be. Has to be." She closed her eyes and said no more. Mary was quiet as well, thinking what a luxury it was that Pearl could keep her mind on the end of the trail and a chance for a new beginning. Mary was aware that end of the trail could and should bring rewards, but she could not afford to let her mind dwell on it. She had a team of cattlehands—more than that, friends—to care for, a herd to guard and move, her family and their land depending on her success. No, it was one day at a time for Mary. She had nearly lost a crew member today because of a single hawk. What would happen if they came upon a gang of rustlers or if the Cherokee tribe in this territory isn't as friendly as Parker intimated? How well would she acquit herself as leader? How well would she protect her people and her property? She studied Pearl's face, now relaxed with sleep, and a wave of determination flowed over her. *I'll get you to that new life*, she thought. *I'll get us all there. We've survived bandits and storms and pure old bad luck, and we'll survive whatever's ahead.*

Her eyes moved to the sky, perhaps beginning to offer a silent prayer for success. The brightest of the stars were beginning to appear in the darkening sky. Soon it would be lush with stars, far more than she could count or would ever try to. She knew they were beautiful and that she should take more time to appreciate these diamonds in the sky. But not now. Later. In her husband's arms. On their ranch. Safe, sound and happy.

Under those same stars, Parker was hobbling his horses for the night. On a normal delivery trip, his mind would be on the food he'd soon be heating up. Since laying his eyes on Katie, though, nothing about this trip was ordinary in Parker's mind. The landscape seemed greener. The sky had been a richer shade of blue, deep like the blue of Katie's eyes. And the stars... how many nights had he rested upon his blanket and stared up at these stars? Yet never had they appeared so crisp, so sharp. They were bright like his future.

He remembered speaking with his uncle after returning from a profitable delivery that had also been his first solo delivery. He was 17 at the time, just a month removed from inheriting his father's half of the business. He had left with a heavy heart, but the combination of youth and business success had brought back his smile. He had said to his uncle that even though he missed his father terribly, he felt that overall his life was pretty good. He was part of a good business, and his job involved travel across beautiful country. Then his uncle spoke words that Parker would never forget.

"Enjoy what you have. But know that your work will have more meaning when it's done to make a better life for a wife and family. That's the only success that matters. Your father understood that."

It amazed him to think that a little over a day ago he had no love in his world and now all he could do was dream of a long life with Katie. And his dreams were fueled with the certainty that wherever she was under these bright stars, she was also dreaming of a long life with him. One day. One chance meeting. One look. Two changed lives.

He thought he had grasped his uncle's words before, but they had just been words of wisdom that his mind comprehended. Now he understood them with his heart. It was true—he wasn't just working for the business. He was working for love, for a shared dream.

To put it as succinctly as I can, Parker may be a rugged young man who rides tall in the saddle, but there is softness in his heart.

Jonas was sure getting tired of eggs. He knew how to cook them and the hens kept laying them, so he kept eating them. He missed Mary's fresh-baked bread and the crumbs that Katie called biscuits. Mostly he just missed them.

Following Doc's orders to exercise his leg and hip—"but not too much or I'll come tie you down!"—Jonas had begun taking morning walks to the henhouse to gather eggs and evening walks around the corral. He was tempted to take a basket of eggs into town to trade for a loaf of bread or some potatoes, but even hitching the wagon was against Doc's orders until his hip was stronger. Doc was probably right, he thought now as he limped around the corral. His knee was better, but his hip burned with every step. His armpit was sore from the crutch, but that was better than putting extra strain on the hip. He'd follow Doc's orders if for no other reason than Doc didn't think he could.

He wouldn't have minded if old Doc came out for another checkup. Jonas wasn't one to get lonely, but he was one to get bored when there wasn't much he could do. He couldn't even hope the neighbors might drop by because the closest ones, Ruth and Prudence, were out on the drive. Besides, Doc might show up with another letter. Waiting for news was a hard thing.

Mary and Katie seemed as far away as the stars above, and he wished he could see their faces in the stars like some people claimed to be able to see figures from old stories. He could maybe see the Big Dipper sometimes, he wasn't quite sure, but when a traveling preacher had pointed to the sky one time and said he could see Orion and Sagisomething and whatnot, Jonas had sent him on his way. He'd heard enough Bible stories to know he hadn't heard those names, and he'd seen enough stars to know there weren't people in them. Yet he supposed it was a pleasant thought that the same stars shining down on him were also shining upon Mary, Katie and the rest of the team. Wouldn't it be something, he thought, if the stars could share sounds? The first thing he'd ask Mary is how are they doing. Then he'd want to know how far they had gone and how much of the herd was still alive. Once he knew that all was well, he would have a question for me: Would it have been too hard for you write who was stolen and what all happened?

He didn't know another letter was on its way that would stir him up even more.

One more person out under the stars that night was Dusty, the nice fellow we had met a while back. He was looping his horse's reins around a hitching post in front of the Frontier Saloon in Dodge City. The stars didn't interest him. He wanted whisky.

If you wanted a lively time with saloon girls in low-cut dresses and gambling and piano playing and brawls and the occasional gunfight, you went to the Palisades Saloon. But if you wanted to shake off the dust of the trail, slug down some whisky and contemplate life, you went to the Frontier. Dusty was more suited to the wild, carefree chaos most of the time, but his long, hot ride had him brooding. He didn't need boisterous companionship right now. He needed a bottle.

Inside the saloon, he slapped four coins onto the bar. "Bottle. Whisky."

The bartender was a stocky, bald fellow who appreciated such direct talk but still found it a bit on the wordy side. He handed Dusty a bottle and a glass, then tilted his head in the direction of an empty table. No sense using words when a nod will do.

Dusty sat at the table, poured himself a drink and swilled it down in one gulp. On an empty stomach—and his was empty—the whisky would start working its magic real soon. He wanted it to loosen the darkness that shrouded his mood. He'd spent his whole life as a happy-go-lucky man, but the long ride under the baking sun had him questioning why he was happy and in what way he might be considered lucky. He was a drifter is what he was. Never stuck with anything. Left farming. Left the livery. Left Leadville after just two days. They likely wouldn't take him back at the livery, figuring he'd just drift away again the next time the wind blew. How was he going to make something of himself if he couldn't stay in one place?

A second drink, this time sipped slowly enough that he tasted it, lightened his load. A third awoke his good nature. He was no drifter! Heck, he was just a fellow that liked a good time and didn't want to work too hard. He was headed back to Ellsworth, wasn't he? He had a home, something a drifter doesn't. His fourth drink was like a beacon, a shaft of light shining down from those stars outside to reveal the truth—it had just been the hot sun getting under his skin. He had plenty to be happy about! Starting with more whisky!

For the first time, he scanned the saloon. There was activity, but the place was none too prosperous. Cowpokes from the herds were likely over at the Palisades. Probably a fair number of regulars had made the trek to Leadville and hadn't been as smart as he was, still digging rather than heading home to a roof and a bed. Then again, this was Dodge City. The so-called regulars might be out robbing a stage or rustling cattle or worse. The whisky had refreshed him enough that he remembered this was no town to be loitering in for long, but the whisky had also made him feel at home right there in the chair. And he still had half a bottle left.

He noticed two men at a corner table back in the shadows, working on a bottle of their own. One of them had his back to Dusty, but from the back alone Dusty could tell this man was a giant. The second man, probably decent sized but appearing puny next to the giant, was doing all the talking. Dusty could hear snatches of words that caught his interest, like "get everyone ready for the next job" and "the money's been good." At least he thought those were the words. The fellow's Irish accent wasn't always easy to follow. It was worth investigating. Perhaps these men had need of short-term help, which was Dusty's specialty. Besides, his lighter mood now called for company.

"Gentlemen," he said as he strolled to their table, "I'll share my whisky if you'll share your company."

If Dusty hadn't had a belly full of whisky, he might not have been able to cover up the stagger he made at the hard stare from the big man. Instead, he just looked a little tipsy. And fortunately the Irishman was more welcoming. "Back home in County Cork we had a saying: 'Only buy your own drink as a last resort.' So join us and pour, my new-found friend."

Dusty chose a chair as far from the big man as possible. "Name's Dusty. And I'm pleased to share your table."

"You can call me Sean. And this talkative little fella here is Brute."

A deep, rumbling vibrated out from Brute's throat, his version of a sigh. Dusty thought perhaps he had swallowed a bear and was busy choking it to death with his throat muscles. He poured the big man a drink.

"Good day to you, Brute. Or good evening, I should say." He watched as Brute's hand engulfed the glass and pulled it to his mouth. Dusty thought the man might have swallowed the glass until he set it back down with a thud. He noticed some scratches on Brute's knuckles.

"Brute's not one to pass the time of day with small talk," smiled Sean. "But I'm always willin' to pay for my drink with conversation. What's your story, lad?"

Sean's charming demeanor was a welcome distraction as Brute rumbled a second time. As Dusty poured another drink for Brute, he shook his head at Sean. "Been out remindin' myself that work and I don't get along. Thought I'd make it big in Leadville, but it was more work than I cared to take on."

"Aye, the streets aren't as paved with gold as we were all led to believe. Or silver in this case."

"Truer words have never been spoken, Sean! It was fine-looking country, I'll say that. Mountains like I didn't know there could be. Like I said, though, diggin' in them wasn't for me."

"We're not ones for laborin' hard ourselves," said Sean, his Irish brogue extending some syllables and adding a musical quality to the words. He raised his glass. "To the easy life."

Dusty raised his glass as well and was partway through his drink when Brute's first words stopped him cold. "Seen any herds?" The deep voice was raw, perhaps from lack of use. It clawed its way through the ear in sharp contrast to Sean's melodic voice. Worse than the sound was the tone behind it. Menacing. As if the wrong answer carried horrifying consequences.

Sean tried to take the edge off. "Oh, let's let the man wet his pipes and tell his story, Brute. I'm sure if he's seen any herds that we'll hear about it." Another rumble. Brute's stare seared through Sean and his tune changed in a hurry. He picked up his own bottle and poured a drink for Dusty. "Still, it wouldn't hurt to move ahead to recent days in your travels. Have you perhaps been on the trail and have you perhaps seen any herds?"

After just one or two drinks, Dusty might have understood the danger he was putting us in, but after seven drinks, his mind was as loose as his tongue. "You can wager your best horse I did! Saw a whole cattle herd bein' driven by women!"

"You don't say?" Sean poured another drink. Even Brute was interested now.

"Thought I was seein' things from lack of whisky, but it was true. Got a man cook. Gave me a biscuit."

Dusty's mouth was off and running about the group of women wearing pants and moving a herd up from north Texas. When he awoke hours later, lifting his heavy head from the table where he had slept face down, his only memory of the night before was engaging in conversation with a polite Irishman and a big, quiet fellow. What had they talked about? No matter, he needed to get moving. Well, after one more whisky for the road.

Under those stars, now fading in the early gleam of dawn, I circled the herd as part of my late-watch duties. I didn't know Parker's thoughts, though I might have guessed them had I been thinking about him. Same for Jonas. I had forgotten about Dusty altogether and had never had a flicker of an idea that his knowledge of us could lead to peril. The meeting—or confrontation, depending on your point of view—with Sean and Brute back at the Bartlett ranch was a distant, faded memory, and even if I had recalled them I wouldn't have let my mind linger on them.

Instead, my mind was on my companions and my future. During the dinners and suppers, I had become more bold as far as asking people about their pasts and their thoughts. They had opened up a little more each time, and I enjoyed learning about them and turning new acquaintances into friends and turning friends into trusted friends. I felt as close to these women—and I mustn't forget Clean Through—as I had felt to my own family. Probably closer, though that was a thought I felt badly about. For Mary's sake, I wanted to see the herd I was circling, even Uncle Angus, get delivered safe and sound to buyers in Dodge. For my sake, I wanted all of my friends to arrive safe and sound as well.

Chapter 17

Pardon my language once again, but, well, doggone it, Clean Through was one heck of a cook. He did more with a wagon of spices and dry goods, some dried beef, a few pots and pans, and a campfire than all of us could do in our own kitchens. Although I have no other experience to compare it to, I have no doubt that we were the best-fed cattlehands in human history. And the most appreciative, too, since we knew what it took to put a meal together.

After his father had died young, he was raised by his mother and his aunt, who were the unofficial doctors in their area of southern Tennessee. They tried to teach him about the medical uses of different herbs and barks and weeds, but it wouldn't stick. What did stick, though, was how those items could change the taste of food and bring out the flavor of meats and vegetables. Perhaps it was the hours he spent grinding up herbs for his mother and stirring up poultices for his aunt, or perhaps it was just a natural talent, but somewhere along the line he became skilled at mixing the perfect blends for baked goods. His biscuits were light, with soft insides that soaked up melted butter and jam. His pie crust was so good we often lapped up all the filling just to save the crust for last.

So it should come as no surprise that we all found ourselves, at times, loitering around the chuckwagon watching him work and asking him questions. He would never let us do any of the work—"it's my job, not yours"—but he was kind about showing us what he was doing. Once Parker had come into her life, Katie became Clean Through's most persistent student. She was determined to learn how to make biscuits that didn't fall apart, and Clean Through was more patient with her questions than Mary had been.

At evening camp two days after our latest river fiasco, the combination of Parker, girlish dreams, and just wanting to talk a little had Katie at the chuckwagon once again. From the way she hesitated, Clean Through didn't need to lift his eyes from the brown sugar and butter he was heating to know that more than just biscuits were on her mind.

"Can I ask you something, Clean Through?"

"Sure. Can't say I'll have an answer 'til I know the question."

"Were you really married almost forty years?"

"Sure was. If my dear Rowena's heart hadn't failed her, it'd be pushing fifty years now."

"What makes a good wife?"

He gave her a quick glance and a quick shake of his head. "Lord, child, you ask a hundred people that and you'll get a hundred different answers."

"What was it your wife, Rowena… what was it she did right, especially at the beginning?"

He raised the creamy sugar/butter mixture from the heat, but kept stirring. "You mean what can you do to make sure that young fella Parker falls all the way in love with you?"

Katie smiled. "I guess I ain't so good at hidin' my questions."

"Here, keep stirring this." He set the pan down in front of her and handed her the spoon. It was the first and only time any of us got to help him. Katie figured that must mean he had something serious to say. "You remember what you were doin' when Parker first set eyes on you?"

"I was walking around the side of the chuckwagon and he was just there."

"Right. You didn't know he was there, so you were natural. You weren't pretending or puttin' on airs." He sprinkled a powdery sugar into the mixture Katie was stirring. "Just keep mixing that together. Easy strokes. There you go." He lifted up another pan that had been cooling in the wagon. "The best thing a young couple can do is relax, let yourselves see each other for who you are. Don't be something you ain't. Now set that pan down and let it cool a little more."

"It's hard to relax when my heart's beatin' fierce just at the sight of him."

"If your heart's pounding, let him know. That's all I'm sayin'. Don't expect any man to read a woman's mind. Just come out and say what's on your mind whether you're happy or sad or mad, because a man don't like to guess." He flipped a two-inch thick cake out of a pan and onto a tin plate. "Now take that stuff you mixed up and spread it on top of this layer."

Katie was surprised by how much the mixture had thickened after cooling for just a minute. She picked up a wooden spatula and went to work. "So you're saying I should talk to Parker as freely as I talk to my friends?"

"He deserves it, don't you think?" He popped out a second cake and placed it on top of the one Katie had frosted. "You want him to be more than a friend, so be more open with him than you are with your friends." He twirled his finger over the cake. "Now spread the rest of that over the whole thing. And listen, what I'm sayin' is don't pretend. Let Parker see who you are, not just the good, but the stuff you want to hide. If you like to wear a crazy color, wear it. If you're clumsy, fall down or drop something. He needs to know, because love isn't built on all the good things. It's built on all the little things that could be annoyin' but finding them endearin' instead."

"Like Pa saying Ma's hands are always cold but still holdin' them anyway?"

"That's a perfect example. Nobody wants cold hands touching 'em. I sure don't. But your pa loves your ma so the cold hands are part of what makes her special. Now if she had started warming up her hands early on, then she'd have to keep doing it the rest of her life or risk surprisin' him with frigid fingers. You learn from her. She didn't pretend or hide any faults, and your pa loves her for it. They can relax around each other." He gave her his near-toothless smile. "I know at the moment you don't think that young man has any faults, but I ain't seen a perfect person yet. He's gonna have faults, and if you love him, really love him, you'll love him *for* his faults, not in spite of them. Understand?"

"I do. Thank you."

"All right, enough of this love talk. Ain't fittin' for a trail drive. Put down that spatula and follow me."

He picked up the cake and carried it to the center of camp where we all were. Prudence and Ernestine had been watching the herd, but Mary had called them in. Katie sat down with the rest of us and watched with curiosity as Clean Through pulled a candle out of his pocket, stuck it into the cake, and lit it with a match.

"Your party from here, boss," he said to Mary.

Mary gave us all a nod and we joined in, facing Katie. "Happy birthday!"

Katie's eyes went wide with befuddlement, then recognition. "Is it August fourth?"

"It is," laughed Mary. "At least according to Laurie's journal."

"I'm sure of it," I added.

Katie skewered a look at Clean Through with mock anger she couldn't hold. "You had me make the frosting for my own birthday cake!"

"That way you'll know it's fresh. And I'm gonna let you cut it, too," he said while handing her a knife. He handed Mary some tin plates, then I helped him fill some cups with coffee. So we started the evening with dessert and a celebration, and we ended it with beef stew and biscuits. All made by a little old man with a talent for campfire cooking even bigger than his near-toothless grin.

Still, I'm getting ahead of myself. All was not well that evening.

As the cake was being served, Ruth was tight-lipped and distant. She took her piece of cake—even in a dark mood, she was smart enough not to turn down cake—and sat down on a good-sized stone that had found its way to the prairie long before us. I strolled over to her with a cup of coffee.

"Get it while it's hot, Ruth."

"Thanks." Her mouth barely opened and I wondered how the cake and coffee were going to get in there.

I sat down on the tall grass beside her, which pretty much made us eye to eye. "How are you feeling, Ruth?"

"Fine."

Uh oh. Ruth has big ups and big downs. She doesn't settle for fine. Another of her lows was settling on her.

I figured I'd better get to the heart of it. "You don't sound all that fine. What's bothering you?" No response. "Still thinking about James?"

"Nope." I followed her eyes. She was staring directly at Katie, Sally and Pearl as they munched on cake and shared a laugh. Fire flared in Ruth's eyes. "I'm thinkin' about what tempted him."

Then like a lightning bolt she shot up and sprinted toward them shouting, "What right have you got to be eatin' cake with decent women!" As the three startled women looked up, Ruth batted away Pearl's fork and plate and then planted her little fist on the left side of Pearl's cheek and mouth. Pearl fell backward off the log she was sitting on, stunned. Ruth was ready to leap on her and keep swinging, but I caught up and Sally and I snatched her by the shoulders and dragged her away, kicking and yelling things about leaving her man alone and how harlots should burn in hell and other terrible things before I held her down and Sally clamped a hand over Ruth's mouth.

Pearl cowered on the ground, not from pain or fear, but from the pit of shame she had fallen into again. Ruth may have slugged her face, but it was Pearl's confidence that took the hit. Ruth was right, she thought. She had no business thinking she could have a future as a decent woman. Her past would never let go. There would always be lusty men who recognized her, angry wives and churchwomen who would despise her for what she had been. Maybe the Lord would forgive her on Judgment Day, but her earthly shame was too great, too oppressive. Could she find freedom from it? Could she find peace? She ran toward the herd, settling at the moment for finding escape.

Mary loomed over Ruth with fury flaming from both eyes. "I wish we were by a river so I could throw you in it! As it is, we can't spare the water so you start coolin' off on your own right now, you hear me!" Ruth continued to wiggle in our grasp. Mary bent down, placing a knee on Ruth's chest and waving a finger in her face. "You said you'd follow my orders and I'm orderin' you to leave Pearl be." Mary lowered her voice, perhaps to offer up a sense of calm or maybe to make the words harder for Prudence to overhear. "I was hopin' this didn't need to be said, but I guess I knew better. So now you listen. It ain't Pearl's fault that your man cats around. You said near as much yourself. He's the one that goes out looking." Ruth was still now, but Sally kept her hand tight over Ruth's mouth. This was no time for interruptions. We all knew Mary was saying what Ruth needed to hear. "You married the man for better or worse, and I understand that his worse has caused you suffering. That's his fault, not Pearl's. You want to hit someone, he's got it comin' and I believe we'd all hold him for you while you wailed away"—true—"but you swat that bee you have in your bonnet for Pearl and bury it, 'cause I'll have no more fightin' on this trip, is that understood?"

Ruth's eyes were filled with water. Mary nodded to Sally to remove her hand. We were now cradling Ruth rather than holding her down. Her voice cracked. "Why's he treat me like he does?" Mary eased down beside her and guided Ruth's head onto her lap. "I always treated him right. Bore his children."

"I know."

"I love him. Always have."

"I know."

"I'm a good wife."

"Of course you are."

"Why ain't that enough?"

"I don't know. It should be. That's the only answer I have. For some men, it just ain't. For some women, too, I expect."

"It ain't right."

"It's a hard way to live."

Ruth's eyes steadied into focus. "It ain't Pearl's fault, is it?"

"No, honey, it ain't."

Sally and I exchanged glances and no words were needed to know that we were thinking the same thing. We were glad to be responsible for our own futures. We were glad we weren't tied down. And somewhere deep inside ourselves, not really as a conscious thought, we were each glad we hadn't been punched in the mouth.

Closer to the fire, Katie and Prudence hadn't moved at all. Katie had watched first in shock as Ruth flew past her with a waving fist and then watched with compassion as Ruth was dragged away to become a sobbing mess. Prudence had continued to eat her cake and sip her coffee. When her mother's anger had turned to tears and she rested her head in Mary's lap, Prudence leaned in to Katie and said, "Still ready to get hitched?"

"It'll be different with Parker."

"Just make sure before you say 'I do,' okay?"

Katie couldn't take her eyes off Ruth sobbing in Mary's embrace. "Promise."

Clean Through, the veteran of trail drives, saw the brief fight in a different light. "Seems like the only one not cryin' is the one that got hit," he mumbled. "Strangest drive I ever been on." He scooped up a bowl of stew and started walking it out to Pearl.

Chapter 18

"Ow!"

The next morning was more painful than the night before for Pearl. Not because of the punch or the heartache, but because it was time for Sally to pull out the stitches in Pearl's head. Unlike when they went in, Pearl was conscious.

"I'm sorry," said Sally. "I'm being as gentle as I can."

"I know you – ow! – are. I don't mean to complain."

"It's not complainin' to say that something hurts when it hurts." She paused a moment to give Pearl a hard look. "You know Ruth was out of line, right?"

"I'd rather not talk about it. I'll try to stay out of her way."

Sally frowned and went back to working on the stitches. "I suppose that's best. You'd be in the right to give her a good wallop and see how she likes it, but Mary might not approve and she has enough on her mind right now. Sure be nice if Ruth apologized, but that's likely asking too much."

A short while later we were riding out to take our places for the day's drive. I paused to watch, expecting trouble, when Ruth stopped at Pearl's usual place at the back of the herd. She just kept her horse there and faced the herd. No gun was visible. Her hands gripped only the reins.

Pearl looked at me and Ernestine as if we knew what was going on, but we both offered shrugs and wary looks. Pearl approached slowly, not wanting a fight. Ernestine was closer than me and kept her eyes on them, ready to rush in if needed. But Ruth surprised us all. "Think I'll ride drag today. Mind helping me out and taking point?"

Pearl was astonished enough that she couldn't speak at all. After a hesitation, she nodded and urged her chestnut mount forward to the pointer position opposite me, all the time wondering if she was hated or liked or if Ruth was just confused. Finally she realized what it was. *She's apologizing*, Pearl thought. *More than that, she's releasing me from blame.* It perked her up. She had a bruised face, a scabbed-over head wound that ached, a lingering fear of an unknown future, and a general feeling of fatigue, yet she hadn't felt this good in a long time. She snapped the reins and her horse trotted forward.

Leave it to Ernestine to lighten the mood for all of us. "Wish someone would pick a fight with me. I could use a day out of the dust!"

At the time, I had no idea how fortunate I had been with the letters I'd sent. I was confident that both Dusty and Parker would post the letters for me at their trading post stops, but I had no idea how long the letters would be there before a rider or courier or trusted cowpoke would come along and be given the letters to deliver. The posts were too scattered and the letters too rare and the riders too few in the open range for any official schedule to be in place. So I didn't know that my first letter had already been delivered and even taken out to Jonas, and I would never have wagered that my second letter would have left the post in such a short time. But the same day that Parker delivered his horses and posted the letter, a cautious army courier traveling from Fort Sill to Fort Elliott had been forced to circle far north due to what he thought was a loud band of marauding Wichitas (which turned out to be three bucks hunting an antelope). His wide loop had taken him to the trading post where he was entrusted to take my letter to Fort Elliott, where my luck continued because a grouchy sergeant was looking for an errand to send a clumsy private on to get him out of his hair for a day or two.

So it was that my letter was delivered to Mickel's General Store in Secluded Springs, where Edward, hoping for news about Ernestine, rushed it to my father at the bank. And so it was that on the same morning Ruth was riding drag, my father was bringing his wagon to a stop at the Bartlett Ranch. Jonas sat on a bench by the front door, his crutch leaning against the house.

"Morning, Jonas."

"Lawrence. Ain't foreclosure time yet, is it?"

"Now don't start off cranky. I'm here to share news and offer up an apology." He got down from the wagon.

"Start with the news."

My father, or I guess I should say Mr. Michaels, held out the letter I'd written. "Another letter from Laurie. Two in one month! Go on and read it. You'll see why I want to apologize."

"I left my spectacles somewhere. Henhouse maybe. How about you just read it?"

Mr. Michaels (no, you know what? I'm going to use "Dad" or "my father" from now on because it just sits better with me) sat down on the bench and read the beginning of the letter out loud. Since it was written after our first river crossing but before the second, they learned about the terrible storm and the difficulties we'd had crossing the Canadian, and that thanks to Mary's leadership the bulk of the herd and all of us were still together and making progress. That's where my father stopped for a moment.

"When Mary returns, I'll apologize to her, but I'm starting with you now. I told her I couldn't extend the mortgage because I couldn't bank on her like I'd banked on you. I felt even more strongly about it when I heard of the women banding together to drive the herd, and I was angry, too, since I felt my daughter was being dragged into it. I'm here to say that I was flat out wrong." (I'm a little jealous of Jonas because I've never heard my father utter such a phrase.) "I didn't know what Mary is made of. Always liked her, mind you, but the resolve she's shown is something I didn't see coming. I also know from the tone of Laurie's letters that she's not only involved by her own free will, but that she feels part of something special. Please accept my most humble apology."

"Oh, hell, Lawrence, no one thought they could do it, not even them. I was against it myself."

"That's kind of you to say."

"I'll admit I wish you'd have extended the loan so that none of this would've happened, but even then I can't blame you for it. And you didn't start the silver strike and get my men held in Nogales and get the Byerlys headin' home and you didn't trample my leg."

"You sure had a streak."

"And it ain't over yet unless that letter also says they arrived at Dodge and sold the cattle."

Dad perked up. "Say, that news isn't in here, of course, but there's more and it's fine." He combed through the letter to the spot where he had stopped. "Here we go. 'The other news I want to pass along is that we were visited by a fine young man and he and Katie could not have fallen in love faster if Cupid had shot them both with the same arrow' —"

"Hold on now. I don't – who's shootin' arrows at Katie?"

"Now don't get your dander up. Cupid is just an old-time god from ancient stories. He'd shoot people with a love arrow and they'd fall in love."

"That don't make a lick of sense."

"Never mind about Cupid. What she's saying is that Katie has a fine young man as her beau."

"She might have met a young man, but he ain't her beau until I say so. That girl and her boy-crazy ways…"

"Why don't you let me finish reading instead of flying off the handle?" Jonas nodded and my father continued. "'It was quickly clear to all of us, Mary included, that marriage is in their future. But the young man (his name is Parker)'—she doesn't say if that's his first or last name—'is very respectful. He asked Mary's permission to court Katie once he finishes the job he's doing. I could tell that both Parker and Mary wished Jonas was there to answer for the family, but she liked the boy plenty and, let's face it, Jonas is back there with you'—Jonas bristled at that and I wish I hadn't written it—'though she held back a complete blessing in hopes that Parker can meet Jonas first. Katie's bubbling over with dreamy-eyed joy. That's all I have time to write as Parker is leaving and has agreed to post this letter for me. I hope it finds you and Mother well. Love, Laurie.'" My father gave Jonas a warm smile. "Congratulations are in order."

"For losin' a daughter to a man I ain't met?"

"Oh now there you go again…"

They continued to poke at each other for a while, but when my father left he knew that Jonas's mixed emotions were perfectly reasonable. He was happy for his daughter and pleased that Mary had stressed that the approval role should be his, but he was frustrated that so much was happening in his family's life without his involvement. Sitting at home gathering eggs once a day while Mary led the herd and Katie was courted by a stranger was in no way how he had envisioned his summer. On top of the frustration remained the fear for Mary's life, Katie's life, our lives, the herd and the ranch.

In his mind, Katie still was and would always be his little girl. A little girl should be home with her father, he thought as he sat there, not traipsing across the prairie crossing rivers in storms, and certainly not meeting young men no matter how respectful. He frowned at the emptiness of the ranch. An image of Katie came into his head, smiling, and he couldn't help but smile himself. "Might as well face up to it," he said aloud as if my father was still there. "She's growin' up." All he ever wanted for her was happiness. If Mary felt the young man was a worthy prospect and his dear Katie, who was smart enough to know her own heart, felt so as well, then so be it. He had taken Mary away from her father. What goes around comes around, and he'd better learn to live with it.

He decided it was time to visit the henhouse. The eggs weren't that important, but he could use the company.

Rains swamped us that day, hindering progress as the trail muddied. Even riding point didn't offer Pearl much relief. She rode with her head down, her body bundled in a blanket. Ruth had expected to eat dust all day, but when the rain came late in the morning, the dust was washed from the air, making it fresh and clean to breathe—for about half an hour. After that the pummeling rain and slogging hooves splattered mud so high it could not be avoided. Ruth was barely visible inside her over-sized coat, water dripping down in a stream from her hat. Ernestine kept her coat cinched around her.

For some reason, I liked the rain. Maybe because that's all it was, rain. No lightning or thunder. Not even endless dark, gloomy clouds. It was just a rainstorm and it didn't chill me like it did some of the others. Before the trail became mud and puddles, I tilted my head back and let the fresh rain hit my face and drip down my throat. Once a muck-filled droplet sloshed up into my nose, though, that was the end of tilting back and enjoying the water. Besides, the rain didn't keep Uncle Angus from wandering off. I had to keep a tight watch on her because I didn't want to take the time to pull her out if she got mired in a mudhole—something that, to the best of my knowledge, my actual Uncle Angus never did.

Mary was up ahead, and despite her black rain slicker she was easy to spot under the light-gray skies. As conditions worsened, she took more time to angle the herd toward the areas where she felt the footing was the most solid.

It was slow going from front to back. Clean Through urged the mules on, keeping steady progress in hopes that the wheels wouldn't sink into any soft spots. Katie was giving Pitch a rest and rode a bay instead. It proved to be a wise decision as Pitch followed Mary and the remuda followed Pitch. That freed up Katie, who had become our best roper, to help out when any cattle—but not Uncle Angus, I remind you—became stuck. She rode back and forth, first helping Prudence free a steer and then helping Sally with a mud-stuck cow.

Long after I stopped finding it refreshing, the rain still refused to let up. The landscape wasn't hilly, but it was rolling, and when Mary reached the top of a gentle slope she didn't see anything ahead that offered cover. It wasn't high ground, but it was the highest ground we could reach that day. She ordered a halt and the herd was happy to oblige. Whether human or cattle, you reach a point where standing in the mud and rain is better than slogging through it. We had all reached that point.

At best, we had made five miles that day. Probably less. Back in Secluded Springs, Jonas had said about fifty days would see us to Dodge City and back. It was starting to look like the horses and cattle would have to sprout wings for us to get to Dodge in fifty days, let alone make the trip back.

If you've ever doubted God's existence, then you should see Oklahoma after a rain. The grass and brush recover fast at the first glint of sunshine, rising to a lush, deep green. Droplets glisten on tree branches and trickle down blades of prairie grass swaying in the breeze. Somehow the reddish-brown mud that had splattered everything eases back down to the ground, hiding beneath the foliage. It's as lovely as it gets.

Until you try to move.

That mud may be hiding, but it's ever-present, and it stuck to us as we walked, a *glop-schloop* sound trailing every step. While the muck and grime slid easily from the grass and shrubs, it was permanently entrenched in our clothes. And though we were doing the work of men, girlish thoughts rose up. As Mary got down from her horse, she noticed Prudence had her hand in the air.

"What is it, Prudence?"

"Do you think this mud will stain my hair?"

Mary smiled a very tired smile. "I think your hair will endure. Can't say the same for our clothes, though."

Still, getting through the mud was another hazard survived, and as the hazards of the trail go, discomfort and a general sense of griminess are low on the list. Somehow Clean Through got a hot fire going—"Wood don't soak through like people"—and our clothes began to dry. The herd was hoof-deep in the muck, which was acceptable. The freshly watered grass filled their stomachs and satisfied their thirst. They were content to stay put. Though we hadn't made much distance, things could have been worse, and to top it off, Ruth didn't try to hit Pearl a single time. In fact, she brought Pearl a cup of coffee and Pearl, sensing a change in Ruth, drank it down without sniffing for poison.

Chapter 19

The ground had been thirsty. By breakfast, only a few scattered puddles remained.

"Let's push it today," Mary said. "The herd's fed and watered. A faster pace for a day shouldn't run the meat off their bones. Maybe we can get in fifteen miles today."

We chose our horses for the day and moved out to our spots. There was a little confusion as both Ruth and Pearl rode out to the drag position on the right, but Pearl settled it. "I'm good right here." Ruth moved up to point and Mary gave the signal to move the herd.

"Aaaaaaaaaaaaaaaaaaaaaa!!!!!!!!!!"

I had wondered if the cattle would get used to Ernestine's yell at some point, but it startled them every time. The screech also scattered three pheasants, a rabbit and half a dozen quail. If storekeeping didn't work out, Ernestine had a future as hunter's helper.

She screamed again throughout the morning whenever the herd showed signs of slowing. We all chipped in some hoots and hollers and the combination of noises and a quickened step by our horses kept the herd rumbling ahead. Clean Through reckoned we made six miles by noon, and if he was correct then that was the most productive morning we had had to that point. "Every bit as fast as men," Clean Through also reckoned.

They came into view just after our mid-day meal. Movement ahead, coming in slowly from the east side of the trail. Then they stopped.

Mary was the first to see them, then Katie and Clean Through. All three signaled to bring the herd to a halt. Ruth and I circled to the front to slow the herd. Prudence came up to help. Sally rode up beside Mary. Even though Sally had spent much of her life staring close at her needle and thread, she had good eyes for seeing far away.

"Up near the bend," Mary said to her, hoping Sally could clarify the situation.

"People. Two of them."

"Rustlers?" asked Katie.

"Maybe," Mary replied before rejecting the consideration. "No. They wouldn't let themselves be seen."

"I'd say it's time to pay the toll, boss," said Clean Through.

"Yeah, could be Cherokee," Sally nodded, still squinting. "Looks like one is leaning on a gun."

Mary swallowed. "You sure?"

"No. Could be a spear or a walking stick."

"Except they aren't walking. They're waiting."

"Jonas said to watch out for tricks."

"But Parker said they were friendly," Katie jumped in.

"Let's hope he's right," said Mary. She gave her reins a gentle shake to urge her horse forward. "Clean Through, keep a hand on your rifle just in case."

"Let me go instead of you."

"No. I'm owner, trail boss and drover. Duty's mine."

"I'll go with you," said Sally.

Mary shook her head and looked back with a half-smile. "Anything bad happens, I'll need you to sew me up."

All of us were gathered now and none of us saw the humor. "Be careful. We'll be watching," said Ruth. Each of us but Pearl had hands on a gun, and it flashed through my mind that about now she was likely wishing she'd brought one after all.

As Mary approached the two figures, she could see that they were men and that one was much older than the other. The older one leaned on a carved walking stick. The younger one, maybe 20, stood to his side. Mary noted the long knife sheathed on his waist. No guns were visible. That offered some relief.

When Mary was within speaking distance, the younger one stepped forward. "My grandfather, Chinmay, 'One of Knowledge,' warrior and elder of the Cherokee, greets the female cowboys."

Chinmay gave a slight nod toward Mary. His long hair was streaked with gray and she thought he was aptly named—there was wisdom in his eyes. She felt her fear lessen and her curiosity rise. She gave a respectful nod back. The old man spoke softly in Cherokee. It was unlike any language she had heard before. It wasn't beautiful to hear. In fact, she thought it might be a harsh language when spoken loudly. But his tone, though firm, carried no menace.

Mary looked at the younger one as he interpreted. "My grandfather believes that trails are not for women. He does not understand why a woman would dress like a man."

Mary smiled. "Tell him —"

"You must speak to my grandfather," the young man was quick to interject. "I will repeat your words for him."

Mary smiled at Chinmay. "Our dresses did not seem right for the work we have to do."

After listening to the interpretation from his grandson, Chinmay nodded approval. Mary could only assume her response had satisfied him. He made a sweeping gesture at the trail and spoke again in Cherokee.

"My grandfather says that women who have traveled so far must be strong warriors."

Again Mary smiled. She spoke with a formal tone. "It is an honor to hear such praise from a great leader." Then she added, "Truth is, we don't always feel very brave."

After hearing the translation, Chinmay again nodded approval and spoke.

"Honesty is bravery," interpreted the young man.

Mary was unsure how to respond, but she didn't need to as the old man squared his shoulders and tapped his walking stick on the ground. She could tell it was time for business and kept her gaze on the old man's deep-set eyes as he spoke.

"My grandfather says that you do men's work and must pay men's toll for travel across our land."

"I understand. What is the toll to cross your honored land?"

Chinmay needed no interpretation. He held up three fingers.

Mary didn't need an interpreter either, but the young man spoke anyway. "For three beef, you may cross."

"Agreed. We will bring you three steers."

Chinmay made a gesture toward the horizon ahead on the trail, held up two fingers, then spoke. This time Mary didn't understand, so she looked at the young man to sort it out for her. "For two more beef, my grandfather will warn you of a danger up the trail."

Mary mulled it over. She didn't want to part with more cattle and wondered if this was just a trick to get more from a woman. Or perhaps to test her resolve. But the old man's eyes were sincere and she remembered his words about honesty. "Agreed. Tell of the danger and we will bring you two more steers."

Again Chinmay spoke. Mary could not understand the words, but the tone was clear. She was receiving a warning of something that caused the old man great concern. It was the longest speech the man had made.

"My grandfather says that bad men wait for you two day's ride ahead. Our hunting party saw them. They are no one's friends. Not Cherokee, not whites. They mean you harm."

A rush of worry enveloped Mary. "What men? Can you help us?" Her questions were cut off when Chinmay held out a raised hand to indicate stop, then crossed his arms over his chest. It was clear to Mary that the discussion was over.

"We have warned you of danger," said the young man. "After you bring the beef, we will involve ourselves no more. We have battled enough."

Mary was pale with nerves, but she regained her composure. "You have done us a great service. I will send the steers."

She nodded at Chinmay, then at the young man whose name we never learned, and then turned and rode back toward us.

It had been a difficult scene to watch. None of us had experienced any run-ins with Indians, but we had heard the stories. Most of the recent conflicts were up north in the Dakotas, and even though there was debate over whether Custer's group had been massacred or stupid, either way it had ended in bloodshed. So it was a relief when we saw Mary turn back toward us. Her conversation had appeared pleasant, yet we could see distress in her face. Our mixture of concern and curiosity rose when she spoke.

"Sally, Laurie, cut out five steers and take them over to the Cherokees. Show them nothing but respect. Then get back." She got down from her horse, glanced at the trail ahead, then looked at us with a face full of worry. "I have decisions to make and I'll be wanting to hear thoughts from everyone."

It was odd that Sally and I now had no fear of the Cherokee men. When we saw the worry on Mary's face but knew it wasn't directed at the Indians, the two men just became part of the job. We needed to get the steers to them and get back to find out what was going on.

If I'd had more time to think I would have given them Uncle Angus, but we simply cut the first five steers from the herd. Chinmay remained on foot with his walking stick, but the young brave had retrieved a painted pony from the brush and sat upon its back. As we neared with the cattle, he rode to meet us and then turned back around to lead the steers. Another brave rode out from the brush and took his place behind the cattle. The steers moved away with the Cherokees without looking back—had they been pets, Sally and I might have been offended. Together with the three men, the steers disappeared into the brush at the side of the trail. There was no exchange of words or even nods between us and the men. It was a business transaction and it was now complete.

Though perhaps five minutes had passed while we delivered the cattle, it felt much longer since we were anxious for Mary's news. As we returned to the group, I realized that it must have felt like an eternity to them. Mary waited for us without a word. Sally and I had had something to do, but the others just had to stand and wait.

Now that we were back, Mary shared with all of us what the men had shared with her. "I don't know how many there are, only that they're waiting for us up ahead."

"You think they mean to take us?" asked Prudence, her hands clutched tight to her chest.

"Maybe they want the cattle, not us," I said. I supposed I opened the floodgates on speculation as everyone started talking at once.

"They might mean to kill us."

"Or worse."

"Maybe steal us and the cattle."

"Think they worked with those men who stole us before?"

"All right. All right," Mary raised her voice to regain control of the group. She was getting pretty good at authority. "We can't waste time guessin'. Fact is, we don't know their intentions, who they are, or how many they are. I know, though, that Chinmay saw no good in them and I believe his warning was sincere. The real question is what we're goin' to do about it."

Ruth shuffled her feet. "We might've learned to be decent cowhands, but we ain't gunfighters."

"Pearl shot those other three," Ernestine offered up.

"We ain't about to take these men by surprise," said Mary. "Nothing personal, Pearl."

Pearl nodded. "Only luck I had on the trip. Can't count on it twice."

"We know they're there," said Clean Through. "That might give us an advantage."

Mary gave a slight shake of her head. "They know we're coming, too. And Ruth's right, we're no match for decent guns, even it's just a few. And it might be a lot."

"So you think we should turn back?" asked Sally.

That lit a fire under Pearl. "I can't go back. I just can't!"

"You'll do what you're told!" bellowed Ruth, her natural inclination toward Pearl overriding the short-lived peace.

"Now don't start!" Mary took a moment and surveyed us all. It was clear her mind was working, but it hadn't landed on a decision yet. "Any other thoughts?"

Ernestine raised her hand like Prudence always did, but she didn't wait to be called on. "I promised my grandfather I wouldn't get killed."

I said, "I think we're all in favor of you keeping that promise."

Mary mulled again, not looking at any of us but knowing that we were staring at her. She had become a trusted leader. We would follow her orders, whatever they were. It still wasn't her way, though, to just bark out orders. Still thinking, still mulling, her frustration showed as she kicked the dirt.

"Going back means losin' the ranch."

"Jonas'd rather have you and Katie than the ranch," said Ruth. "You know that."

Mary again gazed at the trail ahead. "Comin' this far just to go back don't sit well with me."

"Me neither," said Katie. I'm sure her mind was on saving the ranch, but I'm also sure at least a piece of it knew that going back wouldn't get her closer to Parker.

"We've been through too much to turn tail and run," Mary continued. "Even heading back, they might catch us anyway."

Prudence didn't raise her hand, but she did her usual fine job of laying out the situation. "If we can't go forward without getting gunned down or worse, and going backward flat out stinks, what do we do?"

Enough mulling. Mary turned to Clean Through. "How far to the Chisolm?"

At the unexpected question, Clean Through's eyebrows nearly leaped off his forehead. "Ain't close, that's for sure."

"We head due east, we'll hit it?"

"Sure. Miles of hard ground and scrub brush between here and there. Can angle up northeast and save a little time. But Abilene is still a long way off."

"We don't have to get to Abilene. Parker said the railroad goes through Newton now." Despite the tense situation, Katie's lips curled up at the sound of Parker's name. They weren't married or officially betrothed, but her man was already helping. Mary stood tall with the strength of her decision. "Cattle'll sell as good in Newton as they will in Dodge. So we're goin' east. I said before that you were either in all the way or out. Given the new terms, I'm openin' that up again. We're in for harder times than we've known, so if you ain't up for it, I won't think less of you for turnin' around. But do it now."

I wish I could turn this into a big dramatic moment with all sorts of life-changing decisions being weighed and debated, but Katie and Pearl stepped forward at once. Sally and I didn't hesitate—we just weren't as quick as Katie and Pearl. Ernestine stepped up as well, followed right away by Prudence. All eyes were now on Ruth.

"Do I really have to take a step forward? You know I'm still hopin' to shoot a few men."

Mary turned to Clean Through, who nodded his affirmation. "I follow my trail boss."

"Then let's stop talkin' and start movin'. I want as much distance as we can get between us and those men."

She didn't need to tell us twice. We hopped onto our horses and moved in position to turn the herd. Mary mounted her horse as well, but Clean Through stopped her before she rode off. "There's still enough wet ground from the rain that we'll be leavin' a clear trail."

"I know. Have to hope they don't come lookin' for it."

"Aaaaaaaaaaaaaaaaa!!!!!!!!!!"

Ernestine's ability to frighten the herd in any direction was a blessing. Turning the cattle off of the trail and into the brush, however, was a definite turn for the worse. Now that we wanted to drive the herd at a fast pace, unconcerned about how much meat we ran off of them, it was impossible to move quickly through this uncleared land. If there had only been the leafy dogwood trees—their spring flowering long past—moving around wouldn't have proven so difficult since their branches tend to be high up. But add in the eastern red cedar, which is sort of like an evergreen that's chest-high on a cow, other scattered trees and brush and vines, thick grass that hadn't been trampled or eaten by other herds, and the general muck and mud from the earlier rain, and, well, let's just say that our trailblazing did not include blazing speed. I instantly missed the clearing of the trail with its deep green grass, open space and clear view. Once off the proven trail, the going was tough.

"Oh, my throat." The tail end of a breeze brought Ernestine's complaint my way. Her hollers to keep the herd in constant motion had become fainter and less frequent. Sally, Ruth and Pearl whooped and bellowed to fill the gap, but it was a true chore to push the herd. Every time we came upon a tree, which was pretty much all the time, the cattle would split up to go around it on each side.

"One Uncle Angus is enough!" I shouted at a group that sheared off. It took both Prudence and me to drive them back. All of us forced the herd together as tight as possible. It was tiring for the horses, and the long, pointed horns on the cattle meant we had to stay on constant alert.

Still, we kept moving. There were no thoughts of an early camp. We all knew distance was our best ally.

I became a true believer in workpants during that leg of the journey. From the pine branches that scraped across me to the mosquitoes we stirred up to thorns on the brush to the dangers of horns from being so close to the cattle, I could easily have become a bloodied mess. Those blue pants of ours had lost considerable color due to the constant wear, work and storms, but they had lost none of their toughness. From the waist up, I was battered and stung, but at least my bottom half was protected.

While the physical work was hard on Ruth, Sally, Prudence and me, the others had far more weighing on them. Clean Through didn't dare take time to blink, staying alert for holes and fallen trees and numerous other obstacles that disagreed with the chuckwagon's right to forward motion. The high wheels helped the chuckwagon pass above most of the brush, but it wasn't built for use on uncleared land. He drove it with the reins tight in his hands, directing the mules this way and that, his shoulders tightening from the non-stop duress. "Oomph!" was a common refrain as he felt every rut and bump, but he kept that wagon going. If his hair hadn't already been gray, the effort he was making would have done the job.

Ernestine snapped her head around to look back, counted to ten, then looked forward again. Then Pearl did a version of the same. Despite Ernestine's voice growing weak, Pearl could still hear her counting, "One, two, three…" and had begun her own series of look-backs whenever Ernestine reached five. Being at the back of the herd, they felt compelled to watch behind them for the onslaught of rustlers, killers and women-stealers that could arrive at any moment. The rumble of the cattle, breaking branches, snapping brush, hollering women and more meant they would never hear a gang approaching. So their necks received no shortage of exercise, turning from front to back more often than the swivel wheels on my father's fancy desk chair.

Katie rode Pitch and the remuda followed Pitch. How a horse can hold such power over other horses is beyond my knowledge, but whether you call it nature or personality or animal magnetism or just plain luck, Pitch had it. If Katie moved Pitch left, all the horses went left. Same for going right. I think if Katie could have sent Pitch up a tree that the others would have climbed right along without so much as a snort.

Despite the advantage that Pitch gave Katie, she kept twitching her shoulders and jerking her head this way and that. Her wide blue eyes seared into every shadow, sure that a gaggle of marauders hid behind each tree, that bands of unfriendly Indians angry that we turned east to head deeper into Cherokee country crouched low in back of every rise. Like Pearl and Ernestine, she snapped her head around often expecting gangs of outlaws to come swarming from behind, though all she saw were horses, cattle and dust. Maneuvering past a small grove of red cedars, the branches were like bandit's arms reaching out to snatch her. The third time a branch brushed her and she clenched in the saddle, Pitch turned his head back. More than likely he was reacting to a sound, but she took it as a scolding to settle down.

"Sorry."

She squared her shoulders and told herself to calm down and stop letting her mind race with the many, many ways her mother's plan could go awry. She swore at her fears and then swore that she would fall victim to them no more. She knew she had her mother's tendency to worry, but she also had her mother's resolve and her father's strength, and she pulled them to the surface, pushing her qualms deep down inside where she hoped they would stay forever. She had no time for such distractions, and she gained nothing by them. Keep your mind on your duties, she thought. And remember why you're out here. To save the ranch. To be ready for a future with Parker. Above all else, to help her mother keep everyone alive.

Mary did not have the luxury of burying her worries. Lives depended on her and she questioned her ability to protect them. In fact, she questioned everything. We were racing through the terrain, relatively speaking due to the muck and brush and trees, but nowhere near as fast as her mind was racing. Had she made the right decision to turn east off the trail? After all, Jonas had said they'd likely face bandits, then Indians, and then rustlers. They'd survived a rough-go with the bandits and had met only friendly Cherokees. Maybe they should have faced the rustlers head on. That's what Jonas would have done. But, she reminded herself, she wasn't Jonas and the group of women were friends, not hired guns. But avoiding the fight irritated her as a cowardly act. But she didn't know how many rustlers awaited them. But heading east to the Chisolm would take days, probably longer. But... every sentence in her mind started with a *but*. No, she thought, the decision has been made and we'll all just have to make the best of it. She couldn't stop the worries, but she wouldn't let them rule her. She wiggled on her saddle to straighten up her posture and ride tall. There were at least two hours of daylight left and she planned to use every second.

She motioned to Clean Through to keep moving forward, and he acknowledged with a nod. He understood the situation. Then she circled over to Katie. "Keep 'em moving. We don't stop until nightfall." Like Clean Through, Katie gave a nod of understanding. She thought Pitch might have nodded as well, but perhaps she was starting to give the stallion too much credit.

Mary continued back, telling me, then Prudence, then Ernestine of the plan to ride until it was too dark to go farther. The decisiveness and encouragement in her voice belied her inner struggle with her confidence. We fed off it and grew more confident ourselves.

After talking with Ernestine and before moving over to Pearl, Mary took a moment to glance back at where we'd been. The almost straight line of trampled brush, broken limbs and muddy soil imprinted with thousands of hoof prints gave her a moment of pride—we had performed with great skill to keep the herd moving in so direct a course under these conditions. Yet we also left a trail that couldn't be missed by rustlers even if they were blindfolded and asleep. Knowing there wasn't a thing she could do about it, Mary let it go and rode on to Pearl, then Sally, and then Ruth. The message was always the same. Keep moving.

We did indeed push the herd until dark and then some. Had there been a full moon, Mary might have kept us going even farther. I'll tell you something about cattle that I didn't know. They can trot a long way. There isn't a lick of athletic grace in a cow from any angle, but there sure is lung power. Whether it was Ernestine's squeals or they could sense the danger we felt, I don't know. But they kept moving until we said stop. Being every bit as exhausted as we were, they came to a fast stop and we had little fear of them wandering off. A few laid down to rest, but most stood in place and reached for whatever grass they could find to nibble on.

With the herd needing little attention, we made a fast camp. Clean Through made a small fire for coffee, then snuffed it out with dirt to limit the smoke. Dinner was cold beans and day-old biscuits and some jerky, and we were glad to have it. Clean Through had always been such a miracle worker that I half expected him to pull out a pie. Had a long-burning fire been available, though, I still doubt he would have been baking that night. After driving the chuckwagon around hazards all day, his arms had to be aching. Probably his backside, too. Mine was.

The last cup of coffee Clean Through handed out was to Mary, and then he sat down on the ground beside her to rest. Tired and drawn, Mary welcomed the chance to share her thoughts with a veteran of the trail. "Runnin' meat off the herd, but at least we've made some distance."

"We can fatten 'em up later. All we can do now is keep makin' ground."

"Do you think this has a chance of working?"

"Everything has a chance."

"I mean it. Don't dance around. Do we have a chance? Did I make the right decision?"

Clean Through took a sip of coffee and rubbed his whiskers. "It's a lot like believin' in God."

Mary knitted her eyebrows. "How's that?"

"Well, you know, you have faith in God, but you don't know if the faith is justified until you die and see if there's another life. If there is, then you made a good decision in believin' in God."

Mary's confused face brightened to a wry smile. "So we won't know if it was a good decision until we know if it works."

Clean Through smiled back. "Life. Trail ridin'. Anything. It wouldn't be an adventure if we knew all the answers."

"I sure wouldn't mind knowing how this'll pan out."

They sipped their coffee in silence, each staring into the darkness that loomed all around. At last, Mary spoke what was on both of their minds. "They'll come, won't they?"

"Lazy men smellin' easy money. Yep, they'll come."

Chapter 20

As I've mentioned enough times to likely be annoying, I'm doing all I can to maintain honesty and accuracy throughout this book. In that spirit, let me make it clear that this next section is pure guesswork. From what I've pieced together, the gang of men waiting for us on the Western Trail included Sean, Brute and six others. But none of us were there, of course, so please keep in mind that the following conversation and any subsequent writing about these men at times when witnesses weren't present is my best guess at what may have been taking place at the time.

Here, then, is my approximation of what the rustlers may have been experiencing the morning after we turned off of the trail. I'll try not to make it overly dramatic, but I must admit I'm a bit excited about the prospect of making something up.

They were about 20 miles south of Dodge City. Six of the men were spread out, three on each side of the trail, hiding behind trees or rocks or shrubs. Though not expecting us quite yet, they kept their eyes on the trail as anyone could be on it at any time. Rustlers prefer to surprise others rather than be surprised themselves.

Like most ruthless leaders, Sean stayed behind the men where it was safer. He sat lazily behind a large rock, chewing on jerky, his gun and horse handy should he get word that we were near. By his calculations, based on the information from Dusty, it should be a day, probably two, before our herd came over the ridge. Having already stolen two herds in the past six weeks, he was confident in his ability to judge the distances and travel time.

Brute was less confident, or at least less patient. He lumbered up behind Sean, his spacious shadow arriving well before him. "Shoulda seen 'em by now."

"Patience, Brute. We're waitin' on women and cattle, and neither take kindly to bein' hurried."

Scowling, Brute took a long draw on his cigarette and blew the smoke out through his nose like a mythical dragon. "I ain't sittin' and waitin' no more. Gonna go see how close they are." He turned away, not waiting for a reply.

"Don't let them see you."

"I'll get behind a tree."

"Make sure it's a big tree," Sean muttered to himself.

Parker had completed his delivery in Caldwell and, having no idea that we were heading east, was heading west toward Dodge City. But before you think that he was going to ride into our group by accident and save the day, picture that awful map I drew. He was well north of us, riding easy, smiling at the thought of meeting up with Katie again.

It was his intention to meet us in Dodge City and carry out an idea he was quite proud of. Since he wasn't able to meet directly with Katie's father but was anxious to move forward with the courtship, upon arriving in Dodge he would send a wire to Jonas declaring his intentions. It wasn't the same as meeting the man and offering a firm handshake, but it would, he felt, add a layer of honor that the man should and would respect. (And, he thought with a broader smile, it would make him even grander in Katie's eyes, and that could only be a good thing.) What he didn't know, of course, is that a wire could sit in a basket at Edward's store for weeks or who knows how long. Jonas could be a grandfather three times over before learning that his daughter was being courted.

He composed the telegram as he rode, whispering it to himself to see how it sounded. "'Mr. Bartlett'... no, 'Sir. Mr. Bartlett Sir'... Huh uh... Just 'Mr. Bartlett. I wish I could meet you in person to share my intention of courting your beautiful'... no, 'wonderful, daughter, Katie. Stop. However, please know that my intentions are honorable. Stop.'" He etched in his mind the importance of using the word honorable. "'I have met your wife and she looked kindly upon my prospects'... No, that's odd-sounding... 'I am part owner of a horse ranch and your wife agrees that my prospects are good.' That's better. 'I love Katie, sir,' ... Yes, that's when to use sir. 'and she loves me. Stop. I will be a good husband to her if she will have me. Stop. I hope to meet you soon to show you I am worthy. Stop.' That's a good ending. That's all I need right there."

He snapped his reins to pick up the pace. The sooner to Dodge, the sooner to Katie. He continued to compose the telegram as he rode, and with each passing mile he became less convinced that he was as smart as he thought he was. A telegram wouldn't do it. He needed to meet the man.

Chickens. Enough with the chickens. Jonas was part of the way on his walk to the henhouse and had no intention of going any farther. He was a rancher, dammit. He wanted to see cattle, not feathers.

Doc's orders were to take it slow and stay on the crutches, but Jonas reasoned that Doc knew him well enough to know that he'd eventually reach a point where he could no longer stand to take it slow. Therefore, in a logic that Jonas thought best not to dwell on, it could be considered doctor's orders that he *not* take it slow. In fact, if Doc was here right now, he'd likely advise Jonas to hitch up the buckboard and ride out to see how the remaining herd was doing. Yes, sir, he owed it to Doc to go!

The only problem—well, the first of several problems—was that the horses were out in the field. He shifted his weight onto his good leg, then lifted his crutch to study it. Sturdy wood. No visible cracks. Top padding intact.

Time for a real walk.

Two hours later his hip was searing with pain and hot enough he could have fried the henhouse eggs on it, but he had a horse in tow. He guided it into the barn, took a look at the wagon, and decided that tomorrow would be soon enough for a ride to see the herd. He settled the horse in a stall with hay and water, then limped to the house to lie down with a cool, wet towel on his hip, pausing only long enough to collect the day's eggs from the henhouse.

We were up well before dawn. After a long day of hurrying and a short night of rest, the herd was in no mood to get moving again. It took three of Ernestine's now-hoarse screeches to start them stirring and continuous whooping from all of us to maintain any forward motion. As the sun rose and their joints loosened, the pace picked up, not as quick as the previous day's pace, but steady.

Each of us had changed mounts. Katie hated to lose the security of riding Pitch, but she couldn't risk wearing him out after such a hard day. He seemed to sense his duty and trotted along behind her, the remuda following.

All at once the land cleared and what I think of as a miracle happened. We crossed the Cimarron River. Just like that. It was hard to imagine following all the trouble we'd had at the other river crossings, yet this time—with no planning or scouting—we rode up to the river and crossed it without incident. Perhaps not making note of the river was a strategy on Mary's part, or perhaps too much was on her mind for her to even realize the river was there. Whatever the reason, Mary led the herd into the river without so much as looking back. Clean Through followed with the chuckwagon and Katie with the remuda. Ruth and I rode in with the front of the herd, Prudence and Sally moved along with the middle of the herd, and Ernestine and Pearl followed the herd across. No one said a word beyond the normal hollering to encourage the cattle. There were no lightning storms, no hawks scaring horses, no falling in, no problems with a soft river bed, no Indian attacks, no gunfighters, no wandering by Uncle Angus, no bears or panthers or wild elephants, no rockslides, no sudden bouts of cholera or fever or plague.

It was far and away our best crossing. However, it wasn't perfect. Later in the day, Prudence would note that she received a mosquito bite.

Brute was big enough that had he had horns he might've been mistaken for a stray steer on the trail. Hornless, though, he rode his unfortunate horse toward where we should be, all the while keeping his eyes scanning up ahead for any sign of movement. He had traveled far enough that he felt sure he should have seen us by now.

A dark patch to the east caught his eye. He paused on the trail, again studying up ahead, seeking any movement or sign, wary of a trap as people who set traps tend to be. Seeing nothing, he spurred his mount and directed it toward the dark area. Soon he was close enough to see the trampled earth where the herd and us had turned into the brush. With an angry scowl, he spit on the hoof prints etched in the now-drying ground, turned his horse, and galloped back the way he came.

By nightfall we were settled into another dark camp. Using what little starlight and moonlight was available, I scratched away on my paper. With slow movements and creaking bones, Ruth lowered herself down beside me, propping up on her elbows.

"You should put that paper away and sleep while you can."

"I need to get down all that's happened while it's still fresh."

She slid her arms down and dropped her head to the ground. "Ain't nothin' fresh in my mind right now." A second later she was asleep.

I looked around at the others, all asleep. The surprising uneventful river crossing had been the topic during our cold meal of beans (Clean Through was out of bread and biscuits, so it was cold beans and water until Mary gave the go-ahead to build a fire), but even that excitement wasn't enough to overcome the weariness that had soaked us to the core. My pen felt heavier in my hand. My sheaf of paper weighed upon my lap. I wrote "And now to bed" and was asleep within a minute.

Jonas went to bed that night with the fire in his hip replaced by a cold stiffness. As he lay on his back, he raised and lowered his leg hoping to stretch it out and prevent it stoving up any more overnight. Despite his aches, he felt good. He had done something today, even if it was just rounding up a horse, and he would do something tomorrow, even if it was just hitching up a wagon and riding out to see the herd.

Hitching the wagon by himself, with one side of his body hampered by a crutch, would be time consuming, but it was something he felt he could do. He had to, after all, since he didn't have Katie or Mary there to do it for him like they had before.

What really would have made him feel good, what would have loosened up both his hip and his mind, was more news on how the drive was going. The two letters in one month had spoiled him, and he was anxious for more. By his calculation, based on the information in my letters, we should have the herd very close to Dodge City—perhaps even in it— by now. He knew Mary would wire him when the drive was complete, and he had a fair idea that that would be one telegram Edward would feel compelled to deliver.

Perhaps tomorrow he would see how his remaining herd was faring and also hear of the safe, successful arrival of Mary, Katie and the rest of the herd. Well, he thought as he put out the light, it couldn't hurt to dream of good news while he awaited the real news. Yet, as always seemed to be the case, he felt certain his sleep would be troubled.

Chapter 21

"Aaaaaaaaaaaaaaaaaaa!!!!!!"

Starting each day with a scream is more rousing than coffee, which was good since we didn't have coffee. We were off at first light. Clean Through had suggested that Mary ride ahead to scout the terrain and perhaps find a clearer path, but she didn't want to leave the group with one less gun should the gang chase and attack. She remembered how she had been about the last to arrive when that first group of bad men had stolen some of us. If anything happened again, she wanted to be creating survivors, not counting them.

A hot day was in store, despite the slate-gray sky. There had been little cooling overnight, and the air was already thick with humidity. It was tiring to breathe. Even if Mary had found a clear path to the Chisolm, the cattle could not have run far. We felt it best to push them at a steady walking pace.

By the Cimarron River, where we had crossed without incident, the gang of men stopped. Sean examined the drying tracks. Brute scowled as one of the band took a swig of water.

"Drink later. We need to ride."

Sean remained squatted by the tracks. "They aren't far ahead. We should start hearin' 'em by mid-day." He smiled as he rose. "The herd'll be ours by nightfall."

A red-haired man grumbled, "Gonna be a lot more work takin' the cattle back to Dodge from out here."

"Couple more days outside a saloon won't hurt the likes of you," Brute fumed.

The red-haired man wanted no part of a fight with Brute, but needn't have worried. Sean stepped in to calm the group. "Sure, and it's just like ladies to add work where none was needed," he said, his Irish brogue laid on extra thick. "But the herd should be easy pickin's and once you hold your cut in your hands, you'll find it quite rewarding for a few days effort."

"Might find some of those women rewardin', too," laughed the red-haired man.

Brute was lightning quick for a giant. In a flash, he had the red-haired man on the ground. "You get the cattle, not the women. You hear me?"

"Sure, Brute, sure."

Brute gave the man a final shove, then moved to his horse. "Then let's ride. If it's those same women, I'll learn 'em not to run from me, startin' with that girl." Fire burned in his eyes as he spurred his horse to action.

Occasionally the brush and trees would thin, easing our chore of keeping the herd together. During those times, Mary would loop back to check on everyone and, of course, take a long look behind us in search of movement or any sign that we were being trailed.

This time, as we came upon a clearing that extended far to both the left and the right, Mary rode over to Clean Through instead. He had stopped the chuckwagon and she could see that he was pondering their location.

"Looks more like a trail than a clearing," she said.

"Does indeed." Clean Through squeezed the bridge of his nose. Mary said nothing, knowing Clean Through well enough by this time to feel sure he'd do his thinking out loud. He did. "We been goin' northeast... crossed the Cimarron yesterday... this trail goes northwest..." He perked up. "I heard tell that some of the Texarkana ranchers had plans to blaze a branch off the Chisolm that went northwest into Dodge! They must've done it and we've stumbled right into the middle of it! Hot damn! Oh, sorry, Boss."

"Swear all you want once you tell me what this means. You're saying we could still go to Dodge City, takin' this trail in from the east?"

"That's what I think this trail is. We can cross it and continue on through the brush, probably reaching Caldwell in four, five days and on to Newton from there. Or turn the herd here and head back for Dodge from this angle."

"How long to Dodge?"

"Three, four days."

"So it's like a triangle. If the rustlers are chasin' us, we could swing back and maybe get to Dodge with them behind us the whole time?"

"Lotta 'ifs' and 'maybes,' but I reckon so. Don't mean there won't be more rustlers."

"There might be gangs on the main Chisolm, too, for all we know. What do you think? Should we turn northwest back to Dodge?"

The only answer she received was a harsh groan as a bullet pierced Clean Through's right shoulder. Mary snapped her head around to see the gang of men charging us. They were spread out, eight of them, attacking from the side of the herd where Prudence, Ernestine and me rode, bearing down on us with guns drawn. They weren't shooting, perhaps thinking Clean Through was the only one who'd shoot back or maybe hoping they wouldn't scatter the herd. Just in case, by hitting us from the side, they'd effectively protected themselves from half of our guns.

We surprised them by shooting back, though I wish I could say that we hit at least one of them. Prudence fired again and then blended in with the herd, eyes wide with fear. She had no intention of being stolen a second time.

As I fired toward the red-haired man—another miss—Clean Through used his good arm to snap the reins and turn his mules toward a treed area to the south. The scattering and bellowing wails of the herd alerted Sally and Ruth of the attack. With a bravery worthy of soldiers, they raced through the herd, rifles at the ready. We'd been rushing so much that we had no plan, only guts and hope, and just enough smarts to stop trying to ride and shoot at the same time. We stopped. I fired again. Sally fired. Ruth fired. We had all fired at the same man, and whether we all hit him or just one did I don't know, but the gang of eight was now a gang of seven.

Mary had reached us now and she, too, fired. We all did. That the four of us could all miss a target the size of Brute speaks volumes about our lack of marksmanship. The giant of a man rode hard right past us. The one shot he took hit Sally's horse square in the jaw, dropping it and sending Sally flying.

"Follow Clean Through," shouted Mary. "Head for the trees!" She took another shot at one of the men while I helped Sally up to ride double. We sprinted for the trees, Sally's arms shaking as they gripped my waist. Ernestine was beside us, blood oozing from a wound in her arm.

"They're headin' for those trees!" I could hear the red-haired man shout.

"Let 'em run," Sean directed. "Get the herd!"

The gang spread farther to circle the cattle before the herd could scatter completely.

"Come on!" Mary yelled to Ruth, who kept her horse stopped and steady.

"I'll catch up!" Ruth yelled back, her gun at her shoulder. One of the men raced right at her, pistol raised. Boom-boom! came the roar of both guns. The man fell from his horse, dark red liquid staining his chest. Ruth heard the searing sound of a bullet whizzing by just above her ear, taking part of her hair with it. She turned her horse and had no need to do more to send it rushing for the trees.

Katie gave up trying to hold the remuda together. She had her gun pulled, but couldn't find a target in the chaotic movement of the herd. Turning toward the trees where the others were heading, she spotted Brute racing toward her, smiling like a coyote attacking a lame fawn. Her hands quivered. She settled them with a deep breath, took aim and fired, only to have a frantic steer buck up and take the bullet. Brute's beeline toward her was unchanged. She turned Pitch and rode hard, Brute following and gaining ground before Pitch got up to speed.

Pearl, the only one of us without a gun—despite being our best shot—and the last to know of the attack due to her position at the far back corner of the herd, had directed her mount toward the chuckwagon when she'd figured out what was happening. But seeing Brute in pursuit of Katie, Pearl galloped past us and took up a pursuit of her own. "Katie!"

Mary turned at Pearl's yell, just in time to see Brute slow at the top of a ridge, pull his rifle and fire. "Nooo!!" She jerked the reins to start her own pursuit, but the swarming, scattering, bellowing herd was like a wall with no doorway. Seconds later she saw Brute riding away with Katie squirming under his big arm, blood stains smeared across her shirt. "Katie!!!!" Next she saw Pearl continuing her chase and gaining as Brute's horse strained under even more weight. Brute, with Katie flopping like a rag doll, ignored the herd and Sean completely, riding past them on into the prairie ahead. Pearl was slowed by the herd, but would not relent.

Gunshots grabbed Mary's attention. Members of the gang were firing into the air to turn the herd. Ruth and I were firing at them, with Sally and Prudence reloading guns and passing them up to us. Clean Through was weak from blood loss, but dug around supplies in his wagon to pull out more ammunition with his good arm. Ernestine, blood spattered, clutched our horses—no small task as they wanted desperately to bolt.

Torn between duty to us and the desire to protect Katie, Mary hesitated, but the wall of cattle made the choice for her. After one last glance and a quick prayer for Katie and Pearl, she leaped from her horse and joined us. Her mount rushed away before Ernestine could snatch its reins. Mary knew instantly that she had made a mistake. Though she fired her rifle, she couldn't focus on the battle. Her eyes kept going back to where Brute had taken Katie. Her only hope was Pearl, who didn't even have a gun.

She turned back to take another horse from Ernestine, but at that very second a bullet tore through Ernestine's hand. She pulled it back in agony, screaming. The horses sprinted away.

Moments later the attack ended almost as fast as it had begun. The men had turned the herd and were moving it up the trail. The frightened cattle dashed forward, happy to again be all going in the same direction. The last thing we saw was Sean pausing at the back of the herd. He looked toward us and tipped his hat. I wish I could say that my final shot brought him down, but I either missed or the bullet fell short. Sean rode off.

We were alone with our pain, fear, anger and defeat. The torn and trampled trail grew more empty with each passing second as the herd moved away. We were bloodied, robbed, horseless and separated from two of our companions whose fate we did not know.

Mary rushed to unhitch a mule from the wagon. Sally and I lowered Clean Through to the ground to check his wounds. Ruth went to work cleaning and bandaging Ernestine's hand. Prudence loaded guns.

Flailing, kicking, squirming, biting, screaming. Katie's efforts were fruitless. Brute held her in the crook of his arm like she was a sack of sugar. She gave up struggling in hopes of conserving her strength for an escape opportunity. Her only hope was speed. She could never fight the man, but if she could break free and somehow get him away from his horse, maybe she could outrun him. She'd worry about where to run later.

She had heard people say "it all happened so fast" and now the phrase had meaning for her. She was just beginning to sort through what had happened. After the steer had taken her shot and she'd raced away, Pitch— oh, poor Pitch!—had collapsed, blood pouring from his neck. She hadn't heard the shot, but she heard Pitch's shriek and, even now, felt his sticky blood that had seeped onto her shirt. Before she could even rise from the spill, Brute had snatched her right off the ground, barely slowing, then looped to race back past the herd and down the trail. She had caught but one glimpse of his face before he swirled her into carrying position, but that lustful look was etched in her mind. He had no plans to sell her. She wouldn't be that lucky. Whoever named him Brute wasn't lying.

Yet she could not, would not, despair. She was alive and, so far at least, wasn't ruined for Parker. Hope of escape remained.

Sally and I exchanged glances as we pulled off Clean Through's shirt to get to his bleeding shoulder. What we saw were scars from six old bullet wounds. I couldn't resist propping him up enough to look at his back. There was a clear exit wound in his shoulder and six other similar wounds, each scarred over.

"Now I know how you got your name," I said, settling him back down.

"Time I retired," he grimaced as Sally worked to stem the bleeding. "Runnin' out of safe places to get shot."

Any hint that Mary had ever had an indecisive moment in her life was gone. As she unlatched the last strap from the mule and wagon, she barked out orders with a no-nonsense voice that commanded attention.

"Sally, you tend to Clean Through and Ernestine. Laurie, Prudence, take rifles and start walking until you find some horses. Ruth, stand guard. Anyone who ain't female rides up, you blast him."

Then she hopped on the mule and rode off in Katie's direction without another word. She didn't have to tell us her orders for herself. They couldn't be much plainer. Save Katie and Pearl or die trying.

This is it, Katie thought as Brute rode in behind a group of small red cedars and reined his horse to a stop. Escape now or be ruined. Yet Brute wasn't concentrating on her except for keeping her in his grasp as he got down from the horse. He was looking back the way they came, using the trees for cover. Keeping Katie seized under his left arm, he pulled his rifle from the saddle holster with his right hand and held it high by the barrel. Now Katie could hear the fast-approaching clops of a galloping horse… closer… closer… wham! Brute slammed the rifle smack into Pearl's chest, knocking her back enough that her feet pulled free of the stirrups. Her balance was gone and she toppled sideways off the horse as it raced on.

"Pearl!" Katie shouted, surprising herself that her first thought was to wonder how many times the poor woman had been hit on this trip before swiftly moving on to concern over her friend. Then she admired Pearl's bravery and spirit as she rose up, dusted herself off, wiped blood from her lips and faced Brute.

"I'll have your gun," the big man said. "And when I finish with her, I'll have you."

"I ain't armed."

Brute sneered. "Poor excuse for a rescue. Stupid women."

Moments later, Brute had Katie and Pearl positioned one on each side of his horse with ropes around their necks and the ropes tied to his saddle. He had Pearl's hands tied and was tying Katie's hands when Sean rode up.

Sean gazed from Katie to Pearl with a slight grin. "Looks like you got your hands full."

"I'll manage."

"Bet you will." He pointed ahead in the direction the herd was moving. "We'll take 'em another couple hours, then bed down."

"I'll catch up." Brute cupped Katie's chin and made her look into his face. "Somethin' I gotta do first."

Sean gave Katie and Pearl a deeper look. "You could bring 'em along. Some of the boys might enjoy a —"

"Mine." Brute held a steady glare at Sean.

Sean's hand was near his gun. He measured the distance between them, noting that Brute's gunhand was free. Not worth the risk. Sometimes brains are no match for muscle and speed. He held out a placating hand.

"Sure. Sure, Brute. It's fun you'll be havin' and you've earned it. We'll be seein' you later." He tipped his hat. "Ladies." Then with a jerk of his reins, Sean rode off.

Brute pointed to a group of evergreens up the trail with a grassy area beside them. He climbed onto his miracle horse that seemed impervious to his weight. "Start walkin'. And you know what'll happen if you do more than walk." He tugged on the ropes, tightening the loops around their necks.

Their heads down, lifeless, defeated, Katie and Pearl shuffled forward.

Though he had enjoyed his wagon ride out to see the remaining herd, a dark mood had washed over Jonas. As he walked to exercise the ride from his leg and hip the uneasiness he felt had taken him in a different direction. Without realizing it, he had wandered behind the barn near a patch of dirt. The patch had once been a mound, but had settled over the past few months. The grave encouraged a small, wistful smile, for it was the resting place of Sparky the Amazing Hound. At least that's what Katie had called the old mutt. Sparky had excelled at keeping foxes from the henhouse, but in the early spring he had come out on the wrong end of a fight with a cougar. Katie had been inconsolable and it was only when Mary suggested a burial and service that the sobs subsided. He had never heard of burying a dog, let alone saying words over one. But he went along and when he saw the peace that Mary's "long rest Sparky, our fine friend" brought to Katie, he knew the time spent digging was worth every minute.

It was an unusual cemetery for a ranch. Most folks had kin planted in the ground, often lost babies. Certainly not dogs. But it was just him, Mary and Katie. After Katie had been delivered, Doc Galen said that birthing her had messed up something inside Mary. There would be no more children. No sons. Maybe it cost them the joy of a big family or maybe it saved them the heartbreak of more graves. There was no way of knowing. But it made Katie all the more precious and Jonas all the more protective of her—and he was unable to protect her now. "Damn leg," he muttered to no one. He began to limp back to the house, hoping Katie and Mary were well.

Living on hope makes a man feel inadequate. He cursed his leg again.

A quiet, gloomy calm, framed by a watchful wariness, had descended upon Sally. For the moment, the riders were gone, Prudence and I were out looking for horses, and Ruth was scanning the countryside in search of someone to shoot. To keep her mind from dwelling on Katie, Pearl and Mary, Sally concentrated on caring for Clean Through and Ernestine.

The late-afternoon sun cast deep shadows from the trees across the back of the wagon where Clean Through rested. Sally had finished re-dressing Ernestine's wounds—she had been grazed in the thigh and arm as well as hit in the hand—and was again washing the front side of Clean Through's wound.

"Gonna need stitches?" Ernestine asked.

"Don't believe you will," Sally replied, not voicing her thoughts that Clean Through did indeed need sewing up and her sewing things were in her saddlebag on the side now crushed underneath a dead, heavy horse way out in the field. "Biggest thing will be holding off infection, so you keep that hand clean and let me know if it changes color or hurts more than it does already." She smiled at Clean Through. "Guess it'll take more than a bullet to bring you down, huh?"

Clean Through smiled back. "My late wife, God rest her, said bullets pass through me because I'm not a man of substance. Proved her right again."

Sally gave him a pat on his good shoulder and looked up. She was unable to resist an impulse to gaze at the trail ahead. They were hip-deep in trouble in just about every way, but there was no way her mind could stay away from thoughts of Katie, Pearl and Mary for long.

Mary had a gun, but so did that big monster of a man. Even more, he had a big lead on her.

We had had occasional squabbles on our journey, but all in all we were linked together through one purpose and rode with one mind. The purpose and the mindset remained, but for the first time we were separated physically, less able to draw strength from each other. And though not entirely divided from our prospects, there was a definite distance between our reality and our dreams.

Hope, like the trail dust on the horizon ahead, was fading.

PART SIX
RETRIBUTION

Chapter 22

The small, secluded, grassy area would have been a pleasant picnic spot under other circumstances, but to Katie it was a green graveyard. She thought her heart stopped—even hoped for it a little—when Brute kept his hungry eyes on her as he tied his horse to a small tree. Escape seemed all but impossible with her hands tied and a noose around her neck. Her only comfort was Pearl standing beside her, and even then she felt guilty about being glad Pearl was there. She should be wishing Pearl was free, but she couldn't help herself. She didn't want to die alone.

Brute stood before her. Loomed over her. His foul breath watering her eyes more than fear ever could. "Woman gets a man's mind on her, then runs away…" he glowered, "Woman like that needs punished."

"She ain't no woman, just a girl!"

Brute backhanded Pearl across the face, stinging her, extending the cut on her lip. But it was Katie who couldn't hold back tears as Brute reached for the rope around her neck and held it taut. He bent down, leveling his eyes with hers, and spoke with a clear, direct, ominous tone that chilled Katie's very core.

"Now in that soft grass over there, you're gonna get a chance to make up for treatin' me so unkind. For havin' eyes that tease." His hairy lips brushed Katie's ear. "Do me right, you might live. Do me wrong, I'll kill you for sure. Then I'll kill her. Then I'll go back and kill your friends."

Katie, tears dripping from her cheeks, nodded agreement with a whimper.

"Take me first," said Pearl.

Brute raised his hand to smack her again, but stopped when she kept speaking.

"You can do anything you want," she continued with practiced allure in her voice. "Man like you needs an experienced woman. Take the edge off."

Brute looked Pearl's body up and down. The dirty clothes, swollen lip and long history of sadness couldn't hide her beauty. That she appeared to desire him as well added to her appeal.

"Warm-up might be nice at that. Get the fire stoked…" He curled his lip at Katie. "Before the main course."

"No, Pearl, no!" screamed Katie.

Brute shoved her to the ground. "Shut your sorry mouth." He unhooked the neck rope from the saddle and tied it to the tree. "Stay put. I don't aim to tell you twice."

As Brute turned, Pearl fell to her knees beside Katie and put her tied hands in Katie's lap as she moved in for a hug. "It'll all be fine," she said aloud for Brute to hear. Then she pushed Katie's hands down to her boots, connecting them with the shaft of a knife. "Run," she whispered as she saw understanding in Katie's eyes.

Brute yanked Pearl to her feet. "Stop your jabberin'!" He shoved her ahead to the grassy area, smiling as she fell onto her back. With a leer, he lumbered toward her. "Let's get them clothes off." Seconds later Katie heard fabric tearing. She cupped the knife in her tied hands, rose, and began to saw at the rope tied to the tree.

I suppose one must rank God giving his only begotten son as the biggest sacrifice in history, but you'd be hard pressed to convince me that what Pearl did that day was any less inspiring. Just her bravery alone in chasing after Katie with no gun, no plan, just guts… it moves me even now to think on it. But to buy time for Katie's escape by offering herself to that wretched man and his violent, woman-hating ways, risking harm and death to save Katie from the ruination that Pearl had known at such an early age, protecting her like a sister, losing all hope for a better life in order to ensure that Katie's hope still had a chance, and to still have the cleverness and presence of mind to give Katie a knife—that she could have used to free herself while Katie was victimized—well, it shames me to know that I could not have done the same.

Sacrifice.

I ask you, could there be a nobler act?

With the last thread of the rope cut through, Katie worked to loosen the noose around her neck and free herself from its choking bind. Her hands were still tied, but there was no time to cut those ropes now. From the moment Pearl had slipped her the knife, Katie knew what she would, what she must, do. The sounds of slaps and Pearl's groans and more ripping cloth and what must have been a snapping bone had only fueled Katie's conviction.

Brute's big horse had watched her, soundless, while she cut the rope, probably hoping she'd free him as well. It's what Pearl wanted. Take Brute's horse and run, leaving Pearl behind to her fate with Brute.

Like hell.

With her roped hands, Katie grasped the hilt of the knife so that the blade was positioned for a downward strike, then she started running, building up her speed to gain the added thrust she felt would be needed for a deep stab into Brute's thick hide. She saw him move to climb on top of Pearl, now quiet and motionless, and locked her eyes on the coarse hairs poking through the soiled shirt he kept on, marking the place between his shoulder blades. She would aim her thrust there in hopes that a piece of the knife would strike the man's heart.

"Aaaaaaaaaaa!!!" She rivaled Ernestine for volume as she slammed herself and the knife onto Brute's back. She knew that her added weight would intensify Pearl's misery, but also knew it was essential to drive the knife.

The blade seared into Brute and he screamed in agony, blood spraying from his mouth onto Pearl's face. He bucked, throwing Katie off his back like a child's toy chucked from a bronco, then lifted himself to his knees, an unkillable demon rising from the grave. He tried to extend his arms around for the knife, but it was out of his reach. Groaning with effort, he stood, kicking off the pants around his ankles, naked from the waist down, the tails of his shirt not covering nearly enough.

Katie watched in paralyzed fascination as the big man arched his back as if hoping through sheer force to send the knife flying out like he'd sent Katie flying. But the knife remained. Blood seeped from the wound, not pouring as Katie wished. More blood trickled from his mouth. That he was weakened was clear, but that he was still formidable was just as clear.

He staggered a menacing step toward Katie, snapping her out of her inaction. She snatched up a broken limb, the only weapon in sight, wishing her hands were untied so she could swing it with more force. Though it was blunt, she held it out in front of her like a spear, taking comfort in having something between her and Brute. He managed another step forward, his face contorting between rage and pain. She still had an outlet to run, but didn't dare leave Pearl. She thrust the stick at him.

"Stay away from me!"

"Ain't killed me yet," he strained, lumbering toward her, his sheer weight giving his wounded body momentum. Blood continued to ooze from both his mouth and back, and he continued to fight through his weakness. He swatted at the stick. Katie pulled it back, then poked him hard in the chest with it, reeling him back for only a second.

Pearl's entire body felt crushed and her head swam with pain and confusion. Blinking, she could make out Katie trying to hold off the man with no more than a stick. She had no strength to moan as she rose to her elbows. As filthy as the man was, the red-gray sky of early evening and the already-rising moon offered plenty of light, and as the man's naked backside registered in Pearl's mind her head cleared enough for an idea to form. She didn't dare turn her head too fast for fear of passing out, but a slow turn revealed her new goal: Brute's gun belt. Panting, drawing upon strength she didn't know she had, she struggled and stretched until her fingers touched worn leather. She pulled the gun belt closer and reached for the pistol.

Gunshot!

From where?

Katie saw a new circle of blood expanding on Brute's shirt, saw more spill from his mouth. He hovered in front of her, swaying, struggling to hold his balance, the fury on his face replaced by stunned, empty eyes. Katie glanced at Pearl, saw her holding the gun belt with the pistol still holstered. Brute wavered, and she pushed the stick against him to keep him from falling on her.

Another gunshot rang out and Brute staggered again as a bullet pierced his side. This time Katie could track the direction of the reverberating sound and saw a wondrous sight. Pearl squinted and her eyes absorbed the beautiful sight as well.

Mary!

Not too late this time!

With a last gasp of strength, Brute, blood pouring from his torso in red streaks down his naked legs, grabbed the stick and tried to jerk Katie toward him. Sometimes the simplest move is the best, and Katie performed one—she let go of the stick. The momentum of his movement forced Brute backward, his bloody legs unable to check his fall. With a whomp that likely sent prairie dogs scurrying for new homes, he collapsed in a filthy red heap, the knife pushed fully into his chest.

More gunshots rang out, one after the other, six total. Pearl, using the last of her strength in cathartic revenge, had emptied the chamber into Brute. He had been a hard man to kill, but she made sure it was done. The blood flow lessened. Whether from the knife or the bullets or the combination or just plain dumbfoundedness at his fate no one can truly say, but all that matters is that his heart had finally stopped.

Pearl fell back unconscious. Katie rushed to her and cradled her head. Mary rode in and slid from the mule to cradle Katie. For some time, no words were spoken. None were needed.

There were also no tears.

We were done with tears.

Chapter 23

All right, when I say that we were done with tears, I believe I am correct in principle. When Prudence and I came across my horse grazing, I cried. Not so much because of that particular horse, since I rode a different one just about every day and hadn't become attached to any specific one, but because that horse had my saddle and attached to my saddle were my saddlebags and inside my saddlebags were all the notes and thoughts I had written during the drive. I hadn't had time to think of them before, but the sudden sight of them made my eyes well up. I didn't need further proof that writing had become important to me, but I had it anyway. The watery eyes turned to outright tears when I opened the saddlebags to see that all was intact.

However, strictly interpreted and analyzed, I believe that my crying jag came about the same time that Mary's first bullet struck Brute and was over by the time Pearl emptied the gun into him. So, yes, I believe it's accurate to say that we were done with crying at that time. However, when such a statement involves women—and men, too, I'm sure—it's only true until things change.

Still, under that bright moonlight, reunited once again, we were all business.

Mary and Katie had returned, pulling Pearl on a makeshift travois behind Brute's horse, which had not known such a light load for who knows how long. Mary and Katie could have sat there and hugged each other all night, but Pearl was in bad shape. She was unconscious, bloodied and bruised. Based on circumstances, they assumed her ribs were cracked if not broken, and that she was bleeding inside. Warm reunions would have to wait.

There was no thought given to burying Brute. "Leave him be," Mary had said. "A feast for the scavengers."

"Still better than he deserved," added Katie.

They took his guns and, as with the burial, gave no thought to covering him with his pants. If the garment hadn't been so filthy, they might have used it as part of the travois or to help cover Pearl, whose clothes had been torn to shreds. "Even if his clothes were store-bought fresh," Mary said, "we'll never let anything of his touch Pearl again."

Prudence and I arrived back well after midnight, having found three horses, though mine was the only one with a saddle.

It was a time of fast-rising and fast-falling emotions. Each appearance was heralded with hugs and smiles followed almost immediately by stark horror at Pearl's condition. She remained unconscious, and it was likely for the best. Clean Through was also worsening as Sally's bandages hadn't fully stemmed the bleeding and she no longer had her sewing kit for stitches. Throughout all discussions and movement, Mary was never more than an inch away from Katie. She wasn't about to lose her again.

There was no sleeping that night. We stayed awake as much to share all that had happened from our different perspectives as we did to guard ourselves against further attack. Even more, we stayed awake to plan.

After Katie had told us of her frightening experience and Pearl's brave sacrifice and the rescue by Mary, and after Prudence had told of our wandering search for horses, and after Sally had offered up a clear, direct report of the injured—"Pearl and Clean Through need a real doctor or they'll die. Ernestine'll live if she don't get feverish, but that gash in her hand ain't pretty and needs some doctoring, too"—we began to assess our situation.

We had the three horses Prudence and I had gathered, Pearl's horse, Brute's horse, and the two mules. Three saddles, plus the one Katie noted was still on Pitch. All of our guns except for the rifle Katie had left sheathed on Pitch, plus Brute's pistol and rifle. The chuckwagon was full of ingredients, though a little over a day's worth of jerky the only food currently prepared. We whispered the food part because the last thing we wanted was Clean Through to overhear us and decide to pop up and start cooking. Any exertion was likely to increase his bleeding.

Our discussion about our next action was interrupted by Ruth cocking her rifle. "Rider!" she shouted while shouldering the rifle and pointing it at a shadowy shape coming from the woods to the north. All of us with at least one good hand snatched up our guns.

"One of those men would've come from that way," said Prudence, indicating the trail heading northwest toward Dodge.

"Might've looped around," said Ruth.

"Comin' in awful fast," Sally noted. "Not keepin' himself a secret."

"Maybe he's trying to hold our attention," said Mary. "Sally, Laurie, Ernestine, you watch the other directions. The rest of you, if you see his hands move from the reins, start firin'."

A moment later Katie changed the mood from concern to elation. "It's Parker! Oh, don't shoot, it's Parker!"

About that same time, up the trail where the remainder of his gang had the cattle settled for the night, Sean was tired of watching for Brute. He lied down and stared up at the moon. Ruining the first two women must not have satisfied Brute, he thought. He must have gone back for the others. Sometimes when he thought about Brute and women, he smiled. Other times he shuddered, and now was one of those times. Come to think of it, his train of thought continued, no woman had ever satisfied Brute. And none were ever left in any condition to try again. Ah, well, 'tis a sad thing for those women that they crossed Brute's path, and—here his smile returned—a sadder thing for the rest of us that he won't leave us a taste. But, he thought as he pulled his hat over his face and closed his eyes, the money these cattle'll bring from Yankton will buy enough drinks and women to make up for it. Then Brute won't be the only one having a good time.

We lowered our guns only a bit until we were sure that the rider was Parker, but Katie was correct. That they'd only known each other for a few hours and yet his shadowy shape was familiar to her spoke volumes. Perhaps back home we might have teased her a little, but out here we were thrilled to welcome a kind soul. Throwing all thoughts of propriety aside, Katie embraced him and buried her face in his chest. "I thought I'd lost you," he whispered, wrapping his arms around her. She said nothing and simply listened to his heart.

Mary gave them their moment, but there were too many things to do to let that moment linger. First, she wanted answers.

"How'd you ever find us?"

Parker loosened his grip on Katie and turned to Mary, his more formal nature returning. "Chinmay sent his grandson to tell me you were being chased and said I'd find you on the northwestern branch of the Chisolm."

"I guess we made an impression on him after all."

"He also said the beef was good." Then Parker's face clouded. "Guess I was too late to be of any help."

"No," said Mary. "You might've missed out on the first party, but if you're willin' to help, we could use you in the next one."

"Of course I'll help," he said, which in turn made Katie stand just a little taller and prouder.

Up went the hand. "You mean to go after the herd, Mrs. Bartlett?" asked Prudence.

"You bet I do."

"Good," was all Prudence said, but it summed up the feelings of the rest of us. There were nods all around.

"Nobody gets away with hurtin' our people," said Mary. "And nobody sells Circle B cattle but Circle B ranch hands."

We talked more through the night. Katie filled Parker in on all that had happened, and I think he was ready to go empty another gun into Brute's dead body. Mary and Katie assured him that Brute's days of hurting women were over.

Under the first pink light of dawn, we got our first good look at Pearl. My God. She was a rainbow of bruises—yellow, red, green and purple. Sickly colors, not pretty. Where bruises had yet to form, her skin was bloodless and pale. If it weren't for the bruises, she'd have had no color at all. Sally lifted up one of Pearl's eyelids and saw no sign of life. Yet she breathed and had a heartbeat.

"She saved my life," Katie whispered as we stared at Pearl.

"Rescued us from those women-stealers," added Prudence.

"Our first duty is to get Pearl and Clean Through to a doctor," said Mary. "Parker?"

"Closest would be back in Caldwell, I reckon. Doc Evert. Good one, too. Don't hardly drink at all."

"How long in the wagon?"

"Steady pace'll get you there by nightfall."

"I'm not takin' them, Ernestine is." Ernestine raised her eyebrows. Mary kept talking. "Pearl and Clean Through deserve every chance to live, and you need your hand looked at. Can you drive the wagon all right?"

"I'd rather help kill the men that shot me."

"You'll be helping considerable, Ernestine."

Katie spoke up. "It would sure mean the world to me if Pearl got some proper doctorin'."

"She saved my life, too, and Clean Through fed me," Ernestine said. "I'll get them there fast, you can count on it."

Perhaps accepting the inevitable, Mary started treating Parker like a son-in-law—she put him to work. With Katie's help he had the mules hitched and the wagon turned in the right direction in just a few minutes. I filled a canteen for Clean Through, who now drifted in and out of consciousness but was thirsty when awake, and Prudence and Ruth made sure Pearl and Clean Through were blanketed and secured for the ride. There was a little talk about Sally riding along to tend to the wounded, but her wanting to fight and our needing every gun ended the discussion. Before the pink sky had begun its shift to orange, Ernestine was ready to get the wagon moving for Caldwell on the route Parker thought best.

"One more thing," said Mary. "After you get them to the doctor, before you worry about your hand, you send a telegram to Edward to let him know you're all right and to tell him to deliver to Jonas the next telegram that comes through from me. Then send this." She handed Ernestine a folded piece of paper. "It's important that he deliver it."

Ernestine nodded. "I'll make sure." Then she looked at the rest of us, offered a quick "Good luck," and was on her way.

I like to think that at some point during the night Sean was also taking stock of his situation and was taken aback some. After all, he and his gang must have thought they could brush us aside or scare us off with ease, yet we had killed two of the men (plus Brute, though Sean didn't know that). Did he wonder if he had underestimated us? Or overestimated his men? Or did he only care that he was still alive and that fewer men meant larger shares for the rest? He had the herd and we didn't. Maybe that was his bottom line.

One thing was certain, we had made them work. It cost them a fourth of their gang to take the herd, plus they were now three to four days out of Dodge instead of a little over one. That meant more long days in the saddle for people who made their living doing anything but work. Having to do work likely galled them more than having a few of their men killed.

By morning light, they were starting the herd forward. As Sean cinched his saddle, the red-haired man kicked out the remains of their fire. Spotting Sean looking back down the trail, he laughed.

"Ol' Brute must be havin' quite a time." Then he got serious. "Means more work for us. If'n he don't get back, you still gonna give him a share?"

"Would you tell Brute he can't be havin' a share?"

Red gave a sheepish grin. "Reckon not."

"He'll be along. He keeps his own schedule." Sean rode off for the herd, but his thoughts lingered on Brute. Was he finishing off the women one by one? Or had something happened to the big man? No, he shook off such thoughts. Ten men couldn't hurt Brute, let alone a group of weak women.

Still, something didn't feel right and over his years of circumventing the law, Sean had learned that trusting his feelings was often the difference between success and jail time. He called Red over to him. "Somethin' I need you to do."

For once, we didn't have to rush. Let the men move the herd for a while.

With the fresh light of day, a little jerky in our stomachs, and the injured out of sight, our confidence was growing. In the chaos of the attack, we had each seen different men and together our best guess was that there were eight men in total, give or take one. We had killed two during the attack and then Brute, meaning that there were five, maybe six, men left. Counting Parker, and he insisted on being counted, there were seven of us. The men likely shot better than we did, especially with Pearl gone, but at least we had an advantage with numbers. Plus, we were mad.

Mary rode Pearl's horse. I rode mine. After raising the stirrups quite a bit, Ruth and Prudence teamed up on Brute's horse, both fitting easily in his saddle and totaling far less weight than the big man, plus they likely pleased the horse simply by not using spurs. Parker had his horse, of course. Sally and Katie each rode one of the bareback horses. Since neither of them felt comfortable without the control of reins, our next order of business was to ride to where Pitch had been shot out from under Katie. It wouldn't be a pleasant reminder for Katie about her experience, but we needed the saddle and gear. And the rifle in the sheath.

"I'm not looking forward to tellin' Pa about Pitch," said Katie.

"All he'll care about is that you're fine," Mary assured her.

Perhaps because we had time or perhaps because we were delaying our sight of the magnificent Pitch in such a pitiful state, we slowed to a walk as we ascended the ridge leading to the bend where Katie had tried to escape.

Mary was the first to reach the top. "Oh my!" The words were spoken with elation, not sadness, and we all rushed ahead. There was Pitch, standing, grazing, still saddled and ready to ride.

"Pitch!" Katie yelled with delight. She slid from her horse and sprinted to Pitch's side and hugged him.

"Looks like he was creased," Parker noted as he rode over. He pointed to a gash on Pitch's neck, now crusted over with dried blood. "That'll knock a horse cold."

"Will he be all right?"

"Sure, should be. Let's check him out." We watched as Parker got down to examine Pitch. His experience around horses was evident. He had a soothing, casual way about him as he touched Pitch's ears to feel for fever or shock, rubbed his hands down every leg, and checked everywhere for further injuries. "Looks good." He gave Pitch's face a gentle pat. "You're a fine one, you are."

Mary smiled. Jonas would like seeing the way Parker treated a horse with kindness. She hoped Jonas would have the chance to meet this young man; he'd find him to be a good match for Katie. Mary's smile faded as her hopes turned to just wanting everyone to survive as they battled to re-take the herd.

We returned to the main trail and walked the horses all day, not wanting to catch up to the herd and the men until dark. Walking also made the ride easier on Sally, who was not only riding bareback but also had her pistol tucked down her pants in the small of her back since she didn't have a gun belt or saddlebags. Every time I glanced at her I ended up patting my saddlebags to make sure they were there. You don't think about things that simple until they're gone.

By mid-afternoon, the slow pace was becoming tedious, giving our minds time to dwell on re-taking the herd. It would be reasonable, even natural, for fears to build up at the thought of taking on a practiced gang of thieves. In fact, had the time been six or seven weeks earlier when we were still new to the trail, it's a safe bet we would have been traveling the other direction. But we'd changed over those weeks, which felt like a lifetime of learning. We still had our hopes and dreams—part of Katie's rode right beside her—but now, instead of hoping for them, we were determined to make them happen. Those men took what was ours. We wanted it back.

The thoughts made us anxious to move, and Mary had to keep reminding us that it wasn't yet time to attack. Parker was itching to scout ahead, and Katie made sure he stayed with her, out of Ruth's sightline. Ruth was downright eager to shoot a man and the dogged tenacity in her eyes had Katie worried that Ruth would shoot without thinking if Parker got too close. Even Prudence had a steely resolve. Instead of asking questions, she seemed more likely to settle arguments with her gun.

We were going to kill those men.

You can call it flat-out murder if you like. It would be a fair charge, I suppose, since it's what we planned and were on our way to execute. You could call it revenge, since we were going after those who hurt—and for all we knew ultimately killed—our friends, shot at us, stole one of us, and stole our herd. You could call it frontier justice, saying that they had it coming and the only law that mattered was who was standing at the end. You could pick out a dozen Bible verses that condemn it or find another dozen that say it's righteous.

We didn't have a name for it. It was just that thing we were going to do.

Chapter 24

After we located a spring and stopped for water, I made the mistake of offering to switch horses with Sally for a while. I thought perhaps she'd say, "That's all right, I'm used to it now," but instead she couldn't trade fast enough. If you ever want to appreciate a saddle, ride on a horse's bony back for a while. I think the horse appreciates a saddle, too, since I'm sure the seams of our pants dug into its skin.

Just before sundown, Mary rode ahead. Parker had wanted to go, but Mary made it clear who was in charge. "I'm the scout. Period." She was back in a little over an hour, riding toward us silhouetted against the last fraction of the orange sun.

"Went farther than I thought they would, about two miles ahead. Herd looks in good shape."

"Could you see how many there are?" asked Ruth.

"I counted four, but it was dark and I wasn't about to get closer. Four seems low, though."

"Just so one of them has a saddle I can take," was Sally's only comment. I nodded agreement.

"Even if there's another one or two I didn't see, we still have the number advantage," Mary said. "At first light, we'll go in firing. Catch most of 'em sleepy-eyed and holding coffee instead of guns."

While we were planning at sundown, Ernestine was rapping on Doc Evert's door. It was fortunate that the man had returned home from getting his dinner only moments before, because one look at Clean Through and Pearl told him that he was in for a long night.

Ernestine and a burly passer-by called Dutch helped carry the injured into the office. The raucous town was filled with others who could help, since a big group of ranch hands was in town spending the last of their earnings from delivering a herd up in Abilene, but they were too busy drinking and shooting into the air and laughing to take notice of the wagon; it was likely a good thing that Ernestine was wearing pants and a shirt, because they might have noticed a dress and wanted to help her in ways that she didn't wish to be helped. But Dutch was a good friend of Doc Evert's and carried the wounded like someone who had done it many times. He was also kind enough to respect the blanket that the doctor had placed over Pearl and her torn clothes, which we had been hard-pressed to cover.

The doctor quickly determined that Pearl was the worse off, saying only, "My, my, my" before ordering that she be put on the single exam table while Clean Through was propped upon a waiting bench. Doc Evert then had Dutch and Ernestine arrange lamps around the exam table and sent Dutch to the boarding house to bring back Widow Sterling, who helped him with nursing emergencies.

When Ernestine was certain that her friends were in good hands and that there was nothing more she could do at the moment, she left to find the telegraph office.

After another day without Brute's arrival, Sean was now certain that something had gone wrong. As he took the first watch, he did what he had done most of the day—spent his time looking down the trail at where they'd been. There was nothing to be seen, yet disquieting thoughts nagged at him. He tried to shrug them off, telling himself that even if a group of foolish women tried to attack, his gang could pick them off like ducks on a pond. But the unsettling feelings lingered and his concern would rise up strong anytime Brute flashed in his mind.

He hoped Red would return soon.

While Doc Galen was a talker, Doc Evert was a... well, I don't know if there's a word for someone who makes little noises to himself as he mulls things over, but that's about all Ernestine could get from the man as she sat watching him pore over Pearl and Clean Through. "Hmmmm." "Uh huhhhhh." "Huhnnnnn." "Myyyyyyyyy." "Ahhhhh." "Tch tch tch." Occasionally something like "goodness" or "dear me" would crop up, but it was mostly odd sounds of concentration.

Ernestine was worried and feared that she had been too slow in getting them to the doctor. At the same time, his odd sounds gave her comfort. He was clearly a dedicated man who took offense at the mortality of people. She felt confident that Pearl and Clean Through were getting good care.

She stole a look first at Pearl and then at Clean Through, cringing at their bloodless faces and lifeless forms. The doctor's doing his best, she thought, but they sure look beyond saving by any human. She had prayed for her parents, but they died anyway. Still, she supposed there was no harm in praying again. She bowed her head as she heard the doctor sigh a near-silent "eeeeesshhhhh."

If someone asked me to name the most remarkable thing that happened during our journey, I'd be hard-pressed to think of anything more fortuitous than the luck we had with our communications. I had no idea, of course, how swiftly my letters had made it home. Telegrams were obviously faster, but they were subject to delays. Everything from cut or broken lines to an operator being gone for dinner to someone like Edward, who had no interest in deliveries, could slow a telegram by days or more. Yet like my letters, everything lined up just right when Ernestine sent her telegrams from Caldwell. The lines between Caldwell and the relay station at the trading post in Fairview were intact, as were the lines between the relay station and Secluded Springs. The operator at the relay station had fallen asleep at his desk and woke up at the first click to take the message. And Edward was working late at the store, trying to catch up on the bookkeeping that he wished Ernestine was there to help with, so he was ready when the messages came through.

So while we were waiting under the dark sky to re-take the herd at morning's light, Edward had parked his wagon and was pounding on Jonas's door. "Jonas!" Boom, boom, boom. "Jonas! Open up! News from the drive!" Doc Galen stood right behind him.

Lamplight appeared through the window and a moment later Jonas, in his undershirt and hastily pulled-on pants, feet bare, crutch under his arm, jerked open the door. There was no sleepiness in his bright, wide eyes. His heart was pounding. News of the drive in the middle of the night could be damn good or damn bad, but he feared the latter.

Edward rushed through the door and went straight for the table, pulling out a chair and sitting down with a thud. Doc entered just far enough to stand dead-center in the doorway as Edward held up two papers. "Telegrams from Caldwell."

"Caldwell?" That didn't make any sense to Jonas. Could they have taken the wrong trail?

"One from Ernestine. One from Mary."

"Well?" Jonas said, taking a seat himself while still holding the crutch. "What's the news?"

"Ernestine has been injured but assures me she's all right. She insisted I deliver this message from Mary right away." He stuck out one of the papers toward Jonas.

For Jonas, the moment was too important for any pretense. He pushed the paper back. "I ain't good with readin', Edward. Just tell me what it says."

"Sure, Jonas. Sure." He unfolded the paper and read. "'Ambushed, stop. Several wounded but all alive, stop. Katie stolen and herd taken, stop.'" The crutch crackled as Jonas tensed his hand around it. "'Katie rescued, stop. Plan to re-take herd or die trying, stop. Katie met fine young man, stop. Expect they'll marry if we live, stop.'" Edward looked up with a touch of moisture in his eyes. "'Know I love you dearly no matter what. Mary.'"

The fire from the lamplight reflected in Jonas's eyes. "Do one more thing for me, Edward."

"Whatever you need."

Jonas rose and tossed his crutch across the room, slamming it into a wall. "Get me on a horse."

Jonas charged at the door, but Doc Galen and Edward were ready. Doc crouched slightly in the doorway and grabbed one arm as Edward grabbed the other from behind. With two good legs, Jonas might've plowed through, but the two older men held firm.

"You can't go!" screamed Doc.

"You'd never get there!" Edward added.

Jonas pushed on and gained a few inches, his head now out the door.

"Jonas, listen! Listen!" Jonas stayed wild-eyed at Doc's words, but for the moment at least he stopped pushing. Doc loosened his grasp, but he stayed ready to clutch hold again. "Even if you could ride hard, it'd take you a week. It's up to Mary now. The women." He could see Jonas slowly absorbing the reality. "You put your faith in them. Now keep it. It's all you can do. All any of us can do."

Doc and Edward tentatively let go of Jonas. He didn't run. He didn't fall. He simply stood there, shoulder slumped, face clouded. Helpless. No, not helpless. Useless.

Chapter 25

Circumstances change. Thus a good plan in the evening can become a poor plan by morning. Our plan was good because it was so simple. We outnumbered the men, so we would rush them with guns blazing and try to take them out before they could fight back. Perhaps I should also point that we weren't just women, we were *smart* women capable of learning from our experiences. When the men had attacked us, we tried to shoot back from horseback and didn't hit a thing. It was only when we were on the ground, steady, that our shots went true. So when I say that we would rush them with guns blazing, I really mean that we would rush into good shooting positions and then take good, reliable shots while the men were still hesitant due to the surprise. Like I said, smart. All of us were in agreement that the fast, unexpected charge was our best hope for success. Even more, we were confident it would succeed. The odds were with us.

But, as I noted, circumstances change.

During the last hour before dawn we moved closer to the gang's camp, positioning ourselves against a line of trees to the east so that the rising sun would be behind us and in the men's eyes as we rode in. For the umpteenth time, we checked our weapons. Then we watched hoping to see them rise and gather somewhere away from their horses.

"Looks like two watching the herd," Sally said, and we all trusted her eyes. "Rest are just starting to stir."

"Give the word when they start rolling up their blankets," said Mary. "That's when we'll charge. Remember…"—and here's where Mary again turned out to be a lot like Jonas, telling us stuff she'd already gone over a dozen times—"…rifles get in position and take good, steady shots. Everyone else rush in and blast whoever the rifles don't get. Then we all go after the riders."

"Wait! Something's comin'!"

And that's how quickly plans change. As we strained to see in the pre-dawn grayness, we first heard then saw a group of men riding in behind the red-haired man.

"I count five more," said Sally.

"Me, too," said Prudence.

Mary slapped her thigh in frustration. "Pull back. Stay quiet."

Despite being angered that our plan had failed before it began, Mary also knew that we had been lucky. If we had charged just a minute before Sally spotted the oncoming riders, we would have been in a world of hurt.

We could rush five men and like our chances, but ten was too many. And all of them had rifles.

That Sean was a pesky fellow. Somehow he'd reasoned that Brute's absence was cause not to check on Brute, but to send for more men. Apparently there was no shortage of non-working lowlifes in Dodge City. He'd rather divide the profits among more men than risk losing the herd entirely. I always thought that outlaws looked for ways to get bigger shares, but it appeared that Sean didn't think like most outlaws, and that was bad for us.

We had Mary, and that was bad for them.

"All right," she said once we had pulled back a short distance. "They outgun us for sure now, but we ain't done yet." Trickles of yellow sunshine were weaving through the gray morning sky, providing enough light to see the corners of Mary's mouth rise. "We have other weapons that I'm sure they ain't used to fightin'."

The first of our other weapons was me and Sally, or I should say, our feminine appeal with me as the first representative and Sally as the second. We waited until the men had the herd on the move, then we closed the distance to trail them and scout their positions. Two men, including Red and a fellow with a short-brimmed straw hat, rode drag. They were our first targets.

We watched a good chunk of the day, again letting them move the herd—*our* herd—for us, and then put our new plan into action as the afternoon sun hung low in the sky.

I removed the rifle from the sheath on my saddle and left it behind with Ruth, keeping only a pistol within easy reach in my boot. I rode in toward Red at the left rear of the herd, unhurried, trying to think of myself as alluring and hoping the thought shone through in my expression. I stopped when he heard my approach and snapped his horse around, facing me. He was startled, then intrigued as I smiled with all the charm I could muster. We were about forty feet apart.

"Excuse me, sir. I'm lost and it's gonna be cold soon. Do you know a warm place I could spend the night?"

He moved his horse closer to mine, all thoughts of the herd replaced by a lustfulness I found both complimentary and unsettling. "I'm sure I can think of something, little lady."

I snapped up my pistol and pointed it at him. "On second thought, maybe I ain't so lost. Now pick up your gun by the handle and drop it."

He just smiled. "Your pretty hands ain't none too steady. You're not really gonna shoot me."

"I don't need to," I said. "They will."

From directly behind me, having walked in single file behind my horse, Ruth slipped out to the right holding a rifle and Parker slipped out to the left holding a pistol.

I took a moment to glance to the right side of the herd, where Sally had Straw Hat in the same position, backed up by Mary and Katie. Prudence was moving up behind us, the reins of the other horses in her hands.

Red dropped his gun.

"Now turn around, ride straight into the herd, and you just might live."

Red hesitated.

"I was told to count to ten, then fire," said Ruth. "I'm already on six."

Red snapped his reins, spurred his horse and galloped toward the herd. At the right, Straw Hat was speeding into the herd as well. As Mary and the others climbed onto their horses, she shouted, "Now!"

Ruth, Parker, Sally and I fired shots into the air. Our guns didn't have Ernestine's volume, but they had enough of the effect to startle the herd, especially with Red and Top Hat racing forward. All of us rushed ahead, yelling and firing our guns to unleash our other special weapon—the herd itself.

The cattle panicked as if they were in on the plan, and since longhorns tend to be jumpy and skittish, maybe they were. The pounding hooves produced a thunderous rumble like the earth was conducting a symphony of nothing but drums, and the clattering of clashing horns added an angry and ominous beat.

The stampede scared us and we knew it was coming. For the men, it had risen and was upon them so fast and so violent that their only reaction was to run in fear. Straw Hat fell from his mount and his aching scream was cut short by the pounding herd. A choking dust cloud billowed and thickened, making it hard to see. There was another scream from another victim, but I couldn't place its source. The grimy haze both protected and endangered us—it was nearly impossible for any surviving men to see us and shoot, but it was also easy for us to ride right up to them without knowing. Prudence shot one of the riders in the chest after they surprised each other in a small pocket of air. She couldn't remember what he looked like, only that he was "too close to miss."

Frightened longhorns don't scatter. They cluster, slamming into each other in panic and packing tight. They formed a reddish-brown sea rising and falling in swirling waves, a dusty mist hanging in the air. Men caught in their midst had no chance, and we kept on guard not just against the men who were blindly firing their guns but also against any sudden reversals of the herd. I was both excited and terrified to be a part of it, and part of my mind wished that I was off to the side so that I could see how the whole pounding, reverberating, terrorizing, petrifying scene was unfolding.

Finally, we gained some glimpses that confirmed the plan was working. Two men could be seen high-tailing it over a ridge, urging their mounts ahead with both spurs and quirts as if their horses were unaware of the cattle train steaming behind them. Whatever Sean had offered them, it wasn't worth a trampling.

"There's two runnin' off west!" I shouted.

"And baby makes three!" Ruth hollered, pointing at Red as he broke free of the herd and rode hard to the east without looking back.

At the front of the charging herd, Sean's smarts worked against him. He and a second rider had turned one way and then another to escape, but had only managed to corner themselves against a rocky hill. The front point of the herd rumbled past, but the wide remainder was coming up fast and a trampling could not be avoided. The second man, one of the new riders joining the gang that morning after Sean was wise enough to see the need, stopped firing at the herd and turned his gun on Sean.

"You did this! You brought me here!" He pulled the trigger just as a steer gored his horse and knocked the man to a fearsome fate under the running hooves. The shot missed Sean, ricocheting off the stone to clip the back leg of Sean's frightened horse, spurring it straight into the oncoming herd. In a stroke of luck, the herd parted and the panicking horse went untouched. The flurry of movement, though, had nearly thrown Sean from the saddle and he clung to the saddlehorn and the horse's mane to keep from falling. The horse moved on, somehow dancing around the rushing the cattle, guided only by fear, bouncing Sean with every jump. His grip faltered, his hand dropping from the saddlehorn and catching on the butt of his rifle in its sheath. He shrieked as the horns from a surging steer raked his back, yet with one hand clutching the horse's mane, the other grasping the rifle, and one foot twisted inside a stirrup, he managed to stay off the ground until at long last his horse skirted to the side out of harm's way. With his hand that grasped the mane, he tugged back and spoke to the horse. "Whoa... easy now..." The horse came to a stop at last. Exhausted, weak, blood dripping down his back, Sean fell to the ground, his foot still caught in the stirrup, the rifle in his hand.

Parker rode up to Mary and pointed at the two men who had ridden to the west. "Want me to go after them?"

Mary shook her head. "Doubt they'll stop 'til they find a saloon in another territory. Let's try to get the herd under control. Spread the word."

Parker raced ahead, waving for Katie and me to go with him. We picked up Ruth along the way and with no men left in sight to shoot, she consented to join us. The herd showed no signs of slowing, but our horses were worthy mounts and in a short while we overtook the cattle. Ruth continued ahead and fired her gun once again while the rest of us rode across the front to stem the charge. Prudence rode in from the other side and joined us. With effort, we turned the front of the herd to one side and then circled it back upon the remaining cattle, milling it into a reddish-brown whirlpool that tightened in upon itself. It felt like hours had passed, but the entirety of the stampede was likely closer to 15 minutes, 20 at the most.

A gunshot grabbed our attention. There was a collective sigh when we noted that the herd didn't start running again, then a collective gasp as we saw Mary walking her horse up to Sean. The shot that rang out was from Sally's gun. She stood to the side after having shot the rifle from Sean's grip, the bullet continuing through his arm and into his stomach. As Mary approached him now, he was a bloodied, sobbing mess, alternating between fury, pain and fear.

"Cut me loose before this wretched creature bolts!" His boot had slid through the stirrup, now gnarled with the dangling reins, and the stirrup was like a coiled snake that wouldn't let go. He kept one hand pressed on his bleeding gut, pointing the other at Mary with an angry wave. "It's your fault! You did this!" He moaned in searing pain and his voice became reflective. "Father was right. 'Wicked are the ways of women' he always said. Wicked!" The fury boiled in him again. "Wicked women!"

Then Mary lowered herself from her horse and as she walked toward Sean with her gun aimed above the horse, his rage turned to pleading. "No, lass, no. I beg of you. I'm good as dead now, I am. Please. Please! Don't let'm drag me achin' body!"

Mary bent over him. "You ain't worth another bullet." Then she yanked off his boot and let the horse pull free. "But your horse deserves better and one of my ranch hands needs a new saddle." She turned and led the horse toward Sally.

His strength gone, Sean slumped to the ground, dead or soon to be. As with Brute, there was no inclination on our part to bury him. Even if we had the desire, our only shovel was on the chuckwagon that we hoped was now in Caldwell. But I promise you that none of us gave thought to giving any of the dead men a decent burial or saying words over them beyond those I don't think I should repeat here.

They had taken our herd and left us behind. We had taken the herd back and would now leave them behind. Unlike us, they would not rise up again.

Chapter 26

Assessing our situation after re-taking the herd was a lot more fun than when we had counted our wounds and meager belongings after losing the herd. Under normal circumstances, there's not a bit of humor in the words "and then there's the herd," but it made us laugh with delight every time.

"I now count enough saddles for everyone," said Sally.

"And then there's the herd," said Prudence, and bellies shook with had-to-be-there laughter.

"By my count, we now have six rifles," I said, setting up whoever wanted to chime in.

Ruth did. "And then there's the herd!" Comical every time.

We counted horses and canteens and pistols and one potential husband, and, oh yes, then there was the herd that we had snatched back from men who dared to challenge us. We were feeling good and happy and successful, and we lived on those feelings for quite a spell until exhaustion finally set in. It had taken time and effort to round up strays, the darkness of night was upon us, and there was one very important item we were unable to count: food.

More than a day had passed since we'd eaten the last of our jerky. Clean Through had hunted a time or two during our trek, adding mostly rabbits and squirrels to what had started out as beef stew. We'd grown dependent on the chuckwagon, which was natural both because cooking wasn't part of our duties on the drive and because all of us welcomed the opportunity to be free from pots and pans for a couple of months. Now any of us would have been content to knead some dough or stand over a boiling kettle.

"Remember how good Clean Through's biscuits were," said Katie, and her words had our mouths watering and minds hoping that Clean Through and Pearl and Ernestine were all right.

Parker had wanted to hunt earlier, but Mary didn't want to risk losing our surprise attack by the men hearing a shot. Now it was too dark to hunt. I don't know what owl tastes like, but I was willing to risk it if we could have tracked down the hooting calls floating around us. We couldn't. At least the horses and cattle had grass, which started to look tempting as the rumbles rose from our stomachs. We hadn't come across so much as wild berries or something with edible roots.

"Steak dinners for all after we sell the herd," said Mary.

"Bacon for me," said Sally. "The biggest, most heapin' plate of bacon in the history of human life on earth."

"Steak and bacon," I dreamed.

"Steak and bacon and eggs and fried potatoes and more," said Mary. "We'll feast. But for now, fool your bellies with water so you feel full." She turned to Parker who, with a boldness no one objected to, sat holding Katie's hand. "You're sure we're close?"

He nodded. "Barring trouble, we'll be in Dodge tomorrow afternoon."

Ruth held up her rifle. "I dare trouble to find us." The spirited pride we felt rose up again, stemming our weariness for the moment.

"And then there's the herd," Prudence added. It made no sense at all, yet we busted out a fresh set of snickers just the same.

Without Ernestine, it took a few extra hollers for us to start the herd, but we managed. Mary took the lead position. Ruth, Prudence, Sally and I were in our usual spots at each side of the herd. Without the remuda to watch, Katie was free to ride drag. As you likely expect, Parker joined her.

The August air was thick and heavy, adding strained breathing to our hunger, aches and weariness. We didn't care. The end of our journey was near, so near that our minds filled with thoughts of upcoming comforts. Food. Baths. Clean clothes. A bed. More food.

By noon Mary was the first to ride up a gentle rise that led to a bend in the trail. Once upon that rise, she could see our destination. "Dodge City!" she turned and shouted to Ruth and me. "I can see it!" We shouted back to Prudence and Sally and they shouted back to Katie and Parker. The cattle huffed, snorted and bellowed, so perhaps they were spreading the word as well.

For a short time we forgot our hunger, our bodies instead feeding off the excitement of reaching our destination. At our slow-but-steady pace, we were still two to three hours out from front to back. I remember reflecting on what we'd been through and wondering about the fates of Pearl, Ernestine and Clean Through, but I must admit to the selfishness of just wanting a carrot or ear of corn or anything to chew on. Hunger doesn't stay bedded down for long.

A call from Sally shook us all from our thoughts. "Rider! Comin' in fast!"

Like veterans of the trail, which is what we'd become, we pulled out guns in the wink of an eye. "Don't shoot unless you have to," Mary called. "We don't want another stampede."

Ruth moved close to Mary. "Single rider." She put her rifle to her shoulder. "I'll keep his chest in my sight 'til you say shoot or don't."

But as the rider approached, I saw his arms up high and recognized him as a friend. "It's that Dusty! Dusty from back in Oklahoma!" Seeing him made me think of my first letter and it was like a connection to home. "It's him, I tell you. Put your gun down, Ruth."

"Not 'til I'm sure." I think if she chewed tobacco she would have spit right then to emphasize her toughness.

It was Dusty all right, and he came riding in with shouts of joy. "By God! By God! By God!" At last he was beside Mary, panting and wiping moisture from his eyes. "By God, you're alive. I'm thankful for that."

"Reckon we are, too," Mary replied, not sure what to make of the fuss. "Keep 'em movin'," she called out to us. Fuss or not, she wasn't about to lose any more time.

Catching his breath, Dusty paced his horse alongside Mary's and explained how he had been almost back to his home when it occurred to him that he might have said too much to the wrong people when he had stopped for a drink—which turned into many drinks—in Dodge City. He had ridden all the way back to find out our fate.

"I learned about the ones who came after you, who were the ones I'd talked to I'm shamed to say. Then I rode down the Western and didn't find you there. Then I went back to Dodge. It was a mystery how you'd plum disappeared 'til I heard old Yankton talking about the side trail in from the Chisolm. It sure is a relief to know I didn't cause you no trouble."

"We had our share of trouble, but it would've found us whether you talked or not. So don't fret. But tell me about this Yankton."

Dusty spit. "Scoundrel disguised as a cattle buyer. Part of an outfit from back east. He buys all the cattle that Irishman and the giant can round up, payin' half the goin' rate and askin' no questions. Then he ships the cattle and tells the firm he paid full price, pocketing the difference." He scanned the country. "So you ain't seen that Irish fella and the big man?"

Mary told him the highlights of our story, pausing at every "By God" and "My stupid mouth" that Dusty interjected.

"I ain't seen none of those men back in Dodge," he said, referring to the ones who had run off. He smiled. "Reckon they ain't as good around women as I am."

"Reckon not." Mary kept her mind on business. "How many cattle buyers in town?"

"Three that I know of. Yankton. Fellow named Hall. From Chicago, I think. Older man from Pueblo named Dawkins."

"Know 'em enough to advise me any?"

Dusty's smile grew. "Why, ma'am, my advice is to take the best price. You'll be collecting money, not makin' friends."

My father would have liked Dusty quite a bit.

We were a sight. I know this not because of how battered and grimy and weary I felt, but because people began to line up at the edge of town to stare at us in wonder and delight. After all this time, I had forgotten how unusual it was to see women wearing pants. And to the best of my knowledge a female team of cattlehands was about as common as the parting of the Red Sea. Dodge City was a scattering of homes and buildings, and people of all ages came out of them with eyes wide, mouths agape and heads shaking in a well-now-I've-seen-everything kind of way.

Dusty had told Mary of the massive corral at the far edge of the town, near the train depot, and she trotted up ahead of the herd to make sure it was clear. Two lawmen, who were better known back east from stories told about them than they were known to us, rode up to her. One was a sheriff named Masterson. The other a deputy marshal named Earp. Each doffed his hat at her.

"Honor to have you here," said the one named Earp. "Always room for more ladies."

"What route should we take to the corral?"

Masterson laughed and waved his hat toward Front Street. "Lady, you just parade 'em right on through. Ain't a person here won't want to see this."

Mary was almost too tired to smile back at the welcome. She nodded, turned, and waved us ahead.

It was indeed a parade! As we marched the herd down that dirt road through the town, the people who had been watching us joined in and sauntered along. A few of the older women looked at us like we were fallen, shameful females, but most gave us welcoming smiles. As filthy and ragged as our clothes had become, they still had a few of the men palpitating at our curves. Some young girls were happy just to be marching along with us. Most interested of all were the young women in the town, who admired Parker as much as they admired our outfits. A few called out as we passed or as they walked with us.

"You women did this?"

"I like your trousers."

"Where are your men? Who's in charge here?"

"Would you tell my mama to let me wear pants?"

"Bet you're pretty under all that dirt!"

That last one brought a mouth-shutting look from one of the hard-nosed deputies that had been lining up. For a town that carried a lawless reputation, Dodge City seemed to have a large number of lawmen. There was a sheriff and his deputies and a marshal and his deputies. Of course, the main duty of a lawman in a cattle town wasn't so much to stop crime as it was to keep the cowboys from getting so rowdy that they couldn't get up the next morning and spend the rest of their money. These lawmen looked at us with a dubious curiosity, wondering if we would be like most cowhands and spend the night drinking and gambling our money away, and then wondering just how they'd go about arresting a group of women.

It was unnecessary worry on their part. All we wanted was food, a bath and a bed, in that order.

The words that soared through the air like a lovely melody and brought music to Mary's heart, the words that confirmed we were where we needed to be, came from a brown-suited man on the last step of the boardwalk on the railroad edge of town: "I want to buy your cattle."

The words lost their luster a moment later when Dusty said, "That's Yankton."

Then a new round of good feelings stirred up again when a broad-shouldered man called out, "I'll make you a good offer for them cattle," followed by a white-haired man in a pale suit saying, "Not as good as the offer I'll make."

At the large corral, a sandy-haired girl, maybe ten, in a pretty blue dress, opened the gate for us. She looked at Mary with admiration as the herd began to fill the space. I noted with both pride and relief that Uncle Angus was among the first to go inside the fence. Mary dismounted and stood beside the girl. "I'm Mary," the girl said.

"Why, that's my name, too," our Mary replied, making the girl's day even more special. In just short of an hour, Katie and Parker drove in the last of the cattle and, before rushing off to tell her friends that she shared a name with the leader, young Mary closed the gate.

Our job was done.

Chapter 27

"I'm sorry, but I'm just too tired to shake hands." It was the first and only time I heard Mary tell a lie. We had turned our horses over to a nice man who ran the livery stable and had promised to rub them down and get them some well-deserved grain. As we started our walk back to the center of town, there was Yankton holding out his hand. She could easily have slapped, kicked, knifed or shot him, but she settled for not touching the man.

"I understand, I surely do. My name is Sam Yankton and I'm a cattle buyer."

"Yes. We met several of your acquaintances on the trail."

The shine dropped from Yankton's eyes and his grin drooped for only a piece of a second. "I don't know what you mean, Miss…"

"Mary Bartlett. And it's Mrs." She snapped her head to the right. "Ruth! Let it be." Ruth lowered the gun she had raised.

Yankton held out his palms. "Now you ladies don't want to shoot me."

"Not now we don't," Ruth growled. She gave a quick scan of the crowd. "Too many witnesses."

Mary stopped just long enough to look into Yankton's eyes. "You'll have to find a new group of rustler partners, Mr. Yankton. Your others ain't comin' back."

She continued on her walk, which had a burst of energy and a whole lot of backbone to it. As we had for two months, we followed. With pride.

Well, except for Dusty, who felt an urge to quench his thirst and tell some stories at the Palisades.

When we walked into a one-story building simply labeled Cattlemen's Association, it was the first time in quite a while that we couldn't see the sky. Each of us paused in the doorway, startled for a moment by the ceiling. If it hadn't been early evening by this time, we might have been even more unsettled. After the slight hesitation, though, the ceiling became a welcome sight and the final bit of proof that we had returned to civilization. The downside of coming into a room was that it became all the more apparent how awful we smelled.

The two gentlemen in the room were kind enough to ignore our less-than-fetching aroma. Or perhaps they were just used to the stench of sweat and grime and cattle.

They were the two men who had shouted to us about making good offers for the cattle. One was tall, broad-shouldered, with black hair and a blacker mustache. He introduced himself as Tobias Hall from Chicago. The other man, Quentin Dawkins from Pueblo, was older and shorter with wrinkles around his eyes and mouth indicating considerable time spent smiling. He was smiling now.

"I can't tell you how delighted I am to meet you ladies."

"The same goes for me," Hall added. "What you women have accomplished will be stuff of legend."

Dawkins noticed Prudence staring with deep longing at an apple on a nearby table.

"By golly, Tobe, we're being rude as can be. You ladies could use a good meal, couldn't you?"

"Well, sir, yes, we need food and baths and beds more than any time in our lives," said Mary. "It don't even matter which order we get them in. But I reckon we'll enjoy them all a whole lot better if we can conclude some business here right now."

"Nevertheless," said Dawkins. He picked up a small bell and rang it. Almost out of thin air, a cheerful black woman, aproned, appeared in the doorway from the back room. She welcomed us with a smile, then looked at Dawkins.

"Agatha, we need sandwiches and drinks for everyone here," he said.

"Better make it buttermilk," added Hall.

"We thank you kindly," Mary said.

Hall tugged on his jacket and assumed a more formal air. "Very well, while we await the food, let's get down to business. Mr. Dawkins and I each represent different cattle interests. There is also a third buyer in town, a Mr. Yankton."

"We have met and rejected Mr. Yankton."

Dawkins smiled. "You are wise. Mr. Hall and I, though competitors, share a mutual respect for each other and a mutual dislike of Mr. Yankton."

"So you two just make offers right in front of each other? So I haggle with both of you at the same time?"

This time Hall smiled. "Not always, but in most cases we find it saves considerable time for everyone." Then he frowned. "Often a less-than-reputable deal has been made with Yankton by less-than-reputable sellers. We prefer to have our dealings entirely above board."

"Well, Yankton's out and I'd sure like to settle this before those sandwiches get here."

Dawkins gave an admiring nod. "Down to business it is. Tobias?"

"I've looked over your herd and, though some of the steers are thinner than I'd like to see, the firm I represent in Chicago is prepared to pay you twelve dollars a head."

Though arithmetic was in no way my favorite subject, I knew it. And I spent a lot of time around a bank. So it didn't take me long to know that more than 300 steers at twelve dollars a head meant more than $3,600— well over what Mary needed for clear title to the ranch. I could see in her eyes that she knew it, too.

She stayed cool. "I had a higher price in mind myself. Mr. Dawkins?"

"Twelve-fifty a head. Cash money."

Mary's eyes darted to Mr. Hall. "I hear tell that folks back east sure do love their beef."

Mr. Hall sighed. "They do. They do. Therefore, I will up my offer to thirteen dollars a head, which is the highest I have ever paid."

That put the sale at around four thousand dollars.

"I was thinking more in the neighborhood of fifteen dollars," Mary said. Both men looked like she shot them in the stomach.

"F-f-fifteen?" Dawkins stammered.

"Unheard of!" Hall added.

Dawkins had his handkerchief out and was wiping his brow. "I could go as high as thirteen-fifty…"

Just then Agatha walked in with a large tray heaped with bread and meat. Behind her came another black woman, younger, perhaps Agatha's daughter, carrying a tray with two pitchers of milk and a pot of coffee. Just the aroma of the coffee was enough to inspire Mary to bring the negotiations to a fast end.

"I will sell my cattle to whichever of you is the first to agree to pay fourteen dollars a head plus cover our hotel rooms and meals for two days."

It was a stare off. Mary stared at Hall and Dawkins. Hall and Dawkins stared at each other. The rest of us stared at the food.

Silence.

Silence.

Dawkins flinched. "Agreed."

Mary smiled and held out her hand. The rest of us had waited long enough. We went for the food. Then we stopped as Dawkins added, "But with two conditions."

Mary pulled back her hand, but Dawkins raised his hand to ease her mind. "First, the details of the sale are to be kept secret. Neither Tobias nor myself can afford to have cattle prices be so high."

Mary nodded. "Our business is *our* business."

Dawkins's smile returned. "Second, and the primary reason I agreed to your hard bargain, I want to be the first one to hear your story so I can be the first one to start telling it around town."

"Agreed." Mary extended her hand again. "But only after I've eaten, had a bath and slept."

"We have a deal." They shook hands.

Two slices of ham between rye bread and a glass of milk hardly seemed a fitting meal for someone of Mary's newfound wealth, but she cherished every bite like it was a full 75-cent steak. We all relished the meal, and when Agatha, who had watched with pride, spoke, we all relished her as well. Her voice was lovely and direct, and though all the words came out through a smile, there was a definite I-will-not-take-no-for-an-answer tone—the kind of woman who makes you want to reply "yes, ma'am" to everything she says.

"You will all stay with me and it will give me great pleasure to have you in my home. Except for you, boy. You'll be at the hotel. I'll stand for no tomfoolery under my roof!"

Parker was the living definition of taken aback. "Yes, ma'am. I mean, no, I wasn't – wouldn't – I..."

"While you ladies bathe and sleep, I'll see what I can do to freshen up those rags you call clothes. Tomorrow, after you have your cash money in your hands, either I or Mabel here will be more than happy to show you places where you can outfit yourselves with decent, proper wear."

"Yes, ma'am," we said in near unison.

Mary desired to send a telegram to Jonas and also send one to Ernestine in Caldwell to check on the health of our companions, but Mabel talked her into waiting. "Even if you weren't dog tired, the evenin' telegraph operator ain't worth the chair he sits in. You wait 'til you're fresh and 'til Old Man Daggert is on the job. Your news'll keep overnight."

Mary nodded, too tired to offer up a "yes, ma'am."

Agatha's place turned out to be the second floor overtop of a dry goods store. She and Mabel, who was indeed her daughter, lived there for the price of cooking three meals a day for the owner of the store. She called it a palace compared to her childhood shack in Alabama. "Now the only slavin' I do is over a hot stove, and I get paid for that." She was doing well on her own and was making sure that Mabel, who looked to be about 15 or so, was getting an education. I admired Agatha as much as she seemed to admire us.

Truth be told, as tired as we were, her shack in Alabama would have suited us just fine. She split us up into two of the rooms, started handing out blankets and cushions that came from who knows where, and asked us to give her our clothes before we washed up or fell asleep.

"You really don't have to go to all this trouble," Mary said.

"First of all, it ain't trouble. I like doin' it and I'm proud to have you in my home. Second of all," she said with a wink, "I'll be sendin' a bill to Mr. Dawkins."

By mid-morning a considerable amount had been accomplished, very little of it by us. Mabel had kept showing up with hot water throughout the evening until each of us had bathed. Agatha had somehow laundered and dried our clothes. Both Agatha and Mabel had cooked us a fine breakfast. Our efforts had consisted entirely of sleeping, dressing and eating. Katie did a little more, having taken a plate down to Parker, who enjoyed his breakfast behind the store and didn't seem to mind still wearing dirty clothes. He still looked handsome and lovable to Katie.

The real event of the morning was a walk down Front Street. While Mary went to send her telegrams and then meet Mr. Dawkins at the bank, the rest of us took a stroll to see the sights. Dodge City's reputation as a wild cattle town seemed well earned. There was no shortage of saloons and no shortage of men sleeping off their evening activities right on the street. The town was still waking up, but it was busier on a sleepy morning than Secluded Springs was on a Saturday night. The whole town appeared to be hammered together, one building up against the next. The dry goods store was beside a cigar store which was beside a saloon which was beside another saloon which was beside a general outfitting store which was beside a jail which was beside a hat shop—the town just kept going on both sides of the street.

The most important site of the morning was the bank, and we kept our eyes on it while we were strolling through the town. When Mary came out of it, grinning from ear to ear, we were quick to meet her. She led us back to Agatha's and we closed ourselves in a single room.

"Payday," was all Mary said or needed to say.

We had been promised fifty dollars each. Mary gave us seventy-five, plus another five for new clothes or to do with as we pleased. It was more than any of us had ever had in our hands at one time, even me with my banker's-daughter childhood. She gave Parker ten dollars for his help, which he refused, saying that he did it for Katie not the money. That young man never missed an opportunity to impress the woman he hoped would become his mother-in-law, and it was entirely sincere. Mary even saved out five dollars to give to Dusty if we ran into him again. I was sure we would.

Mary assumed the most formal posture she'd taken in quite some time. "Take this money that you've earned and spend it as you see fit in good health. But please know that I will be forever indebted to your kindness, friendship, companionship and especially your bravery. You saved —"

"Oh, shut your mouth and let's go buy things," Ruth snarled. "There'll be time for mush later. I ain't never seen this much money in my life."

Unlike Secluded Springs, Dodge City was big enough to have a full-time telegraph office. Mary walked up to the tall, dark-haired man of maybe 30 at the counter. "I'd like to speak with Old Man Daggert."

"You've found him." He explained, as he had hundreds of times before, that he was born with a patch of gray hair, now long gone, but that the nickname was with him forever. "Even my father and grandfather call me 'Old Man.'"

Mary kept him busy. Her first telegram was an update to Jonas. Her second was sent to "Ernestine Mickel in care of the doctor" in Caldwell, inquiring about the health of our three friends and assuring them (Mary refused to consider that they were anything but alive) that she had their wages and assuring the doctor that she would pay his bill on their behalf. Her third telegram was directed to my father, indicating that the entire mortgage balance was in the Dodge City bank and arrangements would be made to transfer the money to him. Old Man Daggert promised to deliver responses as they arrived (a statement no one in Secluded Springs had ever heard from Edward).

As Mary left the telegraph office, she was met at the door by Parker. "May I speak with you, Mrs. Bartlett?"

"Go ahead. For once I have nothing to do."

"With your permission, I'd like to wire my uncle to let him know that I'll be riding back with you and Katie. I'd like to meet your husband and ask his blessing for me to ask Katie to marry me."

"I should caution you to slow down." She noted that Parker's shoulders only slumped a little. "But I rushed into marriage and it worked out fine. I can see that Katie only has eyes for you. You've done nothing to make me question your character. And the ride back will give the two of you a chance to know each other better." His shoulders were rising again. "So, yes, Parker, you are welcome to ride with us. I can't guarantee a warm response from Jonas, but I can guarantee a swift answer. He doesn't waste words."

"I can't ask for more than that."

When Mary returned to Agatha's, Katie was waiting for her and was much less patient than Parker.

"Parker and I are getting married tonight."

It didn't pack the punch of Brute, but it was still an unexpected blow. It took Mary a moment to recover. "I just spoke to Parker and I don't believe he's aware of your plan. He knows to wait for your father's blessing. And don't tell me you don't know it, too."

Katie lowered her head at the thought of Jonas, but then brought it right back up. Her blue eyes locked on Mary's. "I'd want Pa's blessing if he was here, but he ain't. And I just got to get married right away. I just got to."

"But what's the rush? Why hurt your pa like that?"

The ice in Katie's eyes melted into mist and she fell forward into Mary's arms, burying her face in Mary's shoulders. "Oh, Ma, that big man… so scared…"

Mary patted Katie's back and offered up universal words of comfort. "There, there, now."

"He took me. Was gonna hurt me like he hurt Pearl."

"He's gone now. Can't hurt you no more."

Katie lifted her head and, keeping her arms on Mary, showed her returning determination. "That don't mean there ain't more like him. We killed other women-stealers. All I could think of was gettin' away to Parker or dyin' if I couldn't. I'd have been ruined for marriage even if I'd lived and I won't risk that again. I'm whole and I've got a man who loves me and who I love and I'm gettin' married tonight!" Then the tears came again and she fell once more into her mother's shoulder. Her voice softened to a near whisper. "Please understand."

"I do, honey." Mary tucked a hand under Katie's chin and tilted her face up. "But I don't think you could live with yourself if your pa didn't have respect for your husband, and if you marry Parker without your pa's blessing, there'll always be a distance between you." Mary brushed away a tear and gave her daughter a smile. "I also believe Parker wouldn't marry you without meeting Jonas first, even though he's head over heels for you. You should respect that."

Katie exhaled, then searched Mary's eyes as if they held a deep truth. "He's a good man, don't you think?"

"I believe he is." It's possible that more comforting words have never been spoken.

Despite the fresh money in our pockets, we did more looking than buying. That seemed to irritate the townspeople enough that the novelty of our arrival a day earlier had been replaced by a desire for us to spend money or leave town. From their point of view, that's what cowboys do—get paid, and then spend it all on drinks, women and gambling in the town before heading home penniless to do it all again. When it came to spending money, they didn't expect cowgirls to be any different than cowboys.

But the fact is, most of us had plans and needed our wages to bring those plans to life. Katie, ever the dreamer, bought a nice dress to get married in (and proving that she'd been raised right, it was a practical dress she could wear anytime), but saved the rest for setting up a home with Parker. I bought a soft-leather satchel that hung from a shoulder strap, perfect for carrying around my writing materials. Ruth bought a sky-blue dress as much because she'd never had a store-bought dress before as it was that she liked the dress. Even then, she kept on her pants and shirt, preferring to keep the dress nice for as long as possible. Sally saved her money for future travels. Parker bought a clean shirt.

Prudence's plans were clear early on. The moment Mary had handed her the money up in Agatha's home, Prudence's hand had shot up in the air.

"Yes, Prudence?"

"Do I have to spend this money now?"

"You can spend it whenever you like. It's yours."

"Then I'll just hold it awhile." She had never had spending money before and wanted to hang onto the feeling of wealth in her pocket for as long as she could.

Mary didn't spend a dime on herself. Her pants and shirt, cleaned as best as possible by Agatha's capable hands, suited her just fine. What she really wanted was to be home with her husband.

That evening brought the first response to the telegrams Mary had sent. It was from Jonas. "Proud of you both, stop. Be in front coming home, stop. I'll rush to meet you, stop." She wiped a tear from the corner of her eye, then chuckled as she pictured Edward asking, "Don't you want to tell her you love her?" and Jonas telling Edward to mind his own business. She knew the words meant he loved her. She longed to be home again.

First she needed word about how Ernestine, Pearl and Clean Through were doing. The lack of response made the mind think only of the worst.

She sat in a comfortable chair in Agatha's, distracting her mind by watching Katie primp in front of a small mirror. My, how things change, she thought. Katie had still seemed a girl when the journey began. Now she was a woman ready to marry.

Mary reflected that she, too, had changed. While she had always done what needed doing, she had always been content to follow. Now she was looked to as a leader, and she had earned it. She had taken on a hard task and succeeded. And if God answered her silent prayer and kept Ernestine, Pearl and Clean Through alive, she had brought everyone through. She felt satisfied. And tired. So tired.

"Can we join the others listening to the piano player over the hotel, Ma?"

"We sure can." Tired can wait. She still had ranch hands to keep an eye on.

As they neared the hotel and the glorious sound of the piano—less boisterous than the piano noise coming from the Palisades Saloon—Mary and Katie saw Old Man Daggert hustling up with a telegram. It was from my father: "Thrilled to hear of your success, stop. I will never doubt you again, stop. Please ask Laurie to let us know she is alive, stop."

Mary felt an extra kick of pride at having proved herself to my father, though she had hoped the message would be from Caldwell about Pearl, Clean Through and Ernestine. With Jonas up to date and the mortgage handled, their health was her last remaining worry.

After Mary showed me the message from my father, I almost slapped my head at my stupidity. I'd gotten so used to writing that I hadn't even thought of the telegraph. I rushed out of the hotel lobby to track down Old Man Daggert.

By pure coincidence, the timing could not have been more perfect. As I returned from the telegraph office, I poked my head through the hotel door. Sally was the first to notice me and I motioned for her to bring everyone to the door.

Mary, Katie, Sally, Ruth and Prudence gave me confused looks—well, perturbed might be a better word for Ruth—wondering why I was pulling them away from the music, which is something we don't have in Secluded Springs. "Some folks out here I want you to meet," I said, and then I opened the door all the way.

Clean Through and Ernestine strolled in like they lived here and come in every day. "Glad to see you all made it!" Clean Through beamed. All hurried to meet them. Ernestine's hand was bandaged and Clean Through's shoulder was wrapped, but their hugs were strong and most welcome.

We bubbled over with delight, and our raucousness turned to gasps of utter joy when Pearl eased through the door. She was wearing a hand-me-down dress the doctor must have found for her, she moved slowly, and her face still showed signs of bruises. But she was alive and we were reunited! My God, we had all made it!

Only Pearl's presence could have torn Katie away from Parker. "Pearl!" She embraced Pearl like a sister brought back from the dead, and maybe that's just what Pearl was. "Oh, thank God! Thank God, thank God, thank God!"

"Amen to that," said Mary, tears welling in her eyes.

We all hugged and cried and laughed and hugged some more, likely noisy enough that the drunken cowboys passing by had to wonder what they were missing. Just then Old Man Daggert pushed his way into the hotel with another telegram for Mary. It was from the doctor in Caldwell, who had been gone all day tending to a patient outside of town. It told Mary that Ernestine, Clean Through and Pearl were on their way to Dodge City.

The timing was a fitting end to our journey.

EPILOGUE

Jonas was tossing feed at the chickens when the whinny of a horse got his attention. He gazed up to see Mary, Katie, Parker, Ruth, Prudence, Ernestine and Clean Through approaching in the distance. He cast the feed aside and made his fastest limp their way. Mary snapped the reins and raced toward him. In less than a minute, they were embracing.

"Out front is first one home," Mary said.

"I'll rush to meet you anytime."

The others caught up and Katie scurried to join the embrace. All smiled and cheered at the warmest of reunions, and Clean Through never once considered tossing a ladle of water on them. He didn't need to. The joyful gathering turned to silence as Jonas noted Parker holding out his hand. Katie clutched Mary with one hand and Prudence with the other, looking on with a mixture of hope and fear.

"Sir, I'm Parker Hagen."

Jonas looked him up and down without taking the hand. "Why should I let you marry my daughter?"

Parker kept his hand extended and looked Jonas square in the eyes. "I love Katie and I will cherish her and care for her for the rest of my life."

"And?" Jonas's voice had a hard edge to it.

"And I'll kill anyone who tries to hurt her."

Jonas held his gaze for a moment, then gave a flicker of smile. "You'll do." He took Parker's hand and welcomed him to the family.

Katie exhaled with incredible relief, but it was another round of hugs and cheers and celebration for the rest of us.

"He does say 'you'll do' really well," Ernestine said to Prudence.

"I think my heart stopped."

Mary looked at them both with a see-I-told-you-so twinkle in her eyes.

That evening, after all the celebrating had quieted, Jonas and Mary strolled around the corral, holding hands and sharing intimate thoughts that are neither your business nor mine. Jonas harkened back to where they started. "Guess now we can afford to get you one of Sally's dresses."

"That'd be nice." Mary patted her beat-up pants. "But I'm also gettin' used to wearing these."

"Well," Jonas smiled, "you've earned 'em."

Sally used her wages and savings to continue northwest to Denver, where she opened a clothing store. Word of her fashionable designs spread quickly among the women in town and her business was soon thriving.

Word of the shop's back room also spread among amongst the teenage girls and young women. That's where Sally sells women's pants.

Though her past romantic ills are long gone, they are not forgotten. She learned from them. Men who come calling, taken by both her loveliness and her kindness, must enter by the front door.

As Ruth and Prudence neared home, they were perhaps the least happy of our group. They had a little money in their pockets—more than a little to them—and stories to tell, but they were returning home to the same life in the same shack, though with an unspoken desire to make things better. As they rode around the bend where the shack should come into a view, a deep red color caught their eyes. Two figures were painting the shack.

"It's your pa and Billy!"

During one long, lonely night, sleeping on the ground or at least trying to, James had had an epiphany about the pain caused by his wandering ways. He and Billy had scratched out very little silver, and if he was working this hard for almost nothing, he might as well go home and work hard for his family. They left the next day, and returning home to an empty shack just made firm his commitment to be a better husband and father. He traded his silver and one of their horses for some wood and paint and set about turning the shack into a legitimate house. Ruth and Prudence contributed their earnings to buy a new stove and a few comforts for the home.

Above all, in Prudence's opinion, her father had brought back little silver but he had sure struck gold by also bringing back a rugged young farmhand that she took an instant shine to and was pleased to see that the feeling was returned. They were married the following year.

That same year, word came of a new silver strike in Tombstone, Arizona Territory. Ruth's happiness was never more assured than when James said, "I think I'll sit this one out."

Ernestine only wore a dress again on special occasions. She liked wearing pants, and Edward had gotten used to her wearing them in the store. Even if he hadn't, she was going to wear them anyway because she intended to think for herself from now on. She no longer looked at the floor, and thanks to the confidence she'd gained from the cattle drive—and especially from surviving ordeals with bandits—she looked men in the eye. She didn't even slouch to try to appear shorter.

Above all, though, what shy, quiet Ernestine gained was a reputation for her lung power. She became the official herd-starter in northern Texas. It   was   considered   good   luck   to   have   her   powerful

"Aaaaaaaaaaaaaaaaaaaaa!!!!" startle a herd into forward motion, and many ranch owners in the region pay her well for a ceremonial holler.

During one of her excursions to startle a herd, a tall, lanky cowpoke caught her eye. She caught his eye. And if you've read this book this far you understand why Edward expects a wedding in Ernestine's near future. His biggest wonder is how tall and lanky their offspring might be, and he's happy to stick around to find out.

Clean Through retired to his son's home, figuring the next bullet might just hit something important. He spends most of his time relaxing in a rocking chair on the front porch, staring happily into the distance and sharing stories with his grandchildren and anyone who passes by within shouting distance.

Most people put up with his stories in order to get a bowl of his famous stew, even if sometimes the beef looks a lot like rabbit or squirrel.

When Mary paid Pearl back the $93 she had offered up to join the drive, then gave Pearl her wages and a bonus for all she'd been through, Pearl had the resources for freedom for the first time in her life. Wishing to add more distance between herself and the places of her past, she went west and settled in Pueblo.

A new place and newfound freedom doesn't necessarily mean one knows how to go about starting a new life, and Pearl struggled for meaning. Then one day, as she looked at notices on a bulletin board, a new direction for her life literally hit her in the face when a gust of wind tore free a paper and blew it right into her. She pulled it off and read: "Help Wanted: Woman to care for orphaned girls." She noted the address and strode right to it with purpose in every step.

Now she gives those girls the chance she didn't have when she was young. In the spring, she'll marry the headmaster, a fine man with whom she has shared her story and who believes that what's to come is far more important than what has passed.

Katie will travel there to be Matron of Honor.

Katie and Parker share a cheerful home on their growing horse ranch. Jonas allowed her to keep Pitch, saying that once a horse has been shot out from under you and you both live, you belong to each other.

Belonging to each other is what Katie and Parker embody in every look and touch. They share many duties on the ranch just as they share their dinner table each night—happily. Of course, unlike the couple, Katie's biscuits still tend to fall apart.

Some things just don't change.

Jonas and Mary enjoy riding their horses out to view the herd and check on their four hired ranch hands. The herd is thriving and next summer, when the Byerly brothers have said they'll be back, another cattle drive is planned. Both Mary and Jonas plan to go.

They'll take turns riding out front.

As for me, I went the farthest west of any of us. I rode the railroad to Denver with Sally, then was foolish enough to take a stagecoach from there to Cheyenne to pick up the Union Pacific railroad to San Francisco. After five minutes in a stagecoach, I was sore and getting more sore by the minute. Do not—if you learn nothing else from this story, learn this—do not under any circumstances take a trip in a stagecoach. It is the noisiest, bumpiest, dustiest, most uncomfortable way to travel. You might also be trapped, as I was, with a chatty braggart who wants to make sure you like him as much as he likes himself.

Nevertheless, I made it to San Francisco and soon found work with a local newspaper. A friendly, patient editor helped me learn to polish my writing and after six months paid me the ultimate compliment when he said, "Laurie, your writing has become quite competent."

Along with my newspaper work, I continued to write letters to my parents once a week. I also wrote to my many friends and one summer I retraced my route in order to visit Secluded Springs once again. While there, I completed a few interviews and filled in some gaps in the notes I had taken during the cattle drive. I used them to complete my first book.

I call it The Women in Pants.

Made in the USA
Coppell, TX
06 May 2021

55143398R00111

Acknowledgments

My thanks to Bette Adams, my assistant, who helped me above and beyond the call of duty and who gave her blood, sweat, and tears all through the labor pains and birth of this book.

Carl Furuta was named the best commercial photographer in America in 1983 by *ADWEEK*. When you are working with the best, you know it! Many thanks to Carl and his terrific staff.

Thanks to John Murphy for his great skill and patience.

Illustration on page 198 by Anne Scatto/Levavi and Levavi

POCKET BOOKS, a division of Simon & Schuster Inc.
1230 Avenue of the Americas, New York, N.Y. 10020